Waiting for You

Joshua buried his nose in the side of her neck. She was wearing a light, flowery perfume that, when combined with her own scent, produced an enticing aroma that did crazy things to his libido.

Erica's body relaxed in his warm embrace initially. Then she felt his breath on her neck, and her nipples immediately hardened. She put her hand on his chest with the intention of pushing him away from her. Once her hand touched the hard muscles of his chest, though, she could only think of one thing: making love to him. His ban on sex had been hard to abide by these past six weeks, especially when a mere touch sent her desire for him spiraling out of control!

Other Books by Janice Sims

AFFAIR OF THE HEART
"To Love Again" in LOVE LETTERS
ALL THE RIGHT REASONS
OUT OF THE BLUE
FOR KEEPS
A BITTERSWEET LOVE
"The Keys to My Heart" in A VERY SPECIAL LOVE
A SECOND CHANCE AT LOVE
THIS TIME FOREVER
"Teacher's Pet" in LOVE IN BLOOM
FOR YOUR LOVE
DESERT HEAT
TO HAVE AND TO HOLD
"A Love Supreme" in CAN I GET AN AMEN

Published by BET/Arabesque Books

Janice Sims

Waiting for You

ARABESQUE

BET BOOKS

BET Publications, LLC
http://www.bet.com
http://www.arabesquebooks.com

ARABESQUE BOOKS are published by

BET Publications, LLC
c/o BET BOOKS
One BET Plaza
1900 W Place NE
Washington, DC 20018-1211

All Kensington Titles, Imprints, and Distributed Lines are available at special quantity discounts for bulk purchases for sales promotions, premiums, fund-raising, and educational or institutional use. Special book excerpts or customized printings can also be created to fit specific needs. For details, write or phone the office of the Kensington special sales manager: Kensington Publishing Corp., 850 Third Avenue, New York, NY 10022, attn: Special Sales Department, Phone: 1-800-221-2647.

First Printing: April 2005

10 9 8 7 6 5 4 3 2 1

Printed in the United States of America

This book is dedicated to Gwendolyn E. Osborne and Christa Jackson, who, when I told them I was writing a trilogy about a family of winemakers, promptly sent me books, magazines, and articles on the subject of winemaking. Ladies, I was able to absorb a lot of information from that material.

Many thanks!

ACKNOWLEDGMENTS

I would like to thank my editor, Evette Porter, for her enthusiasm when I suggested a trilogy about a family of African-American winemakers from California. I'd also like to thank my publisher, Linda Gill, for giving the project the go-ahead. As a writer, I couldn't ask for better support.

In love, as in life, I
am often reminded

That joy is a *choice*, and you
should take it where you find it.

The Book of Counted Joys

Chapter One

Erica Bryant looked around the crowded room for her escort, Hubert. She smiled when she thought of his name in English. In French, it was pronounced *Hugh-bare.* The French language made everything sound sexier.

Her lower lip protruded a bit when she didn't see him. Leave it to Hubert to abandon her in a roomful of strangers, especially since she'd been in Paris less than four hours. Luckily, she'd slept on the plane so she wasn't tired after the flight from northern California to France. She *was* excited, though. After two years of begging her father to allow her to go to Burgundy and train under Sobran Lafon, Hubert's father, she was finally here! Burgundy was known for being the region whose land produced the best pinot noir grapes in the world. Hence its reputation for making superior red wines.

Erica's family, the Bryants of Glen Ellen, California, in the Sonoma Valley, were premier makers of Sauvignon Blanc and Chardonnay white wines. However, their land also had the potential to nurture pinot noir grapes, and Erica wanted to get the best training possible before embarking on the Bryants' new enterprise—making the rich red wine. It made good business sense.

Winemaking was in Erica's blood. When she was born, her father snuck a bottle of Bryant Winery chardonnay into the hospital room where Erica lay in her mother's arms and put a drop between the newborn's lips for good luck. By the time she was five, she was piggybacking on the tractor with her dad while he worked in the vineyards. It wasn't surprising that she'd majored in enology, the scientific study of wine, at UC Davis and thrived on the winemaking analytical work such as monitoring yeast cultures, the care and maintenance of the barrels, and fermentation of the wine. Now, at twenty-seven, she was a lab rat to the core. She would not rest until she came up with the best winemaking formula for discriminating palates.

That's why she was at this intimate wine-tasting hosted by the Etienne Roumier Winery. In her opinion, they made the best pinot noir in the world. She had heard the astounding rumor that the winery had pinot noir vines on its *domaine*—its property—that were more than a hundred years old. She meant to see those vines before she left Burgundy.

The event was relaxed, with tables set up around the ballroom of one of Paris's grand hotels. There was a different vintage from Etienne Roumier's cellars at each table, where individual waiters graciously served the guests. Erica was standing at one of the tables being poured one of the younger pinot noirs. She smiled at the waiter. "*Merci*," she said, her French not even close to being fluent. However, she could manage in a pinch. The waiter returned her smile and his dark eyes swept appreciatively over her shapely form. She pretended not to notice and turned away.

Secretly, she was pleased that he thought she looked attractive in her short pale yellow dress. It was springtime in Paris and she felt very festive in it. Her new short hairstyle made her do a double take every time she passed a mirror. For years she'd worn her black tresses long and in braids. But she'd wanted something different for her three-month stay in France; so Estelle, her stylist, had relaxed her thick hair and cut it in a layered do that required very little upkeep. She could finger-comb it in a rush.

Erica patiently allowed the wine to sit for a few minutes so that the sediments would have time to settle to the bottom of the glass. There was a tall black man in his midthirties standing too close behind her, muttering to himself.

Curious, Erica strained to hear what he was saying. "This tastes like swill," he grumbled in French. She was pretty sure she had understood him correctly. She watched him out of the corner of her eye, not daring to look at him directly for fear he'd try to strike up a conversation with her. Although he had declared the wine more suitable for porcine consumption than human, he continued to drink it with relish.

Erica swirled her wine around in the glass, contemplating its color. She brought the glass to her nose. It had a nice, fruity bouquet. She continued to monitor the strange man with her peripheral vision. He stopped at a nearby table and was served another glass of red wine. She observed as he swirled the wine around in his glass as she'd done and brought it to his nose to sniff. He wrinkled his nose in distaste, then looked directly into her eyes and smiled at her. Erica nervously smiled back, lowered her gaze, and moved farther away from him. He followed her.

The hairs stood up on the back of her neck. Where was Hubert when she needed him? Was she going to have to handle this creep on her own?

He murmured something else in French, and she realized he was talking to himself.

She walked a few feet away from him, putting more

space between them. She was wary of people who talked to themselves in public, thinking they might be unhinged. When he didn't follow her she breathed a sigh of relief and finally brought the wineglass to her lips.

He slipped up behind her. "I could make better wine than this in my basement!"

This time he spoke in perfect English.

Erica nearly choked on the wine. Sputtering, she gazed up at him, irritated. He merely smiled and peered down at her with such an innocent expression in his thickly lashed, dark brown puppy-dog eyes that she suddenly forgot the rejoinder she had on the tip of her tongue. He reminded her of someone. *Whom*, she didn't know, but his eyes were very familiar to her. He was good-looking in a disheveled way. His charcoal gray-striped suit hung well on him, his white silk shirt open at the neck, and he had stubble. While the trend for men nowadays was neat cuffs with cuff links, he wore no jewelry. She liked that. She also liked how his wavy black hair was shorn close to his head. And the long, sharp-tipped sideburns he wore were sexy.

She glanced down the length of his body. *Nice muscles under those clothes*, she thought. *Too bad he's a nut!*

Finding her voice, she said, "So, you know what swill tastes like?"

"No, thank God. But it can't taste any worse than this. It'll turn into vinegar within a year in the barrel," he stated as he stood there slowly rubbing his unshaven chin.

That was too much! She was a winemaker and they were a superstitious bunch. How dare he make dire predictions for the life of this wine? She took another sip and rolled it around on her tongue. It was full-bodied, sweet, but not too sweet, with a nutty aftertaste. It was delicious. She felt that after some time in the bottle it would be quite good. "At any rate," she told him with authority, "you're wrong. This wine is young, but shows a great deal of promise. Now, would you please keep your negative comments to yourself? I'd like to enjoy the tasting in peace!"

For the next couple of minutes she thought she'd struck him dumb with her rudeness, because he simply stared at her. She didn't regret a word of what she'd said. He had it coming, denigrating his host's wines. He'd been rude first!

"You are right, I really should watch what I say, I might get fired," he said with a twinkle in his eyes. He held out his hand. "Hello, I'm Joshua Knight of the Etienne Roumier Winery."

Erica's mind raced. Yes, he was the head enologist at the winery. She'd been hearing about him for years, but had never met him on her rare trips to Burgundy. The Lafons and the Roumiers were not the best of friends. Their enmity went back at least three generations. Something about Sobran's and Etienne's fathers once being best friends and falling out over a woman. Erica didn't know the particulars of the feud, just the basics. Etienne Roumier had taken on Joshua Knight as his apprentice more than ten years ago after his only son, Christian, had died in a skiing accident. Some said he loved Joshua like a son and was going to leave him in charge of the winery when he died, which was unheard of in Burgundy, a rather insular society of winemakers. Usually the winery went to a son, and only a son. Etienne had a daughter, if Erica remembered correctly. Why wasn't he preparing her to take over for him? Tradition, she guessed. In Burgundy, the men worked the vineyards and the women kept house. *Thank God I'm American,* she thought. She had every intention of one day running her family's winery. Her brother Franklyn was a chef and owned a restaurant in San Francisco. Her other brother, Jason, was an attorney in Bakersfield, California. She was the only one left to run the winery when their dad was ready to retire. She refused to think of his dying. Even entertaining the thought caused her distress because she adored her father. She'd wanted to be just like him ever since she could remember. As for her dad, he'd taken one look at her in the hospital and announced to his wife, Simone, "Okay, sweetheart, you finally win, we'll name this one after me."

Simone had grinned. Two older boys and he'd refused to allow her to name either of them Eric Jr. A girl comes along, and it's suddenly all right with him. Or that's how her mother had put it to her in retelling the story countless times over the years.

Erica smiled at Joshua as she shook his hand. "It's a pleasure to meet you, Joshua. I'm Erica Bryant."

They allowed their hands to fall to their sides. "Yes, I know," Joshua said warmly. "Hubert told me all about you. You're here in France to learn how to make good pinot noir. In which case, you should be under my tutelage, not his."

His grin was infectious. Erica decided the way his white teeth shone against the dark richness of his skin was a definite turn-on. She couldn't let an invitation like that go overlooked.

"I accept. You can show me around your *domaine* while I'm here."

Joshua reached into his inside coat pocket and retrieved one of his business cards. Handing it to her, he said, "I'd be delighted to show you around any Sunday. I have the whole day off and we could have a picnic on the grounds while I instruct you in the time-honored tradition of fine winemaking."

Erica's cheeks grew warm when he pressed the card into her palm with his thumb and held her hand a bit longer than was necessary. Their eyes met. His gaze was intense, as though he were committing her face to memory. "Call me."

"I will," she said.

Suddenly a young woman around Erica's age, late twenties, pounced on him, literally. She wrapped her arms around him from behind and hugged him tightly. "There you are, darling!" she purred in heavily accented English.

She sighed with satisfaction as she sinuously moved around his body to face Erica. Petite with beautifully tanned skin, she had dark brown hair that fell to her waist and looked as slick as sealskin. She gazed disapprovingly at Joshua with doe eyes that were a velvety shade of brown. "We've been looking for you. Father is ready to give his *boring* speech and, of course, he wants you beside him."

Joshua quickly made the introductions. "Erica Bryant, meet Dominique Roumier, my employer's daughter."

"Hello, Miss Roumier," Erica said politely.

"Miss Bryant," Dominique said coldly, her eyes never leaving Joshua's face.

"Why don't *you* stand beside him tonight?" Joshua asked, miffed at her rudeness.

"I would love to," Dominique said, tossing her hair. She moistened her lips. "But you're the one he's grooming to take his place; therefore you're the one he wants by his side, not me!"

Erica suddenly felt sorry for her.

Across the room, a short man in his midsixties, moving slowly as if he might be experiencing some discomfort, approached the podium. "Good evening, ladies and gentlemen," he said. "I am Etienne Roumier."

Enthusiastic applause ensued. Joshua gazed regrettably into Erica's eyes. "Promise me you'll stay right here until I return," he said, his eyes pleading.

"I won't leave this spot," Erica agreed with a warm smile.

Joshua tossed a sharp look in Dominique's direction, then hurried to the stage. Erica watched him go, her heart thudding in her chest. Her gaze settled on Dominique and the smile on her lips disappeared. The other woman was frowning at her.

"Don't waste your time," Dominique said with a smirk.

"I beg your pardon?" Erica was the type of woman who felt women were supposed to be a sisterhood, a support system for one another. She'd never engaged in warfare over a man, and never would. This little Frenchwoman had been antagonistic toward her from the start. Perhaps she should set her straight right away!

"Don't misunderstand me," Dominique told her. "Joshua doesn't belong to me, and I know it. He belongs to my father. That's what I meant. He is devoted to his work, and he doesn't have time for romantic intrigues. So if you're looking for something lasting, look elsewhere."

Erica laughed softly. "We only met five minutes ago. You're reading far too much into this. There's nothing going on between us."

Dominique snorted. "I've never seen Joshua look at anyone the way he was looking at you. There *is* most definitely something going on between you!"

Erica didn't comment as they turned their attention to what was being said on the podium. Etienne Roumier was beaming at Joshua with pride. "My English is not as good as it should be," he told the guests. "I will speak from my heart and have my partner and friend, Joshua Knight, translate."

He began speaking in French, his dark eyes animated, his tone of voice full of emotion. After a while, Joshua smiled at him and said, "Etienne wants to thank you for coming. God has blessed us with a good year. No losses from hail this year."

Everyone laughed. Tales of hail and the subsequent effect on the grape crops were notorious in Burgundy where any winemaker could tell you horror stories about almost being ruined by hail, or miraculous stories of

```
           W A L D E N B O O K S

SALE          1872  102 0930  04-30-05
                REL 7.8/1.07  150 19:36:03

01 1583145656                         6.99
02 1583146261                         6.99
03 0689877048                         7.99
04 0681024054          40  0.25       1.00 N
            SUBTOTAL                 22.97
GEORGIA  6.0% TAX                     1.32
            TOTAL                    24.29
XXXXXXXXXXXX8037 VISA                24.29
            AU# 0020930

   Visit www.WaldenbooksStores.com

==========CUSTOMER RECEIPT==========
```

Returns to Waldenbooks Stores:

If you are unhappy with your purchase for any reason, simply return it within 30 days accompanied by your receipt for a full refund. Without a receipt, only an exchange or a Customer Return Gift Certificate will be given. Returned merchandise must be in saleable condition. Magazines and newspapers may not be returned.

Waldenbooks
BRENTANO'S

Returns to Waldenbooks Stores:

God allowing them to make the best wine of their lives with the grapes that were left undamaged after a severe hailstorm.

Etienne spoke again, this time his animated eyes somewhat sad.

Joshua translated. "Etienne announces that due to ill health, he will be stepping down from the day-to-day running of the winery. He will miss functions such as these, and seeing the faces of dear friends."

Expressions of disappointment arose among the guests, many of whom had known Etienne for decades. They were genuinely saddened to hear of his failing health.

Etienne raised his hand, requesting their silence. Then he spoke again. When he'd finished, Joshua appeared reluctant to translate. He bent low, whispering something into the older man's ear. Etienne looked sharply at him and motioned to the microphone, evidently insisting that Joshua translate exactly what he had said.

Joshua evenly said, "Etienne has put me in charge of running the winery."

The applause was immediate and spirited. Everyone started talking at once about the exciting turn of events. Etienne hugged Joshua, who, resigned, it seemed, fondly returned his embrace.

Wondering if Dominique had known what her father was planning to do beforehand, Erica looked at her to gauge her reaction to the news, but all she saw was Dominique's back as she ran from the room. Erica thought of going after her, but decided against it. She didn't think Dominique would accept comfort from a woman she barely knew. So she stood with the rest of the guests and applauded the two men on the podium.

She was almost blinded by the flashbulbs from cameras brandished by at least five photographers she hadn't noticed among the crowd until now. She stepped backward, shielding her eyes, and ran into someone behind her.

Hubert steadied her. "Hold on, don't fall on that cute fanny of yours."

"Never mind my fanny, where have *you* been?" she asked accusingly.

"There are some very nice-looking women here tonight," he said. Hubert was five-eleven, solidly built, with dark curly hair that he wore too long, full lips that the opposite sex found irresistible, and soulful brown eyes that had melted many cold hearts. He considered women to be his calling. As a priest considers God's work to be his, Hubert was just as devoted to the study of women in all their delightful forms. Or, that was the impression he gave. Erica thought it was all a cover for the very sweet man underneath his playboy demeanor.

Erica grimaced at the photographers. "Where did they come from?"

"This is big news," Hubert told her. "The Etienne Roumier Winery has been tops in its field for more than thirty years. They've maintained a standard of excellence that many wineries will never achieve. And now he's turning over the reins to someone who isn't a blood relative. It's unheard of!"

"It speaks volumes about his opinion of Joshua," Erica said.

"Oh, then you two have met." Hubert sounded pleased. "Yes, Joshua is a good man. But I do not think Etienne's surprise went over well with him. He has dreams of his own."

Erica was silent. She'd unwittingly stumbled into a family drama. A daughter who appeared to be angry with her father for not taking her seriously. A devoted employee who was so good at his job that his employer rewarded him with the top position with the company. How would all of this play out? She had noticed some hesitancy on Joshua's part when Etienne made his announcement.

She looked up at Joshua now. He was dutifully posing with Etienne. Smiling that wonderful smile of his. Then he politely asked the photographers to wrap it up. After a few more pictures, the photographers did as they were asked. Joshua helped a frail Etienne off the stage and walked him to his table. Then he bent and said something to the woman who was sitting beside Etienne, his wife perhaps, Erica thought. The woman laughed delightedly, then Joshua excused himself and made his way back across the room to her and Hubert.

"Do you want me to get lost?" Hubert jokingly asked Erica before Joshua joined them.

"Don't you dare," Erica said. "This man is far too appealing to be alone with."

Hubert laughed. "You Americans and your inhibitions."

"Let's not resort to stereotypes," Erica warned lightly. "I've known you since you were five. I happen to know that you didn't even kiss a girl until you were sixteen."

"Keep your voice down," Hubert cried. "Do you want all of Paris to hear?"

"They will if you leave me alone with Joshua Knight."

"Did I hear my name?" Joshua asked upon his arrival. He smiled down at Erica. "Is this man bothering you?"

Erica eyed Hubert. "He always bothers me, but I still manage to love him anyway."

Joshua laughed shortly. "You've been friends that long, huh?"

"Unfortunately," Hubert offered with a pained expression on his handsome face. "I know all of her secrets."

"Oh, please share," Joshua said, enjoying their conversation immensely.

Erica narrowed her eyes at Hubert and cocked her head as if to say "do and die!"

Joshua laughed because he was delighted to once again be in the company of a sister. Black women had a unique array of body language that he never saw women from other cultural backgrounds display. One such movement Erica had just expressed with her eyes. It was a threat directed at Hubert without even saying a word.

To help Hubert out, Joshua said, "Is anyone else as hungry as I am? Why don't we go somewhere and grab something to eat?"

"I could eat," Erica said, brightly.

"So could I," Hubert said, glad Erica had stopped piercing him with her eyes.

"How about Pierre Gagnaire?" Joshua asked, mentioning a popular Paris restaurant.

"You have to reserve a table there way in advance," Hubert said doubtfully.

"I phoned and asked them to save me a table," Joshua said, his eyes on Erica's face. "Have you ever been there, Erica?"

"No, I haven't," she replied.

"Then it's settled," Joshua said, gently taking her arm.

Outside, Hubert spotted Dominique standing alone wiping her eyes with a tissue. He'd known her all his life. Kept apart when they were kids because of the family feud, they rebelled as teenagers and started secretly seeing each other in their social circles. They'd never dated. Hubert had wanted to date Dominique. She simply preferred older men, and he was two years younger than she was. Sometimes he thought she only dated older men to irritate her father who continually admonished her to get married and gift him with a houseful of grandchildren. Dominique would be twenty-nine on her next birthday, and didn't appear to be in any rush to take her father's advice.

"Give me a few minutes?" he asked Joshua. "I want to see if Dominique can be persuaded to join us."

"All right," Joshua said. He was glad to have more time alone with Erica.

In Hubert's absence, he helped Erica into the limousine. He sat across from her. In the close confines of the backseat, Erica could smell his cologne, a masculine scent that assailed her senses. It was a cool May night, but his body heat made her forget the chill.

"Where are you from, Joshua?" she asked, hoping to break the spell his nearness had cast. She leaned toward him, awaiting his reply.

"I grew up in California," he told her.

Erica sat back on the seat, crossed her arms over her chest, and regarded him with an expression of utter delight. "*California?*"

"That's right," he confirmed, an enigmatic smile on his full lips.

"I knew I'd seen you somewhere before!" she cried triumphantly.

Joshua grinned, enjoying the intimacy of the moment. "California's a big state. We could have lived there all our lives without running into each other."

"No, there's something about your eyes," Erica insisted, looking into them. They were dark, almond-shaped, and expressive. The kind of eyes that could sweep you up into the stratosphere one instant, and send you crashing back down to earth the next. In their depths she imagined a world of possibilities and, as now, a modicum of pain and loss. The sadness she'd glimpsed had been fleeting, but definitely there.

"We have met before," Erica said, adamant that they had met each other.

Joshua's gaze shifted away from her eyes. "I don't know what you mean, Erica. We met for the first time not more than twenty minutes ago."

Erica smiled slowly and shook her head. "It's funny how you didn't look at me when you said that."

Joshua met her eyes once again. He leaned forward and grasped one of her hands in his. They stared into each other's eyes for several seconds, after which Joshua cleared his throat and said, "Okay, we *have* met before. But it was many years ago, and I would prefer that you recall our meeting on your own without any prompting from me. I think that the memory will then be more meaningful for you."

Erica breathed deeply and exhaled, gathering her thoughts. She had been right. With one good look into his brown eyes she'd known they'd met before. Curiosity was eating her up! Naturally inquisitive, and a lover of mysteries, she didn't know how she would survive the evening not knowing where they'd met, let alone having to wait for his revelation or, as he'd requested, for it to finally dawn on her when and where they'd previously run into each other.

Looking at him now, how his sensual lips peeled away from his straight, white teeth, how the lines around his eyes crinkled when he smiled, how his very presence filled the limo, she knew that getting to know him would be well worth the effort.

She leaned forward. Taking his cue from her, he leaned in as well. "All right," she agreed. "But if I can't recall where we've met, you've got to promise me that you'll tell me before I have to go back home in three months' time. Deal?"

Their hands were still clasped. He bent his head. Now their cheeks were nearly touching. He whispered, "Very well. But you *will* remember me, Wendy."

Erica fairly melted when he called her Wendy. *Peter Pan* was her favorite childhood story. How could he have known that? He was giving her a clue. Her golden brown eyes eagerly raked over his face as she willed herself to remember. Nothing came.

Joshua inhaled the heady fragrance of her cologne. It took every ounce of his strength to resist pulling her into his arms and kissing her soundly. To believe that fate had brought them back together after all these years. He would never have sought her out. It would've been unseemly, perhaps even profoundly inappropriate to do so. He would be lying if he said he hadn't thought about her over the years, though. He credited *her* with his choice of a career. Would he be a winemaker today if the two of them hadn't encountered each other earlier in life?

Now here she was. She'd grown into a beautiful woman. But, somehow, he'd known she would. Her mother had been an exceptional beauty and he'd figured, like mother, like daughter. *But to actually set eyes on her!* He could not slow his heartbeat, he was so excited. Although most of his memories from the summer he'd met her had been happy ones, others had also surfaced upon coming face-to-face with her again.

The summer they met was the summer his mother died.

Chapter Two

"Why did you call me Wendy?" Erica asked, now so intrigued that she regretted promising that she would allow the memory of where they'd met before to come to her unaided. She never should have made that promise.

They were still alone in the backseat. She could hear Hubert and Dominique exchanging heated words in front of the hotel. She hoped they would be just a while longer so that she would have time to wrench the truth out of Joshua.

For his part, Joshua was watching her with a smile curving his lips, thoroughly enjoying himself. "That's for me to know, and you to find out," he told her lightly. "Where is the fun in disclosing everything to you all at once? I will give you clues. You're a smart woman, you'll figure it out."

Erica sighed. "Okay, be that way!"

Joshua laughed shortly. "You're not long on patience, are you?"

"I've never been good at waiting," Erica admitted.

"Then this will be an excellent exercise for you."

She turned narrowed eyes on him. "I think you're having a little too much fun at my expense."

"Don't pout."

"I'm not pouting," Erica declared. Her lower lip *had* protruded a bit though. She drew it back in and moistened her lips.

Joshua observed her, wondering if the movement was calculated on her part or simply an unconscious act. Whichever it was, watching her tongue caress her luscious lips had made him harden. Frankly, he'd been in a semi-aroused state from the moment he glimpsed her winsome form in that pale yellow deadly weapon she had on, commonly referred to as a dress. He'd noticed several men eyeing her tonight, with good reason.

"Do you always look so delectable in a dress?" he asked suddenly.

Erica was so startled by his comment she gave a sharp intake of breath. "My only concern was to look presentable."

"Well, you exceeded your expectations. You were the most attractive woman there tonight. You weren't aware of all the attention you were getting from the men in the room?"

"No, my interest was only in the wine." She shifted in her seat.

"Am I embarrassing you with this kind of talk?" His dark eyes bored into hers.

Erica's hand went to her throat. She could feel her heart pounding in her neck. "Of course not. I love discussing male-female courtship rituals."

"You sound so clinical," Joshua accused her.

"A man sees an attractive woman and his senses are engaged. With further perusal, he gets a physical response. That's entirely clinical," Erica said reasonably.

"On the contrary, it sounds perfectly natural to me. Tell me, if you weren't physically attracted to me, would you have joined me tonight?"

Erica laughed shortly. "What makes you think that I'm attracted to you?"

Joshua held her gaze. "I know when a woman finds me attractive, Erica."

"Maybe I agreed to go to dinner with you because I want to pick your brain," Erica suggested. "You *do* work for Etienne Roumier."

"Erica, my dear, your eyes are dilated. You can't sit still. And, excuse me if I'm getting graphic, but your nipples are hardening as I speak. You are attracted to me, admit it."

"You first," she returned, with a glance at his crotch.

Joshua laughed. "Touchè."

Erica started to say something but had to hold her tongue because at that instance, Hubert and Dominique piled into the back, Dominique beside Joshua and Hubert beside her. They were still arguing as Joshua gave the driver, who was visibly relieved to be under way, their destination.

After a quick ride through Paris, they arrived at the restaurant, which was located at the top of the avenue des Champs-Elysées, by the Rue Chateaubriand. They were greeted by a solicitous maitre d', who became even more solicitous when he heard who the party he was seating was. Joshua Knight was warmly welcomed in the best restaurants in Paris because Etienne Roumier supplied them with exquisite wines from their cellars.

They were shown to a choice table for four, whereupon the maitre d' bade them a good evening and assured them their waiter would be with them shortly.

Erica looked around the elegantly appointed room. Muted autumnal colors in deep reds and browns gave the room a relaxed atmosphere. Though most of the tables were occupied, only a murmur of voices and the tinkling of cutlery against bone china were audible.

Joshua had made certain Erica was seated next to him. He looked over at Hubert and Dominique, who had their heads together, deep in conversation. He didn't know why Hubert didn't bite the bullet and simply ask

Dominique out on a date. It was obvious he was besotted with her. Joshua sincerely wished Dominique would hook up with someone who would be a good influence on her. She was in dire need of a shot of self-confidence.

He turned his gaze on Erica, who was looking around the restaurant with great interest. He smiled, happy that she appeared to be the sort of woman who enjoyed new experiences.

Erica turned around and caught him staring at her. She smiled at him. Giving him a sultry look, she said, "This is a beautiful restaurant."

This woman makes me itch, Joshua thought. It had been a long time since a woman's nearness affected his libido so powerfully.

He cleared his throat. "Yes, it is. I have yet to have a bad meal here."

"What do you suggest?"

"The kidneys are good," he said. "Although if you're not used to rich organ meats they may be too much for you on your first visit. The beefsteak is excellent as well and so tender you can cut it with the edge of your fork."

"That sounds good."

"Tell you what," Joshua suggested. "I'll get the kidneys and you order the steak, and we'll share."

"All right," Erica said.

"Hubert, Dominique, are you ready to order?" Joshua asked the couple, getting their attention.

Hubert looked up, appearing reluctant to draw his gaze away from Dominique's face. "Yes, whenever you two are ready."

"Dominique?" Joshua said, concerned. "Are you all right?"

Dominique raised her gaze to his. "Of course. I know you were as surprised as I was by his announcement tonight."

"Things can't go on as they have been," Joshua told

her with finality. "I only went along with Etienne tonight because I saw no other way out. It's your birthright. You have to step up to the plate and claim it. You and your father have one thing in common: you both stubbornly refuse to hear anything you don't want to hear. I've told Etienne time and time again that I want to start my own winery one day. He doesn't want to hear it. And you sulk because he does not take you seriously. Well, *make* him take you seriously."

"How?" Dominique cried, her eyes flashing. "I have gone behind his back for years learning everything I could about winemaking. If not for you and Hubert instructing me, I would know absolutely nothing about my heritage. My father thinks women ought to tend hearth and home and be content doing it! He's stuck in the Middle Ages."

"Then it's time for you to bring him into the twenty-first century," Hubert said. "Show up for work every day, even if he ignores you, and keep doing it until he can't ignore your presence. Dog his steps. Impress him with your knowledge. You're his only child, Dominique. What do you suppose he'll do to you, disinherit you? He wants you to get married and have children. Tell him, you'll do it if he cooperates with you. Give him a time frame. Say, within six months, if you haven't proven your worth, you will get married and give him grandbabies."

Dominique sighed heavily. She turned her gaze on Erica. "What do you think?"

"Me?" Erica said. "We've just met. I thought I would do well to stay out of the conversation."

"No," said Dominique. "You're a woman, and I want your opinion. Hubert tells me you never had this problem with your father. That your father actually expects you to take an active role in running the winery."

"My parents trained all of us—I have two older brothers—to help with the family business. It's how we grew up. My father inherited the land from his father, and that's how it was done for at least six generations of Bryants. I've never known anything else. I've never wanted to do anything except make wine. If my father were opposed to my one day running the family business, you'd better believe I would fight him until I won. My question is, how badly do you want it, Dominique? Do you feel it in your gut? Will you be miserable the rest of your life if you don't go into the family business? Because that's what it comes down to, isn't it? You've got to make your father believe that you're totally committed to maintaining the same standard of excellence he and his ancestors have maintained for generations. That's important to your father, and it should be important to you."

Dominique laughed. "I'm almost sorry I asked." But she looked at Erica with respect in her eyes.

Joshua and Hubert laughed too.

"American women," Hubert joked. "Ask them one question and they recite the Declaration of Independence!"

"That's what's so wonderful about them," Joshua said of American women. "They're so passionate."

Erica was glad the waiter arrived at that moment, because she dearly needed a glass of ice water. Joshua's proximity and the piercing manner in which he watched her were making her body heat rise. To say nothing of the fact that she was reading more into what he said than he probably intended. American women were *passionate.* What was up with that? A true statement, but did he have to let the word roll off his tongue so sensually? Or was that her imagination?

The waiter filled their glasses with sparkling water before leaving to give their orders to the chef. In his absence, Dominique turned to Hubert and asked, "How did you and Erica meet?"

Hubert secretly hoped she was asking that question

because she was jealous of his relationship with Erica. It would indicate she actually had some interest in him.

"Erica came to visit my family when she was five years old," Hubert began. "Her father, Eric, and my father met ten years before when my mother and father honeymooned in California. They wanted to investigate California's burgeoning wine industry on the sly. They were driving around in northern California, had a flat tire, and who would come along but Eric Bryant? He was not married to his wife, Simone, then."

Hubert smiled at Erica. "Would you like to pick up the story?"

"My dad is this big, tall guy. Anyway, when he stopped to help Sobran change the flat, Sobran was, at first, wary. He thought this guy might try to rob them, or something!"

Everyone laughed.

"But with the first word out of Sobran's mouth, my father knew he was French, and he started speaking to him in rapid French. My dad and mom are both fluent. My dad because his parents insisted he learn it in school. My mother is from Louisiana, where she grew up speaking it. In the course of their conversation, Sobran learned that my father's family owned one of those California wineries he was so interested in. My father invited him and Fabienne to dinner and they've been friends ever since."

"They wrote letters and phoned one another for years," Hubert put in. "My folks visited them soon after Erica and I were born. Then, when we were five, they came over here. By that time the Bryants had three kids, and the Lafons also had three. Erica and I didn't really become aware of each other until then, and when we met—"

"We hated each other on sight," Erica said, laughing.

"Yes, it was mutual hate," Hubert confirmed. "She was taller than I was at five."

"Girls sometimes grow faster," Erica countered.

"And she was better at sports, too. I made the mistake of showing her how to play soccer and she kicked my tail up and down the football field, my older brothers laughing at me all the way."

"So, what was the turning point?" Dominique asked. "When did you become friends?"

"Oh, it was near the close of our visit to France," Erica told her. "I loved to climb trees. Hubert and I were always competing with each other. He dared me to climb the tallest tree on their property. To prove I wasn't scared, I did. But when I looked down, I froze. Terrified, I clung to the tree's limb for dear life."

"Being the gentleman that I am," Hubert joked, "I climbed up and coaxed her down."

"To top off his gentlemanly act, though, he never mentioned it to my parents, who would have punished me severely. And I mean a whipping, not a talking-to. My parents didn't believe in sparing the rod. And we turned out just fine, thank you. Not a serial killer in the bunch! So, after Hubert's kindness, I fell in love with him and have only learned to love him more over the years." She smiled warmly at him.

Hubert blushed. "Don't get mushy on me, Bryant!"

Joshua felt a twinge of jealousy when she gifted Hubert with such a smile. However, he knew she and Hubert were merely friends. Hubert had told him as much earlier that evening. The two of them had not even entertained the thought of dating each other, fearing they'd ruin their friendship, which was fine with Joshua.

"I see you got started climbing things you couldn't get down from at an early age," Joshua said to Erica. He gave her another one of his enigmatic smiles.

Erica returned his smile. *Another clue*, she thought.

She was getting a headache trying to recall where she'd met him. Now she knew, or perhaps he was trying to mislead her, that he might have been around for one of her climbing mishaps. But that could have been any year up until her thirteenth, when she finally stopped climbing trees in favor of succumbing to adolescence and everything it entailed, including a keener interest in boys.

Over dessert, they discussed their travel plans.

"We're taking the train to Dijon in the morning, where we'll have a car waiting," Hubert said of his and Erica's plans. "Erica loves the train. I prefer driving and offered to drive to Paris to pick her up, to avoid a train trip, but she insisted on the train."

"It's the best way to get to Burgundy," Joshua agreed. "Of course there's not much to see in Dijon, but the drive to Beaune is scenic. I'm afraid I have to stay in Paris a couple more days."

"I'm returning to Beaune in the morning," Dominique said. She had regained her calm over dinner and was in a reflective mood. She kept glancing at Hubert as if she were seeing him in a whole new light. "Father and Mother will expect me to travel with them. I would prefer the train."

When the check came, Joshua signed for it.

"Thank you for a delicious meal," Erica said.

"It was my pleasure," Joshua told her, his gaze holding hers.

"Dominique and I would like to thank you, too," Hubert joked. He waved his hand in front of Joshua's eyes. "If you could tear your eyes away from Erica for a moment."

"Why?" Joshua asked. "I see you two all the time."

His comment only made Erica's smile widen.

"Don't you dare forget to phone me," Joshua told her. "I could come take you for a drive on Sunday? We'll visit some of the sights."

"It's a date," Erica said.

Joshua smiled indulgently.

Then he finally regarded Hubert and Dominique. "Hubert, old buddy, would you be a gentleman and see that Dominique gets to her hotel safely? I'd like to escort Erica to her hotel, if it's all right with her?"

"It is," Erica said.

Hubert leaned close to Erica and whispered, "I thought you didn't want to be alone with him."

"I changed my mind," Erica said.

"Don't invite him in," Hubert warned.

"What is he, a vampire?"

Joshua laughed. "You two can't whisper to save your lives."

"You are far too overprotective," Dominique said to Hubert. "Erica can take care of herself. I, on the other hand, will have to guard against *your* considerable charms."

It was settled. Hubert was suddenly eager to get a cab and see that his lady fair arrived at her hotel.

The couples parted in front of the restaurant.

Erica and Joshua sat a couple of feet apart in a late-model taxi. They were turned toward each other, both of them acutely aware of the tenuous thread that held them together this early in their acquaintance. Neither of them wanted to make a misstep and spoil what could very well be the greatest love affair of their lives. They intuitively felt the ripe potential of something truly wonderful happening between them.

Erica broke the silence with, "Are you my Peter Pan? Will you take me on an adventure I'll never forget?"

"Come over here and find out," Joshua challenged her.

So she did.

He pulled her firmly into his embrace and Erica wrapped her arms around his neck as she tilted her chin upward, offering him her mouth. Joshua took it.

Their kisses were salty and sweet, tasting somewhat like the chocolate mousse they'd had for dessert. At first it was a test of how well they fit together. Tentative touches that only fanned the flames. Exhalations mingling. Bodies finding the right position. Ah, *yes*, there it was. Rhythm found. A series of soft sighs, tongues meeting in a sensual dance of pure pleasure. Bodies yearning for more closeness.

When they were able to draw apart, their breathing ragged from the intensity of the kiss, Joshua knew one thing: he was done waiting. She was here now and he would do everything within his power to make her his.

Erica knew that when they'd met before, they certainly hadn't kissed. His kiss was an experience she would never have forgotten.

Chapter Three

The train trip to Burgundy took under two hours. Erica sat in the forward-facing seat while Hubert sat across from her, not at all interested in the passing scenery.

"You are far too jaded where your country's concerned," she told him.

Hubert yawned. "When you've seen one cow, you've seen them all."

Erica, on the other hand, delighted in the pastoral countryside. Nature's greenery was evident all around them: rolling fields of sunflowers, wine-producing slopes covered with vines painstakingly trained to grow uniformly on a stake. Gone were the days of the arbors that grew naturally. Growing grapes was a science some knew better than others. Burgundy winemakers liked to credit *terroir*, or the coming together of the climate, the soil, and the landscape, with their success. They claimed that there was no place in Burgundy for trends, and they were loath to change. Why try to fix what wasn't broken? Theirs was a formula that had worked for hundreds of years.

Erica agreed with that way of thinking in some instances. Her family, too, made wine the Old World way. As little mechanization and fertilization as possible was used in the process. Winegrowers spend most of their time tending the vines, because good wine begins with good grapes.

"Does Sobran still get up at five every morning to work in the vineyards?" Erica asked. She crossed her jeans-clad legs, slid her sunglasses down to look at Hubert.

He was wearing jeans this morning, too. And his eyes were bloodshot. Erica wanted to ask him how late he and Dominique had stayed out last night, but refrained from doing so. He'd tell her, eventually.

Hubert raked a hand through his curly hair and smiled at her. "Sobran Lafon will probably be getting up at five o'clock to tend the vines when he's a *hundred* and five."

"That's tradition for you," Erica said with admiration.

"That's obsession for you," Hubert countered. "Where are the vines going? They'll still be there at seven."

"It's you youngsters' lackadaisical attitude that scares your father's generation," Erica joked. "They're afraid once they're gone, you all are going to let the traditions and their tried-and-true methods of making good wine go down the drain."

"We love this land as much as they do. We simply believe in working smart, not hard," Hubert explained. "And whether they like it or not, things are changing. It used to be that winegrowers sold their wine to *negociants*, or merchants, who then finished the wine, bottled it, and sold it worldwide. Today, we're bottling our own wines and distributing them worldwide ourselves. The old ones had to resign themselves to that. They will get used to other necessary changes."

Erica was aware of what he was talking about. Her family had also used a middleman in the past. Today, they sold directly to distributors. The ability to communicate on a wider scale had made the world smaller in a sense. They shipped wines to customers in all corners of the world.

Erica sighed wistfully. "Still, for me, coming here is like going back in time. The sense of timelessness is comforting. California is so fast compared to the Cote d' Or."

The Cote d' Or, the slope of gold, was the region in Burgundy they were passing through. Beaune, Hubert's hometown, was considered the capital of Burgundy wines and perhaps the most beautiful town in Burgundy. Dijon, where the train was heading, was at the top of the Cote d' Or. They would have to drive farther south to reach Beaune.

"You are a born romantic," Hubert said with a smirk.

"So are you," Erica replied. "You're smitten with Dominique. Why haven't you two ever gotten together?"

A pained expression screwed up Hubert's handsome features. "Am I so obvious?"

"Yes." Erica didn't lie to him. "I couldn't miss it. I'm sure she knows. What's the problem?"

"The problem is, Dominique is so intent on confounding her father's plans for her she's cutting off her nose to spite her face. Is that the correct saying?"

"Yes. She's hurting herself with her actions more than she's hurting her intended victim, Etienne."

"Exactly!" he cried. "I would settle down if Dominique would only recognize how perfect we are for each other."

Erica shook her head sadly. "Romeo and Juliet."

"What?"

"You and Dominique. Your families don't get along."

"Oh, that," Hubert said, dismissing the whole idea. "My father never talks about the feud. I'm sure it's all forgotten. After all, his father and Etienne's father are both dead now."

"I hope you're right," Erica said. "You know how you Burgundians are about your traditions."

Hubert grimaced. "Can we stop talking about the past?" He leaned forward in his seat. "What I want to know is, did you kiss him?"

Erica laughed shortly. "Did you kiss *her*?"

"Yes," Hubert said softly, a dreamy smile on his face.

"Yes," Erica replied. There was an equally dreamy expression on her face as she sighed. "We're a couple of romantic fools."

"Yes, we are," Hubert agreed.

Jean-Marc Lafon, Hubert's older brother by two years, met them at the train station. He and Hubert were the only siblings still at home. Their older brother, Luc, owned a winery in Stellenbosch, South Africa, a region becoming known for its red wines.

While Hubert struggled with Erica's bags, Jean-Marc swept her into his arms for a warm hug. He wore his dark hair cut close to his head, and he had a short beard that was kept the length of a day's growth. Tall for a Frenchman, he stood nearly six feet. Muscular arms flexed as he effortlessly lifted her from the station platform.

"*Mon Dieu*, you become more beautiful with each passing year," he said sincerely. "When are you going to marry me and put me out of my misery?"

"If she married you, you'd really be miserable then," Hubert joked.

"Was anybody talking to you?" Erica asked. She kissed Jean-Marc's cheeks.

Afterward, she and Jean-Marc clasped hands and he led her to the waiting Jaguar.

Loaded down with Erica's luggage, Hubert followed slowly. "I could use a little help."

Jean-Marc regrettably let go of Erica's hand to lend assistance. He took the largest suitcase and grabbed Erica's hand with the other one. Beaming down at her, he said, "*Mere* cannot wait to have another woman in the house. You should have seen how she was bustling about the kitchen, preparing lunch for you. She's making your favorite, *boeuf Bourguignon*."

"Mmm," Erica moaned. "Nobody makes beef stew like Fabienne." She glanced back at Hubert. "Hurry up!"

The Chateau de Lafon was built in the sixteenth century. It sat in the middle of three hundred acres and was a few kilometers on the outskirts of Beaune. The white stone it was made of had turned gray over the years, and the roof was a darker shade of gray. Turrets hugged all four corners of the main house, and several smaller structures surrounded it: a gatehouse, a dovecote, and a kennel. Sobran raised pigeons, and Fabienne was very fond of dogs.

Jean-Marc expertly drove the Jaguar around the curves that led to their house on the hill. A clay-covered half-mile stretch of road, made smooth from so many vehicles traversing it, led up to the chateau. On either side of it, the rolling landscape was neatly mown and tall, spindly trees stood like sentinels heralding their arrival.

When Jean-Marc stopped the car a few feet from the front entrance, two beautiful spaniels bounded down the steps to greet them, followed by Fabienne, looking cool and collected in a chic sleeveless white blouse and a pair of slim black pants. On her small feet were black leather flats that looked like they'd been inspired by ballet slippers.

At fifty-seven, she was still trim from daily walks with the dogs and her various duties around the house. Her dark brown hair had silver streaks in it and was cut in a sleek bob that was tapered at the nape of her neck.

Dancing brown eyes welcomed Erica as she opened her arms to her. "*Mon petite*, I am so happy you have come to pay us a visit."

Erica allowed herself to be enveloped by Fabienne's arms as expensive French perfume wafted around them. Fabienne was only five-two, so Erica had to bend down to receive her embrace.

"Thank you, Fabienne. I'm thrilled to be here. I have missed you all so much!"

There were tears in Fabienne's eyes when she straightened up to regard Erica. "I was just talking with your *maman* this morning." She placed her arm about Erica's waist and directed her toward the house as she continued. Pausing at the first step, she turned to look at her sons. "Come on, come on, your father will be in from the vineyards soon and we will sit down to lunch."

Her attention again fully on Erica, she said, "Your mother and I were just talking this morning, reminiscing, catching up. Between us, we have six children. I told her she was the lucky one, she has a daughter. And she said that for the next three months I should consider you a loaner." She laughed delightedly. "So, young lady, you are not a guest in this house, you are our daughter."

"That can't be!" Jean-Marc jokingly lamented. "If she's my sister, I can't marry her."

"Wouldn't that be wonderful?" Fabienne enthused. "A merging of the Bryants and the Lafons: the best wine-making families in the world."

"Don't you think you're being a tad grandiose?" said a masculine voice from behind them. "*Two* of the best, perhaps."

They all turned to smile at Sobran, who stood there in his work clothes and work boots, his hat in his hand. He came and hugged Erica, after which he kissed both her cheeks. "Welcome. I plan to work you as hard as I work any of the other men."

"I wouldn't expect anything less," Erica told him.

Sobran laughed, his suntanned face crinkling around the mouth and eyes. He was Erica's height, and solidly built. Fifty-two years working in the vineyards must have been good for him, because he was energetic and had rarely been sick a day of his life.

Erica figured there must be something to the adage *do what you love and love what you do*, because Sobran was a prime example of someone who obviously adored what he did for a living.

They all continued inside.

"I don't have to ask how your parents are, because we spoke with them this morning, and I know they're fine. But how are you, my dear? How was your trip? Did Hubert pick you up on time at the airport? And did you attend Etienne Roumier's tasting? Were you able to keep his wine down?"

Erica laughed at his comment about Etienne Roumier's wines. "Yes, I was able to keep his wine down, although I wasn't there long before he made the announcement about his replacement. Hubert and I left soon afterward."

"Ah yes," Sobran said. "Joshua Knight. A good man. Etienne was lucky to hire him right out of school." His brows rose, as though he'd just thought of something. "He went to the same school you did. He and Christian were in the same graduating class. And then Christian went skiing in Montreux and had that terrible accident." He gently shuddered, the thought of losing a son horrifying to him.

In the foyer, Fabienne slipped into command mode as the mistress of the house.

"Hubert, put Erica's things in the big corner room. She'll be comfortable there, and she'll get the southern exposure in the mornings. Everyone else: wash up for lunch. The meal will be on the table in five minutes."

"I'll help," Erica immediately offered. Like she did with her mother, she enjoyed being with Fabienne in her element, the kitchen. Both her mother, Simone, and Fabienne were excellent cooks. Simone was a trained chef, while Fabienne simply picked up her skills from her mother and grandmother.

Fabienne accepted her offer and the two of them headed to the kitchen while the men went upstairs.

The house was furnished with antiques that had been passed down from one generation to the next. Wooden floors were polished to a high luster. While the house was huge, it was also homey and in some respects reminded Erica of a large farmhouse. There were few luxury items, simply good, solid furnishings, the wood gleaming with the patina of age, and upholstered in the French Provencal style.

The kitchen, however, was a study in modern efficiency. Big, with dark red tiles on the floor, the cabinets in a light colored wood with glass insets. The counter surfaces also consisted of tiles, but in white instead of red, and Fabienne had every conceivable modern appliance including a Sub Zero side-by-side refrigerator/freezer any restaurant would have been proud to have in its kitchen.

Copper pots hung on the wall next to the stove. No pots hanging from the ceiling for Fabienne. Small of stature, she would have had to call someone every time she needed a saucepan.

Erica went to the sink to wash up. Drying her hands on a paper towel, she watched Fabienne stir the *boeuf Bourguignon*. "May I ask you a question, Fabienne?"

Fabienne looked up at her and smiled. "Anything you wish."

"Has a woman ever headed a Burgundy winery?"

Fabienne paused a moment, thinking. "I've heard of two women who purchased wineries in Burgundy and are doing quite well. One was a woman in her thirties whose family makes wine in Bordeaux. The other is an Englishwoman in her late fifties. I've met her, a charming woman."

"But no homegrown women?"

Fabienne frowned. "No, and that doesn't sit well with me, either!" She lowered her voice conspiratorially. "I know what you're getting at. My baby boy tells me everything. It's Dominique Roumier, am I right?"

"Yes," Erica said. "She went to dinner with us last night, and I liked her. She wasn't very friendly at first, but she grew on me."

Fabienne laughed softly. "Yes, that's Dominique. She's always been a complicated child."

"Then you know her well?"

"Her mother and I grew up in the same village near here. Berenice Leroux-Roumier. We meet for lunch at least once a month."

"But I thought your families were on the outs."

"What the husbands don't know won't hurt them," Fabienne said. "Berenice and I think it's a silly feud. Etienne's mother was in love with both his father and Sobran's father. She chose Etienne's father. The two men were best of friends before she came along, and apparently they could no longer be friends once she chose one of them over the other. Personally, I think things turned out splendidly. I adored Sobran's mother, Chantal. She was a lovely, lovely woman."

The men came into the room, holding a loud conversation in French. Hubert walked up to his mother, took the spoon from her hand, and licked the gravy off it. "*C'est délicieux, Mere.* We're famished!"

Fabienne took the wooden spoon from him and put it in the sink. "Off you go to the cellar to get two bottles of wine."

Hubert immediately went to do her bidding, calling out over his shoulder, "A man could starve around here."

Sobran and Jean-Marc took seats around the large kitchen table that Fabienne had set earlier. She met Erica's eyes. "We'll continue this conversation later. Would you get the bread out of the oven and put it in that basket?" she asked, pointing to a basket on the counter next to the stove with a clean red-and-white-checked cotton towel in it. "Then get the butter from the refrigerator. It's in the top shelf of the door."

By the midday hour they were all seated around the table with their heads bowed.

"Father, thank you for this bounty from your earth. Thank you for giving us such a beautiful world to play in. And thank you for allowing our daughter, Erica, to arrive safely. Amen," Sobran prayed.

Erica had to surreptitiously wipe tears away with her cloth napkin.

In Paris, Joshua was having lunch at a sidewalk café. His companion was Lucy Harmon, an American fashion model whom he'd been dating off and on for the past six months. Lucy was five-eleven and from Texas. A sweet girl whose looks had propelled her to the top of her field almost in spite of herself. She was so humble she thought her success was the result of sheer luck. Anyone looking at her knew that it was because she had that certain *je ne sais quoi* that made her stand out in a crowd. The modeling world grabbed her and ran with her.

She was picking at the food on her plate. She'd been unusually quiet during the entire meal. She had also seemed unable to hold his gaze for any length of time.

Joshua ate with gusto, as always. After finishing, he placed his fork on the plate and cleared his throat. "Lucy, I need to speak with you about us."

Lucy raised her eyes to his. She smiled tremulously. "Yeah, I think we do need to talk. I, um . . ."

"It's not working out between us," Joshua said, guessing that's what she was trying to say to him.

She sighed sadly. "I'm sorry, Joshua. It's just that you're rarely in Paris, and you never invite me to Beaune for visits. You say you're too busy with work. And, well, I've met someone."

Joshua couldn't even muster a modicum of regret at her announcement. All he felt was relief. He liked Lucy, and she was fun to be with. She had an enthusiasm for life that had attracted him at first. But then he realized that at twenty-three, she was too young for him. For the past three months, he'd been trying to find a way to let her down easy. Now she was giving *him* the heave-ho.

He smiled at her. "That's great, Lucy. I wish you all kinds of happiness with your new boyfriend."

Lucy narrowed her eyes at him. "You're taking it pretty well. You've met someone too, haven't you?"

Joshua nodded. "Yeah."

Lucy breathed a sigh of relief. "I'm glad, because I didn't want to hurt you, Josh. You're a really great guy when you're around. Just out of curiosity, is she another model?"

"No, she's in the wine industry."

"A sister in the wine industry?" The few people in the wine business that Joshua had introduced Lucy to were invariably French and not of African heritage. She was genuinely surprised.

"Yes, she's a sister, and she's from California. She'll be in France only a few months. And what does your new paramour do for a living?"

"Oh, he's a musician," Lucy said nonchalantly.

Joshua smiled. Models and musicians were usually matches made in hell. They looked glamorous together but the model usually got the short end of the stick in the relationship.

"Be careful," he said. "Don't do anything to shock your mama in Houston."

"Don't worry," Lucy said. "On the inside, I'm still that girl from the projects. He ain't gonna play me!"

"All right then," Joshua said, satisfied. "Dessert?"

"Why not? Order me a strawberry tart."

Chapter Four

I will never complain about getting up early again, Erica silently vowed as she trudged through the vineyards alongside Sobran at five fifteen the next morning.

The sun had barely kissed the sky. The air was chilly. She was dressed similar to Sobran, pants, long-sleeve shirt with a jacket over it, and work boots whose tops came up to her knees.

She had to admit, the purpling sky was gorgeous this time of morning, and the scent on the air was loamy with a hint of ozone. She'd grown up on that smell, and it was very pleasant to her.

"The land you're going to grow your grapes on," Sobran asked, "is it high or low?"

"High," Erica answered. "And it gets more cool days than warm days."

"Excellent," Sobran told her. "I don't suppose, in California, you have to worry as much about hail." He stopped walking and sniffed the air.

Erica laughed softly. "No, sir, although we can occasionally get some violent rainstorms." Erica stopped too, her nose upturned. The humidity in the air portended rain.

"Rain is good for the grapes," Sobran said. "But not too much rain. We're going to get some this afternoon."

Erica congratulated herself. She wasn't Eric Bryant's daughter for nothing.

They walked on.

"A lot of people claim that we grow good grapes here because of the happenstance of our location," Sobran said. "Burgundy gets a lot of bad weather. But it's what we do in combination with the rain, the cold and the heat that helps us grow good grapes. It's by the grace of God that we have good crops from year to year. That's why some winemakers stockpile during good years. They are not at all certain they will have another one." He sounded wistful. Then he brightened, and said, "I'm going to show you the proper way to prune a pinot noir vine today!"

Erica felt in her coat pocket for the gloves Fabienne had pressed into her hand before they'd left the chateau. Sobran must have mentioned his intentions to his wife.

He stopped at a group of vines and withdrew a large pair of pruning shears from the deep pocket of his coat. Erica noticed that he was not donning gloves. His hands had toughened from years of doing this.

The sun had risen enough so that there was now enough light to see by. The leaves of the vines were wet with dew. Sobran grabbed hold of a small bunch of grapes that were clustered extremely close together. "You see how some of the tiny ones are hemmed in by the larger grapes?"

"Mmm-hmm," Erica answered, her eyes on his hands.

He snipped away the larger grapes that were impeding the growth of the smaller ones.

To a novice, it might appear that he was cutting away the wrong grapes, that he should sacrifice the smaller, ones instead. Erica understood his reasoning, though. Her father pruned in the same fashion.

"It is months before the harvest," she said. "And the smaller grapes will grow, while the larger ones you cut off will enrich the soil beneath the vines."

"Your father taught you well," Sobran said, obviously impressed. He handed her the pruning shears. "Now you do some while I start on the second row."

Erica took the shears and began working.

At around seven, other workers began appearing in the vineyards, all with the objective of pruning the vines. Erica was introduced all around, and soon everyone fell into an age-old rhythm that farm workers had followed aeons ago.

They chatted while they worked, and the sun was high in the sky before Sobran said, "*Le dejeuner?*" It was lunchtime.

Dominique carefully siphoned wine from a cask using a long glass tube called a wine thief. She emptied the wine into a glass, set the wine thief aside, and tilted the wine in the glass this way and that way, observing the opaque liquid, heavy with sediments.

Before the wine would be put into bottles it would be strained first for clarification and removal of as much of the sediments as possible. No matter how well you strained it, some of the sediments remained.

As she brought the wineglass to her lips a sharp voice cried, "What is the meaning of this, Dominique!"

Dominique turned to find her father standing with the aid of a cane near the entrance to the cellars. He continued walking toward her. "Henri told me you had taken over the testing. I did not authorize you to do this. You have no right to be here!"

Dominique suddenly felt like a child caught with her

hand in the cookie jar. She climbed down the short ladder that had given her the extra height she'd needed in order to reach the casks on the upper level. Gathering her nerve, she looked her father straight in the eyes. "I have every right to be here. I am your daughter! Would you have me look a fool when in conversation with your business associates? I must learn all I can about the business. I do not wish to embarrass you in public!"

She'd shrewdly appealed to his vanity.

Etienne pulled himself to his full height of five-six. He nevertheless had to lean on the cane, which put him in a foul mood. He hated having to bow to his body's limitations. "Dominique, I had no idea you felt this way." He looked astonished.

Dominique let out a grateful sigh. She had been holding her breath. "I have a confession to make, Father. I have been secretly learning the business because I had hoped that you would allow me to take a small part in running it. I'm more than pleased you have chosen Joshua to step in your shoes. However, I do believe that someone in the family should *also* take an interest in the running of the business."

Etienne was silent as he looked into her eyes trying, perhaps, to discern if she was sincere. Dominique knew how he felt about women taking part in the business. They had argued about it on numerous occasions. He'd tried to get her to learn enough about making wine, and of their heritage, in order to pass on the knowledge to her children (whenever she settled down to have any!). But she'd refused on the grounds that if she were not good enough to work with him, she didn't want to know anything about their so-called heritage. She had been obstinate and willful.

He sighed deeply. It must have been his illness that had made her soften toward the idea of learning about their heritage.

He smiled at her. "Dominique, are you afraid your

old man is going to die soon, and that's why you've suddenly taken an interest in the family business? Because I am not going anywhere for a while, hopefully! I'm retiring now in order to spend more time with you and your mother. I promised her that we would spend our golden years together, not in the pursuit of more wealth. We are already rich enough never to have to work another day in our lives. Now we should enjoy our hard work. Joshua will make certain the business continues to prosper."

"No," Dominique objected. She closed the distance between them, the wineglass still in her hand. She held it up so that the light filtered through it. Looking at it, she said, "In this glass is the culmination of all your hard work, Father. And I'm proud of you. I don't think I've shown that enough in the past. Maybe your illness had something to do with it. I don't want to lose you. Ever."

She set the glass atop a nearby barrel and went to embrace her father.

Etienne hugged her tightly. "Okay, okay. Learn all you want. Tell Joshua I said you have access to everything."

Dominique kissed his cheek. "Thank you, Father!"

In the shadows of the cellars, someone listened and took note of everything that was being said. Over the years hate had festered in his heart, and now he could no longer stand aside while Etienne Roumier reaped all of the rewards. Where was Roumier's sense of honor? No man was an island. Like many other rich men, Roumier had gotten where he was by treading across the backs of those he'd callously used and tossed aside.

The listener watched as Etienne graciously accepted kisses from his adoring daughter. *You will get what you deserve*, he thought, directing his anger at Etienne.

After lunch, Erica ran into Hubert on the landing as they were both heading to their bedrooms. She had removed her sweater and now wore only dark pants, a long-sleeve shirt, and boots. Hubert wore a gray T-shirt, a pair of well-worn jeans, and a pair of work boots.

"Hubert, is there an electronics store nearby where I can buy a cell phone? I didn't bring mine, since my carrier doesn't operate over here."

"You don't need to buy a cell phone," Hubert said. "You're only here for three months. You can use mine."

"You don't mind?" Erica asked. "What about your girlfriends?"

"What girlfriends? I'm too busy obsessing over Dominique to think about any other women."

"You poor baby," Erica sympathized.

"Yeah, I've got it bad," Hubert said. "And I can't talk to anyone about it except you and *Mere*. If I talked to Jean-Marc, he'd go straight to *Pere* with the news. I don't want *Pere* to know."

He grinned suddenly, completely transforming his face from solemn to jovial. "You want a phone so you can speak with Joshua privately, don't you? You can't make calls to the States with it."

"Okay, so you figured it out," Erica said. "Listen, love-boy—"

"Love-boy!" Hubert cried indignantly.

"You're in love, hence, *love-boy*," Erica explained. "Don't worry, I'm not going to call you that in public. It'll be between you and me, but yes, I'm having fun at your expense. You're the one who told me you'd never fall in love. I come to France and find out that you're pining after the enemy's daughter. This is rich!"

"Keep that up and you won't get the phone," Hubert warned. He started walking in the direction of his bedroom.

Erica followed. "Oh, don't get upset, love-boy, I'm happy for you!"

Hubert opened his bedroom door and allowed her to precede him inside. He closed the door behind them.

"If I'm love-boy, I suppose that makes you horny-girl. Because you're definitely not in love with Joshua, you're just trying to 'get some.' "

"I think you watch too much American TV," Erica said as she plopped down on his bed. Hubert's bedroom was like a small apartment. It had its own bathroom, a splendid view of the grounds, and every electronic device known to man.

"I never knew you were such a techie," Erica said, looking at all the digital equipment, cameras, and computers. "What do you need with two computers?"

"One is personal. The other is exclusively for the business. I create and maintain our Web site."

"Oh, you did that? Great job!"

"Thanks." Hubert walked over to his desk and picked up his cell phone. He reached in the desk to retrieve the charger. "Listen, no dirty language. The phone company keeps records of cell phone conversations."

Erica laughed as she took the phone and charger from him. "You're kidding, right?"

He shook his head. "'Fraid not. I learned that from one of my friends who's a hacker."

"We have no privacy anymore!"

"We never did," Hubert said cynically.

Erica smiled at him. "I hope Dominique comes to her senses about you soon, love-boy. You're becoming melancholy."

She pecked him on the cheek and hurried out of the room. "Thanks for the phone!"

In the privacy of her own room, she sat in a chair in an area she'd dubbed the reading corner because in it was a comfortable overstuffed chair with a floor lamp right beside it.

Taking Joshua's card from the pocket of her shirt where she'd put it this morning with the intention of finding an opportunity to call him, she dialed his number. Today was Wednesday. He'd said something about taking her for a drive on Sunday, but it wouldn't hurt to phone him and give him a number where she could be reached, just in case.

The number rang three times, her trepidation mounting with each ring. Why was it such a nerve-racking thing to phone a man you were eager to get to know? There were so many opportunities at the beginning of a relationship to make a fool of yourself. You wanted to make a good impression. But sometimes, you failed.

She was almost relieved when his voicemail kicked in. After she listened to the recording in French of how to leave a message, she pressed the appropriate button and started talking. "Hi, Joshua, this is Erica. As you know, I'm staying with the Lafons. Hubert was kind enough to loan me his cell phone while I'm here. So that's his number on your caller ID. I'm the one you'll reach when you dial it, though. The ball's in your court now."

Once she was finished, she rose, clipped the phone to her belt, and trudged downstairs to find out what Sobran had planned for her afternoon. She felt energized and raring to go!

Joshua didn't listen to his messages until midafternoon. He had just concluded a meeting with Roumier's American distributor, James Arensen, and was on the way back to his hotel in order to pick up his bags, which were already packed in preparation for his train trip to Burgundy later that afternoon. He sat in the back of a cab and listened to his messages.

When he got to Erica's, he immediately recognized her voice. Her introduction had been totally unnecessary. He thought it was sweet nonetheless. He smiled, hearing her voice as the message played into his ear.

Nimble fingers quickly dialed the number she'd given him.

Miles away, Erica was once again pruning vines. When her cell phone rang, several workers paused to look down at their own cell phones clipped to their belts before resuming their snipping.

The sun shone brightly, but the temperature was only in the sixties, so she hadn't worked up much of a sweat. Her face had a glow to it anyway when she heard Joshua's voice on the other end of the line.

"Hello, Wendy, what are you up to?"

"I'm pruning vines," she answered, smiling.

"They've got you hard at work already?"

"And I'm loving every minute of it!"

He laughed softly. "What are you going to do after your shift ends?"

"Go home and luxuriate in a tub of hot water."

"And after that?"

"A quiet evening at home."

"I live seven miles from the Lafons. I could pick you up and we could go for a stroll in the town square. Stop at a café for a coffee. Take a ride with the top down. There's supposed to be a full moon tonight."

"All the more reason to stay in tonight," Erica joked.

"But you won't." He sounded confident.

"No, I won't," she said.

"*À bientôt.*"

"All right, I'll see you later," Erica said huskily.

When she hung up several of the men and women looked at her knowingly and others made hooting noises as if they'd understood her conversation perfectly and were good-naturedly ribbing her. One young man kissed the top of his hand, making sound effects as if two lovers were locked in an embrace.

Erica joined in the laughter. It was good to be accepted as one of them.

Chapter Five

The sky opened up at around four in the afternoon and drenched everyone working in the vineyards. Used to inclement weather, they quickly donned their raincoats and hats and walked back down the hill to the chateau. Erica walked with Sobran, who told the others, "Go home, we're not going to get anything else done today."

To Erica, he said, "If you work that hard every day I might not send you back to your father once your time's up here."

Erica laughed. "I love it here, Sobran. The sun, the easy camaraderie of the people, even the rain. I'm having a ball!"

"Wait until the harvest," Sobran said. "*Then* tell me that!"

They chatted during the walk back to the chateau. As soon as they stepped onto the chateau's back patio, Fabienne came out of the kitchen and greeted them.

"How was your first day, Erica?" she asked. She and Sobran briefly kissed.

"Apparently, she thought she was at a day spa instead of getting blisters on her hands," Sobran joked. He had a mischievous gleam in his eyes when he added, "I think it must have something to do with the mysterious phone call she received this afternoon."

"Phone call?" Fabienne asked as she ushered the two of them inside. "In the vineyards?"

"Darling," Sobran informed her, "half of the workers have cell phones. What did we do before the advent of the cellular phone? I suppose people had to keep phoning until they got us."

"He doesn't like electronics," Fabienne said as an aside to Erica. "The phone call wasn't from your parents, was it? Everything's all right at home?"

Erica told them about her plans to go out with Joshua later that evening.

Fabienne seemed delighted. She moved about the kitchen, preparing cold drinks for Erica and Sobran. "I am surprised you and Joshua haven't met before now. He and Hubert have been friends for about four years. He's visited several times."

Erica's eyebrows rose in surprise. Seeing her expression, Sobran said, "What? You don't think we can be civil to the enemy?"

"Sobran!" Fabienne cried. "Don't joke like that. You'll have Erica thinking we don't trust Joshua, when that isn't true."

Sobran laughed shortly and sat down at the kitchen table, his hands wrapped around the glass of lemonade Fabienne had given him. "Well, he does work for the enemy."

"You and Etienne haven't been in the same room together in ages. How can you consider him the enemy when you don't even know him? That silly argument between your father and his happened before you were born," Fabienne said passionately.

Sobran rose and went to his wife, his love for her shining in his eyes. "Do not get yourself upset, my dear,

I was kidding! I don't know about Etienne, but I don't care about an old feud! It just amuses me to poke fun at him now and again. He's so staid, so aristocratic. He thinks his winery is the best in the Cote d'Or."

"Don't you think yours is the best?" Fabienne asked.

"With good reason!" Sobran said seriously.

Fabienne threw her head back in laughter as she hugged her husband. "You are as conceited as he is." She wiped tears from the corners of her eyes. Looking up into Sobran's eyes, she asked, "What if I told you our son is in love with his daughter?"

Sobran's mouth fell open in astonishment. "What?"

"Hubert is in love with Dominique Roumier," Fabienne said, pronouncing each word with care. She wanted to be sure her husband heard her correctly.

"It's about time the boy picked one woman instead of chasing every female who crosses his path."

"I'm glad you feel that way, Father, because I'm going to ask Dominique to marry me," Hubert said from the doorway.

Erica's heartbeat accelerated at the tone of his voice. Her friend had decided he would no longer be patient where Dominique was concerned. He meant war!

She didn't know how long he'd been standing there, because her attention had been riveted on Fabienne and Sobran and their conversation. But he had her full attention now as he walked into the kitchen and stood before his parents. "She might turn me down, but I don't think so. I've loved her a long time. Ever since I was seventeen. But, of course, I was too young and scared to say anything to her about my feelings then. I'm not now, and I'm going to tell her exactly how I feel, and *have* felt, for all these years."

Erica suddenly felt as if she should give them privacy, and she rose to leave the room, only to be called back by Hubert.

He went to her and pulled her into his arms. "Where are you going? You're the one I have to thank for helping me make up my mind to tell Dominique how I feel."

Erica's eyes widened in horror. "Me?"

"Calling me love-boy? Asking what's taken me so long to ask her out?" Hubert said, grinning. "You inspired me, little sister."

He happily rocked her in his arms, while Erica prayed that all would go well between him and Dominique. She would hate to have been the one to instigate all of this only to see it blow up in his face! What had she gotten herself mixed up in?

"Whoa, love-boy, don't count your chickens before they hatch. First, see if the lady is amenable to spending the rest of her life with you. Then you can thank me. Make me the godmother of your first child. Build a monument to me, for all I care!"

Hubert laughed. "I'm way ahead of you. I'm seeing her tonight."

"*All* of my children are going out tonight?" Fabienne asked. "Jean-Marc told me this morning he'll be having dinner at Sophie's. Then, Erica told us she's going out with Joshua. Now you!" She looked at her husband. "Looks like we're going to have the house to ourselves tonight."

Sobran pulled her close to his side. "The better to have my way with you, my dear."

It was dusk when Joshua drove onto the stretch of road leading to the Chateau de Lafon. He knew the way well, since he'd been a guest in the Lafons' home on numerous occasions. But he never imagined he'd be coming here to pick up a date.

The weather had turned cooler following the afternoon showers, and he'd wisely put the top up on the Mercedes. As he got out of the car and walked up to the portico, his black wing tips making a crunching sound on the gravel in the driveway, he inhaled deeply then exhaled. He didn't know why he was nervous. She was only a woman.

He ran a hand across his damp forehead and rubbed his hands together. He stood there, a tall man dressed in a dark blue suit with a white silk shirt open at the collar, his hair neatly cut, and a day-old beard he'd trimmed with clippers before coming over, smelling of soap and water and cologne that were easy on a woman's olfactory senses.

He felt like that boy she'd known instead of the man he'd become.

He stood awhile longer on the portico until he had decided that there was nothing to be nervous about. He had done nothing wrong in the past. He had nothing to be ashamed of except, perhaps, being overly fond of a girl who was much too young for him then. Seven years separated them. Those seven years that had seemed so insurmountable then, posed no problem now.

He used the old-fashioned knocker.

A few seconds later, Sobran came to the door attired for dinner. Joshua remembered that the Lafons always dressed for dinner. Some customs were good to keep.

"*Bonsoir,* Joshua," said Sobran pleasantly.

"*Bonsoir,* M. Lafon," Joshua said respectfully.

"Erica is upstairs," Sobran told him. He stepped aside to allow Joshua to enter.

"Won't you join me and Fabienne for a drink while you wait?"

"That's very kind of you," Joshua said.

Sobran closed the door, and with the finality of the thud of the door closing behind them, so went the formality that had stood between them. He had known Joshua for four years, but he had known Erica all her life. Joshua might be in Erica's life for only a short while, or he could be a permanent fixture. Wherever their relationship went, Sobran needed Joshua to know that Erica's welfare was of utmost importance to him and his family.

They stood in the foyer facing one another. "Joshua, I don't know if Erica told you that our families have been friends for many years."

"Yes, sir, she told me."

"I held her in my arms when she was an infant. She and Hubert were born the same year. We visited her family in California that year. We stayed more than a month in their home and we were like one big, happy family. Fabienne and Simone, Erica's mother, are like sisters they are so close. We would feel somehow to blame if Erica came to visit us and got her heart broken."

Joshua smiled. He'd seen it coming. Sobran Lafon was a man who took his responsibilities seriously, especially when it came to family and longtime friendships. What Sobran didn't know was, so did he. Loyalty was second nature to him, and it had always been. Though he'd come from a poor family, they were good people, solid people who taught him honor and self-worth in the face of adversity.

"I would never do anything to hurt Erica," he told Sobran, his voice even.

Sobran believed him. "I simply wanted you to know how I felt."

"And I thank you for telling me," Joshua said sincerely. "But Erica will probably break my heart before I'd ever break hers."

She'll break it if she doesn't remember me, he thought.

"Shall we?" Sobran said, leading the way to the library where Fabienne waited.

Fabienne was not in the least bit formal with Joshua when she saw him. She'd liked him since the first time they'd met. In his dark eyes she saw a very sweet soul who had worked his way to the top of his field with fierce determination. She knew there was an inspiring story in his background, but dared not press him for it.

She went to him and kissed both his cheeks. "Good to see you, Joshua. It's been too long since your last visit."

"It's always a pleasure," Joshua said, smiling warmly at her. Fabienne possessed the kind of charm that put you at ease the moment you found yourself in her presence. He had never felt anything but welcome when he came to her home.

Fabienne gestured to the couch. "Won't you sit down?"

Sobran was at the bar. "What can I get for you?"

"A glass of whatever you have uncorked will do nicely," Joshua said.

Sobran poured him a glass of last year's pinot noir. In fact, he poured three glasses of the wine, placed them on a tray, and carried them over to the group. He served Joshua, then Fabienne. Finally, he set the tray on the coffee table in front of the couch and sat down next to Fabienne.

The three of them raised their glasses. "*À votre santé,*" said Sobran.

"*A la votre,*" Joshua said, returning the well-wishes.

When you get three wine people together, of course the topic turns to wine.

Sobran bemoaned the fact that so many new wine frontiers were springing up all over the world. Places where you would not dream of finding a winery suddenly had wineries producing good wines. "Mexican merlot," Sobran said. "Mexico was known for tequila. Now fine restaurants offer Mexican merlot."

"Not so surprising when you realize that the oldest winery in the Americas, Casa Madero, which was founded in 1597, is two hundred and fifty miles south of the Rio Grande. Mexico has been making wine longer than most people know. Now the Baja Peninsula is making really good chardonnay, sauvignon blanc, and several other varities," Joshua said. He liked nothing better than discussing the future of wine.

"South Africa," said Fabienne. "We can't forget how successful Luc and others have been there. We went for a visit last winter. Beautiful country!"

"Walla Walla, Washington," Erica said, coming into the room. "The winemakers there make great merlot and syrah."

"Walla who?" asked Sobran.

"It's a remote location in southeastern Washington State. It's very rural and there are only a handful of growers there, but they're making a name for themselves. Their wines are reasonably priced, and they're starting to make California winemakers sit up and take notice," Erica continued, her gaze fixed on Joshua.

Rising, Joshua couldn't take his eyes off her. She was wearing a sleeveless short black dress with a square neck. Very little cleavage was showing, but that was not where his eyes had been drawn.

Her beautiful brown skin was a feast for the eyes. Her shoulders, her arms and legs, and her neck. When they'd met, he thought she looked like she worked out. Now he wasn't so sure. Working in the vineyards could have wrought those sculpted arms and legs. He knew that when he'd worked daily in the vineyards he'd never been in better shape. Now he had to do free weights in order to stay in tip-top form.

His gaze rose to her sweet mouth. Pale red lips that were ripe for kissing, with a beauty mark next to her mouth that he wanted to nibble on. She had full, sensually contoured lips that a man could spend a lifetime finding ways to appreciate.

"Do I need to introduce you two?" Sobran joked, referring to the fact that Erica and Joshua were simply staring at each other without saying a word. "Erica, Joshua. Joshua, Erica."

Erica parted her lips to speak, showing straight white

teeth, and Joshua had to restrain himself from stepping forward, sweeping her into his arms, and kissing her right there in front of Sobran and Fabienne.

"Hello, Joshua," she said, going along with Sobran's joke and offering her hand.

"How are you, Erica?" He was surprised his voice sounded so calm. He took her hand, bent, and planted a dry kiss upon it. Her skin smelled like freshly cut roses. And it felt as smooth as silk.

"*Amusez-vous bien,*" Fabienne cried, watching the reaction of the two of them to each other. *A nuclear bomb has less combustible power,* she thought with a smile.

She and Sobran walked them to the door and watched as they descended the steps to the Mercedes.

Fabienne would have stood there until they drove away, she was so pleased, but Sobran pulled her away and firmly closed the door.

Alone, he said to his wife, "I don't think you had to tell those two to have a good time. Did you see the way he looked at her?"

"Did you see the way she looked at *him*?" Fabienne countered. She blew air between her lips, as if letting off steam. "I don't know if I should have let her go out with him. What if she can't resist him?"

"Darling, I do believe we're way past that question having any significance. It's obvious they will *not* be able to resist each other. The question is, how long will they be able to avoid the bedroom?"

Chapter Six

Erica wrapped her shawl around her shoulders as they stepped outside. Joshua opened the passenger-side door and helped her in. After closing it, he glanced up at the indigo sky. The moon was still low and shone through an opening in cumulus clouds so white and fluffy they looked like meringue.

Erica reached over and unlocked his door for him.

Joshua slid into the leather seat and closed the door. Alone, they found their nervousness apparent in the form of excessive chattiness.

"Nice car," said Erica a little too cheerily, as she fastened her seat belt.

"Thanks, it's very maneuverable," Joshua replied. *Maneuverable?* He could have kicked himself. *Why did I say that? I should have said it's fun to drive.*

He buckled up and started the engine, then turned his head to meet her eyes. "You look exquisite, and you smell wonderful."

"Thank you. You're doing things to my heartbeat too," she returned with a smile.

Joshua relaxed somewhat. "I don't know why I feel as

though I've never been on a date before." He put the car in drive and pulled away from the chateau.

"You've never been on a date with *me*."

"We went to dinner together night before last."

"Do you count that as a date? We weren't alone."

"Is that so?" he asked, unconvinced. "We were quite alone in the cab when I took you back to your hotel."

Erica blushed, remembering their kiss. "I want you to know that was an aberration. I don't usually kiss on the first date."

"You said it wasn't a date, so I guess it was okay. Will I be penalized tonight since this is, officially, our first date?"

"I sincerely doubt it. I've wanted to kiss you since I walked into the library and saw you sitting there," she told him frankly, observing him closely for his reaction.

Willpower and desire struggled within Joshua. Willpower won. He wanted to stop the the car and kiss her for that admission alone. She had a way of surprising him with her candidness that he found very refreshing.

"The feeling is mutual," he said. "I'm afraid I embarrassed myself in front of the Lafons, staring at you like an idiot. But I've thought of nothing but you since Monday night, and once I had you in my sights again, I forgot that I am a sophisticated man of the world who's capable of coherent speech."

Erica reached over and placed her hand on his thigh. He put his right hand on hers, grasped it, and gently squeezed. "Let's talk about something less volatile, shall we?" he said jokingly.

"What do you want to talk about?"

"Tell me about your childhood in Glen Ellen. And I'll tell you about mine in Oakland."

Erica sighed softly and glanced up at the moon. The clouds had drifted, giving the moon its rightful place at center stage in the night sky. "Glen Ellen's a small town, but charming. At least *I* think so. Besides winemaking, it's known for the Jack London State Historic Park. He lived there during the last years of his life. In fact, he was the one who started calling Sonoma Valley 'Valley of the Moon' because of the moon's tendency to hide behind the mountain peaks when he'd go horseback riding at night. Did you know he was only forty when he died? Every schoolkid in Glen Ellen knew that by the time they were in kindergarten."

Joshua loved the sound of her voice, so he wanted to keep her talking.

"I suppose your family's farm is on famous Highway 29?"

"Of course. Practically every winery in Sonoma Valley is on H-29. Like the wineries here in the Cote d' Or are located off of the N-74."

"Was your place open to tourists?"

"Signs were posted telling them the days and hours we were open. But a lot of people just showed up and knocked on the door, expecting to be shown around and given a personal wine tasting. Mom's pretty easy-going about unexpected visitors, but Dad has been known to go ballistic with people who were rude. That's the easiest way to set him off, not showing respect for other people's property. It's an inherited streak that affects the males in the Bryant family. Apparently Great-Grandpa Jonas, who bought the property in the late eighteen hundreds, was nearly chased off the land by his neighbors who didn't think a black man ought to own prime real estate next to them. The widow who sold it to Great-Grandpa hightailed it to San Francisco right after the sale. She must have known what was going to happen. Anyway, some men on horseback with hoods over their heads came calling one night and started shooting up the house. Jonas and his wife, Beatrice, shot several of them. Jonas was an ex–buffalo soldier, and by the time Beatrice was ten, she could outshoot her brothers. The next day, Jonas went into town and reported the incident to the sheriff, who, suspiciously, had his arm in a sling. Based on his gut feelings that the law in town was corrupt, Jonas put his cards on the table and told the sheriff that if anybody came on his property threatening him or his family again, he was going to shoot first and ask questions later. Surprisingly, nobody else came calling in the middle of the night. They tried every legal and not so legal ploy to try and get the land, but Jonas was too wily for them. He managed to leave the land to his son, and so on down the line. That's the version Dad has been telling us all our lives. It takes an iron will, and a good shotgun, to hang on to your property."

Joshua laughed. "I like your dad's version."

"So do I. But back to your question, which I never answered, by the way: I had a happy childhood in Glen Ellen. I knew my folks loved me, and my brothers tolerated me; they didn't try to drown me or anything. I could rip and run to my heart's content. I *loved* living on a farm. I loved everything about it, which, I think, surprised my folks. My brothers complained about chores like any normal kids. I followed my dad around as if I were attached to him at the hip."

"You've never wanted to do anything except be a winemaker?"

"Oh, when I was a teenager I wanted to be Janet Jackson for a minute; otherwise, no, I had no desire to be anything except a winemaker. What about you?"

"When I was a kid, my family moved around so much I never stayed anywhere long enough to get interested in anything. My folks were migrant workers. They would go wherever the 'season' would take them. Meaning they would go wherever a major crop was in season. In fall, it would be New York State for the apples. In late summer it would be California for the grape harvest."

His tone was quiet, reflective.

Erica knew not to express surprise or sympathy for his humble beginnings. For one thing, she'd known migrant workers all her life, and she'd loved and respected many of them. Her earliest friendships had been formed with children of the farmworkers who'd come in late summer to help with the harvest.

In fact, her first crush had been on . . .

"Oh my God," she said, her voice filled with awe, as she turned in her seat to face him. Tears formed in her eyes. She remembered it all now. How Joshua and his family had come to join in the harvest the summer of 1988. She was ten years old then. Joshua must have been seventeen. She'd made a fool of herself following him around, asking him all sorts of questions.

"I thought your family's name was Jenkins!"

A tumult of emotions ran through Joshua. Joy at her finally remembering him, a bit of shame for having been exposed as the poor boy whose parents had been farmworkers, and bitter sadness when his mother's sweet face appeared in his mind's eye. "Dan Jenkins was my stepfather," he explained. "Knight was my real dad's name."

"No wonder," Erica said. "I've been hearing about you for years. If I'd known your last name was Knight, I would've put two and two together before now." She sighed contentedly. "*My* Joshua! I adored you. I thought you were divine!"

"I thought you were *magnifique*," Joshua told her, his voice husky. "You made me feel as if I were the most special person in the world. That summer, you were reading *Peter Pan* for the first time, and you talked about the story constantly. I jokingly started calling you Wendy, and you called me Peter."

"I remember," Erica said, picking up the story. "I took that book with me everywhere. It was a dog-eared mess by the end of the summer. My brothers hated the story because I pestered them about it so much. I'm sure they would've torn it up or thrown it in the fire if I'd ever let it out of my sight, but I slept with it."

Joshua laughed. "You didn't!"

"Yes, I did. I knew Jake and Frank had designs on it," Erica said, laughing too.

She sighed and fell silent. She felt humbled in the face of what fate, or God, or the powers that be, had done: reunited her with the first boy she'd ever had romantic feelings about. Even if they *were* entirely innocent.

Joshua had treated her like a kid sister. There had been nothing untoward between them. She knew he probably would have avoided her like the plague if he'd ever had improper thoughts about her. And she was so young she didn't know what improper thoughts were, let alone why people had them!

But she had loved him nonetheless. She had loved him with a pure heart. When he left with his family following the harvest, she had cried herself to sleep, convinced that she'd never see him again.

However, she did recall hearing something about his family a few days after he'd gone away. She'd overheard her parents in conversation one night as she passed their bedroom door on the way to the bathroom down the hall.

"It's a shame about Antonia," her father's voice had said.

Erica had stopped outside their door. The door was cracked, so they couldn't see her standing in the hallway. However, she could hear them clearly. She wouldn't have paused, but Joshua's mother's name had caught her attention. It was unique. She'd never known anyone else by that name.

"It's sad, is what it is," her mother had said. "She was only in her midthirties. Susan said it was a burst aneurysm that killed her. She died instantly. Daniel and the kids must be devastated. I'm going to the funeral, Eric. It's going to be in Oakland. That's where she was from."

When Joshua heard Erica's soft sobs, he thought she'd simply been overcome with emotions brought on by good memories. But when she didn't let up after several minutes, he pulled the car into the parking lot of a nearby parish church and turned off the motor. Unbuckling his seat belt, he reached over and tilted her head up, looking into her eyes. "Darling, if talking about the past is going to upset you this much, we won't talk about it."

Erica unfastened her seat belt as well and threw her arms around his neck. "Joshua," she said softly in his ear. "I just remembered you lost your mother that summer."

He held her tightly against him. He had not known she was even aware of his mother's death. The day of the funeral had been a blur. Grief had made him blind to everything else except the fact that his mother was gone forever.

"How did you find out?" he asked, his breath on her cheek.

"I overheard my parents talking about your mother dying suddenly. My mother said she was planning to go to the funeral in Oakland. . . ."

"That's right, the service was held in my mom's old church in Oakland. My dad went back to work soon afterward and left me and my sister, Joslynn, with Aunt Dee."

He kissed her high on the cheek, tasting her tears.

Erica pressed her lips to his cheek as well. "My parents went to the service, but they wouldn't let me go with them. I think they were afraid I'd say, or do, something that would embarrass your family."

"I wish you'd been there," Joshua said.

"Me too." She didn't understand what was happening to her. Why did seventeen-year-old memories hurt so badly? She could imagine, even now, the pain he must have endured when his mother died and then, soon afterward, his father went away to earn a living in a job that required long absences from home.

She had cried herself to sleep for days after hearing of Antonia's death, wondering how Joshua was faring. Her mother had told her that she was experiencing those emotions because she'd allowed herself to get too attached to Joshua.

Puppy love, she'd called it. "*It's a normal phase of growing up, sweetie,*" she'd said. "*Joshua was much too old for you. He will always have a special place in your heart, but you will meet many handsome boys in your lifetime.*"

Her mother had been right. Many handsome boys had come and gone over the intervening years, and her memories of Joshua had remained deep in her heart.

Joshua took her face between his hands, wiping her tearstained cheeks with the pads of his thumbs. He kissed her forehead, then peered into her eyes. "Stop that, this is supposed to be a reunion. It's not a time for sadness," he said gently.

Erica closed her eyes, trying to stanch her tears. She sniffed, opened her eyes, and gave him a beseeching look. "I was remembering how badly I wanted to see you back then to tell you how sorry I was about your mother."

"Now you've told me, and I thank you," Joshua said with a smile. "Come now, let me see that beautiful mouth curve into a smile."

Erica gamely smiled for him. She wasn't finished telling him how she felt, though. "I will never scoff if my ten-year-old daughter comes to me one day and tells me she's in love. My emotions were real, and they ran deep. I didn't understand them, but that didn't make them any less real!"

"Your mother was right, I was too old for you back then. I felt the inappropriateness of our situation. That's one of the reasons why I stopped you from throwing yourself in my arms every time we ran into each other."

Erica laughed softly. "I *did* do that, didn't I?"

"Yes, you did, and it was my mother who pointed out to me how it would look to others if they saw us. But I want you to know that my feelings for you were completely innocent. You were a child, and I was nearly a man. However, it was your warmth, your zest for living, and your family's kindness to my family that helped me decide that, perhaps, one day I'd like to live like you all lived. Your family made me see the possibilities that life offered and, from that summer on, I set my sights on learning everything I could about making wine."

Erica sat in his arms, taking in his words, deriving great pleasure from the sound of his voice and the intensity with which he spoke. She couldn't believe he was telling her that he hadn't forgotten her, that he'd carried her memory with him, and that it had inspired him, in times of self-doubt and indecision, to go for his dreams.

She snuggled closer. "That is the sweetest thing anyone has ever said to me."

She smiled up at him. "Be forewarned, I'm still enamored of you, Joshua. Even when you were being a rude beast the night we met, I was still drawn to you."

"*You* be forewarned, Miss Bryant. Before summer's end, you will be mine." He said it with such conviction that she had no doubt he meant it.

"I can't wait!" Erica cried happily, and threw her arms around his neck.

They kissed with slow deliberation to seal the bargain.

Chapter Seven

"Eric, wake up, you're snoring like a motorboat!" Simone Bryant said as she none too gently elbowed her six-foot-three husband in the side. Eric murmured an incoherent sentence and went back to sleep. However, he automatically rolled over, and the snoring ceased. Years of doing his wife's bidding had made him capable of doing it in his sleep.

Simone smiled and fluffed her pillow before lying back down. Thank God her husband didn't snore every night, only when he was truly exhausted, or she'd never get any sleep.

Her mind was going a hundred miles an hour anyway. She probably wouldn't be able to sleep even if her lovable motorboat were not keeping her awake.

Erica had phoned her with the stupendous news that she'd been reunited with "her Joshua." Her daughter had sounded so excited Simone had been convinced that the child was already half in love with him. Simone remembered Joshua and his family. How could she not? Antonia Jenkins had been a lovely lady. Gentle of spirit, hardworking, and devoted to her family. Her death had been a tragedy. Simone also recalled how her little girl had gone on about Joshua when she and Eric told her that she could not attend Antonia's funeral with them. It was the only tantrum her usually even-tempered child had thrown. Yes, Lord, that girl had shown out, demanding to be allowed to come along. She'd held a grudge against them for months afterward.

Simone and Eric had made their decision based on their experience as parents. They were aware of how she felt about Joshua. They were fond of the boy too. But that didn't mean they were going to allow her to attend his mother's funeral where she would probably do something she would later regret, like proclaiming her undying love for him. What did a ten-year-old girl know about everlasting love? If she had been closer to his age they might have considered allowing her to go pay her respects.

Simone sighed and sank deeper into the pillow, sleep still eluding her.

Being a parent was the hardest job on God's green earth. You never knew whether you were making the right decisions or not. You just had to have faith and let love guide you. She wondered, now, what would have happened if they'd let Erica attend Antonia's funeral. Would she and Joshua have made a permanent connection? If they had kept in touch, would they be married, with children, by now?

Simone sat up in bed. Just as she'd suspected, she wasn't going to be able to go to sleep until she talked this over with someone. She glanced at her slumbering spouse. No dice. When Eric was asleep, he was *asleep*! An alien invasion, with little green men storming into their bedroom, wouldn't rouse him.

She swung her feet off the bed and rose.

Five feet three and 120 pounds, she nevertheless had an inner strength that belied her physical size. She ran a hand through her short, tousled hair. It was dark brown with golden highlights. Simone never missed a hair appointment. Not because she was vain, but because she had been taught at an early age that women who took care of their bodies lived longer, happier lives. Looking good on the outside worked wonders for your emotional health. She didn't know why that was true. But she'd seen a new hairdo transform a woman, make her step livelier, her attitude sassier.

Her mother, Monique, was seventy-nine years old, looked at least ten years younger, and was a living example of the theory. For years Monique Toussaint had had a standing ten o'clock hair appointment each Friday morning in her New Orleans, Louisiana, beauty parlor and, come hell or high water, she made it on time.

Simone walked barefoot downstairs to the kitchen. Their hacienda was more than three thousand square feet and made of thick stone. In the summertime, the temperature was cool inside. In winter, the place could get drafty and the fireplaces throughout the house got a workout.

Tonight, the temperature was in the high sixties, so the cool tile on the kitchen floor felt wonderful on her warm feet. She switched on the overhead light and dimmed it.

Sitting on a stool at the breakfast nook, she reached for the phone and dialed her eldest son's number. Franklyn never went to bed before midnight. Sometimes he couldn't sleep either and spent the night painting. He was quite a good artist and could probably make a living at it if he needed to. His first love was the culinary arts, though. He got that from his mother, who was a cordon bleu chef. In some ways, and she hated to admit this, Franklyn was the child of her heart. She loved all of her children equally, but Franklyn had been the first. They'd practically grown up together because she had been so young when she'd had him—twenty. He was thirty-five now. From day one, it had been undeniable that Franklyn was attached to his mother. As an infant, he would wail if anyone else held him. When he started walking, he would waddle all over the house, following his mother. She couldn't turn around for him and decided to put him to work. He started learning to cook at four. By the time he was seven he was preparing meals for the family. Not just meals. Delicious meals.

His father expressed concern that Franklyn might take after his mother *too* much. His mother laughed it off and told him not to worry. She had been right, of course. Today, Franklyn was a strapping six-foot-two heterosexual man with a successful restaurant in San Francisco and all the female attention he could stand. Which was way too much since he was also painfully shy around the opposite sex due to a permanent limp he'd gotten when he was kicked by a horse at twelve. His limp made him self-conscious about his appeal to women.

Simone sighed as she waited for him to pick up the phone. If only he'd recognize that his limp was so slight that most people didn't even notice it. And the women who did didn't care, because Franklyn was quite dreamy if the truth be told. There had been many times when Simone and Eric had had dinner at The Vineyard, Franklyn's eatery, and she'd observed women, and men, giving him sensuous looks. Franklyn, God bless him, was oblivious to it all.

The only woman Franklyn had eyes for was Elise, his pastry chef.

Simone was just about to ponder the thorny subject of Franklyn's unrequited love for his pastry chef when Franklyn picked up.

"Hello, Mom, what are you doing calling this late? There's nothing wrong, is there?"

Simone laughed. "I can never surprise you anymore, what with that caller ID gadget on everyone's phone. No, sweetheart, nothing's wrong, except your sister has been in France less than a week and she's already falling in love with someone."

Franklyn laughed too. "Good for her."

"I'm glad you feel that way. You know the lucky guy."

"Oh? How do I know him?"

Simone reminded him of the summer of 1988. He was a freshman in college then, but he'd been home for the summer break and had helped with the harvest. She was certain he would remember Joshua.

He did. "Joshua Jenkins is Joshua *Knight* who works for Etienne Roumier? Small world." He sounded genuinely intrigued.

In his apartment overlooking the San Francisco Bay, Franklyn held the cordless phone to his ear and walked across the living room to the south window. He had the lights off. There was a full moon and the beams danced upon the surface of the bay.

"Looks like you and Dad couldn't keep them apart after all," he joked.

"So you remember that too," Simone said with an amused tone to her voice. "She was only ten. What were we supposed to do?"

"Exactly what you did. What will be will be," Franklyn said. "This sounds like one of those stories you hear about on reality TV."

"We'll have to wait and see what happens, but it sure is remarkable, isn't it? After seventeen years, they meet again."

"And there's no problem with their age difference this time," Franklyn observed.

"No, the only thing that can keep them apart this time is themselves," Simone wisely said. She yawned. "Okay, Frank, tell me how you're doing on that front. Are you seeing anyone?"

She wanted him to say, *Yes, I'm dating Elise.* But she didn't hold out much hope. Franklyn's sous chef, Lettie Burrows, who was a friend of the family, and an inveterate gossip to boot, kept her informed about what went on in the kitchen of The Vineyard. Lettie's last report had Franklyn still gazing at Elise with pent-up longing, but no luck on his asking her out yet.

Simone had never let Franklyn know she was aware of how he felt about Elise. She didn't want to be the type of mother who snooped in her children's love lives. However, Franklyn was taxing her patience.

"No, Mom, I'm not seeing anyone, but when I do get serious about somebody I will bring her to meet you and Dad."

Simone bit her tongue. Franklyn had never brought anyone home.

"Umm, Frank, what about that cute pastry chef? What's her name? Elaine?"

"Elise, Mom."

"Oh, what a pretty name, for a pretty woman. Is she married?"

"No, she's divorced. She put him through law school and he left her when he passed the bar exam."

"What a louse!"

"Yeah, I hear he really broke her heart. She's not exactly man-hunting right now. In fact, some guy tried to hit on her at the restaurant and she gave him his head on a platter."

"Sounds like my kind of girl," Simone said with a laugh.

"Yeah, she's something else," Franklyn said, unable to hide the affection in his voice. "She's smart, and funny, and talented. Our desserts have been selling very well since she joined us."

On her end, Simone smiled. Even though Franklyn owned the restaurant, lock, stock, and barrel, he always referred to it as if it were a joint enterprise between him and his employees. His attitude garnered respect and loyalty among those who worked for him. He was generous with his time, his praise, and his profits. Those who worked for him received great benefits, and the better The Vineyard did, the fatter his employees' pay packets got. She admired that in him. Any woman would be exceptionally lucky to get him.

Why couldn't Elise be that lucky girl?

"You sound like you like Elise a lot," Simone said, hoping she had kept the eagerness out of her voice.

"I do," Franklyn admitted. "But I don't think she'd be interested in me."

"What makes you say that? Have you asked her out?"

"No," Franklyn said softly. "I just don't think I'm her type. I overheard her talking to another woman about men one day, and she likes athletes. She likes men with perfect bodies."

Simone couldn't help it: she let out a long-winded sigh. "Franklyn, *you're* an athlete. You lift weights, you cycle, you climb mountains, for God's sake!"

"But I'm not perfect. I have an injury that's never going to go away."

"Boy, I'm hanging up now because you're getting on my nerves. Ask the girl out!"

Simone calmed down and said, "The injury that's doing you harm is not in your leg, but in your head. If you let something like a limp keep you from pursuing a woman you're interested in, you're a fool, Franklyn. And I didn't raise no fools!"

"You're wrong, Mom. To some women, it matters."

"Yes, dear. But not to the women who matter."

Franklyn had no argument against his mother's reasoning.

"If she turns me down, I'll be devastated."

"If you never ask her, you'll be worse off."

Franklyn was quiet for a long while.

"Honey, this is long distance," Simone said.

"Okay, I'll do it, but if I'm shot down, I'm coming home for the weekend and you'll have to bake your no-flour chocolate cake to comfort me."

"It's a deal," Simone happily agreed. "I'm going to bed now. Good night, sweetheart."

"Good night, Mom. I love you."

"I love you too. And I'll love Elise too if you marry her and give me some grandchildren."

Franklyn laughed. "I'll see what I can do."

"Bash his head in! Kill him!" Dominique cheered on Hubert, her new fiancé, as he tackled the opponent who had the ball. Erica and Dominique were standing on the sidelines of the soccer field with what appeared to be half the occupants of the town of Beaune and the opponents' hometown, nearby Pommard.

Erica had seen many soccer matches on TV, but this was ridiculous! These people were insane! Mothers, fathers, children, grandmothers, grandfathers. They were all passionately involved with the game, shouting at the players and the referees, jumping up and down with glee when their team scored, and angrily stomping the ground when they were scored on.

Erica's heart was in her throat as she watched Joshua, a midfielder, play. He'd tried to explain his position to her in the car on the way to the game, but she was lost. She noticed that he always seemed to be in play, moving up and down the field, assisting other players, especially when they had to defend against the other team making a goal. He had scored the first goal of the game and she'd been inordinately proud of him. But she had to admit she was more interested in how sexy he looked, muscles flexing, in his shirt, shorts, kneesocks, and cleats, than she was in the game.

"Kick him in the balls!" Dominique shouted.

"You're a bloodthirsty little thing," Erica joked.

Dominique laughed. "You don't understand. We live for soccer here. It's the national passion. This is just your second week in Burgundy, you'll get used to it."

"It's how you get the aggression out of your system?" Erica suggested.

Dominique smiled at her. "Soccer is no more violent than your American sports of football and basketball."

Erica gave her that much. "I suppose you're right. My dad and brothers get kind of crazy at football games too."

"And soccer's not a contact sport," Dominique said, satisfied she'd won the debate.

Hubert was dribbling the ball down the field, running while controlling it with his feet. He passed the ball to a teammate who headed it, bumping it with his head, to another teammate who leaped into the air and drop-kicked the ball toward the goal. The goalkeeper dove for it, but his reaction time was too slow and the Beaune team scored.

Both Dominique and Erica cheered loudly, but their screams were drowned out by the crowd's. Beaune had won the game!

Spectators ran onto the field to congratulate or console their respective teams.

Erica jumped up and down, trying to see Joshua over the heads of the frenzied masses. She saw him jogging toward her. She met him halfway and he picked her up and swung her around. He was covered in sweat, but she didn't mind as her body slid down his and their mouths met in a salty kiss.

"You were *masterful*," she told him, unable to take her eyes from his face.

Joshua beamed his thanks. "Come on, let's get out of here."

They hurried through the crowd, and once they had a straightaway, they ran the the short distance to the parking area where they got into the Mercedes and peeled away from the soccer field.

"We'll go by my place, I'll shower, we'll relax, and then I'll make dinner for you," Joshua told her as he drove.

Erica was turned toward him, her legs folded beneath her.

Joshua glanced at her out of the corner of his eye. She was wearing jeans and a short-sleeve white blouse. Low-heeled sandals covered her lovely feet, and her nails were painted seashell pink. Such simple attire. But even simple attire on a voluptuous body could be sexually explicit. Her full breasts appeared to be about to rend the seams of her modest blouse with each exhalation. The ripe swell of her thighs enticed him. He imagined how heavenly they would feel wrapped around him.

Erica smiled when she caught his gaze on her body. Hadn't she been looking at him in the same way a few minutes ago? She reached up and massaged the side of her neck, tilting her head to the side, just so, giving him an exquisite view of the area, a newly discovered erogenous zone for her, which he knew drove her to distraction whenever he nuzzled her there.

Joshua's mouth watered, remembering the taste of her skin.

"You're going to spoil me," she said in reply to his offer to cook dinner for her.

"I want to spoil you," he said, his voice a bit hoarse. *I want to strip you naked and make love to you right now.*

Erica moistened her lips and smiled at him. "We'll spoil each other." *I can think of many ways to spoil you, baby. And all of them involve both of us being buck to the bone!* She grew warm at the prospect, grasped a corner of her blouse at the chest, and fanned herself with it, allowing air to circulate between the crevice in her breasts.

"What's the matter, are you warm?" Joshua asked. "I'll turn on the air." *Or I can take you home with me, put you in a tepid bath, and slowly bathe you.*

Erica's breathing had quickened with desire. "No, I'm okay." *I just want you so badly I'm about to have a meltdown right here and now!*

"All right," he said much more calmly than he felt. *Dear God, it's only been a fortnight, it's too soon to take her to bed. Make me steel.*

He was praying for the strength to resist her. But the only thing that remotely reminded him of the hardness of steel at that moment was his erection.

They fell silent.

The hum of the Mercedes's motor, the displacement of air as they sped toward the outskirts of Beaune, and the sound of their breathing were all the noise they heard for the next few minutes.

Erica looked out the window, her mind not on the sights, but on her tumultuous thoughts. If Joshua asked her, she would gladly make love to him. She was certain of it. Yet, if she had met another man, a man whom she had not known in her childhood, she would never dream of taking such a step this soon in the relationship.

Was she letting her emotions cloud her judgment?

With Joshua, she felt a sweet pain deep inside her that could not be alleviated by anything except complete surrender to him, and complete possession of him. A giving and taking of everything that they were.

On some level, she felt she knew him to the core. And yet, logically, she was forced to concede that she did not know him at all.

She turned to watch his profile. He seemed deep in thought.

Ahead she saw the turnoff to the house he owned near the river. It was a neat, rather large cottage, built more than a hundred years ago. Ivy covered the stone wall that surrounded it. An ornamental iron gate, an example of the traditional craft of Burgundy metalwork, encouraged privacy.

He parked in front, but didn't immediately turn off the engine. Regarding her with a grave expression, he said, "Erica, let's be frank, shall we? We have a past, and because of it, we're inclined to romanticize what's developing between us. But the fact is, you don't know me. And I don't know you." He paused. "Wait, I shouldn't make assumptions." He unbuckled his seat belt and reached over to undo hers as well.

He moved closer to her and grasped her face between his hands. "Am I interpreting your body language correctly? Do you want to make love to me?"

He saw the surprise mirrored in her eyes before she lowered them.

"Look at me," he gently urged her.

She met his gaze.

"Yes," she said. The volume of her voice was barely above a whisper.

Joshua bent his head and brushed his lips against hers. He let out a groan as she opened her mouth, welcoming him. She tasted delectable to him, like a peach left out in the sunshine, warm, sweet, and delicious.

He felt her surrender to him. Knew that if he picked her up now and carried her inside to his bed, she would willingly give herself to him and not regret one moment of it. Closing his eyes, he surrendered too. He gave up the notion of right and wrong. Could this be wrong when they both wanted it so badly? And who was to say it was too soon to make love? Knowing someone was never an exact science anyway. Couples who have been married for decades don't really know their partners.

He knew this about Erica: she had loved the boy that he used to be. Why couldn't she also love the man he'd become? There wasn't much of a chasm between man and boy, really. He still valued family and friendship. He still thought that life was what you made it, and that if you weren't happy with the person that you were, you could reinvent yourself. He'd done that.

It was this revelation that gave him the willpower to break off the kiss and hold Erica at arm's length.

"I want you too," he told her regretfully. "But when

we make love, you're going to be making love to the man I've become, not to an image of me that you've carried in your heart all these years."

He reached over and refastened her seat belt. "I'm going to take you home."

Erica closed her eyes and sat back on the seat. A small sigh escaped from between her lips. She knew there was no use arguing with him. Some things never changed. Joshua Knight had been a proud boy, and he was a proud man. He would not deign to have a woman desire him for anything other than who he truly was.

Chapter Eight

From late May to early July there were frequent rainstorms. None so severe that extensive damage was done to the vines, thank God. Erica began to see the wisdom of Sobran's habit of getting up at five each morning to work in the vineyards. By the middle of the afternoon, rain made it impossible to work. They got in enough work in the sun, however, for her to acquire a very noticeable tan that turned her golden brown skin a shade darker.

Her hair was growing out, too, and Fabienne suggested they take a girls-only day trip to Paris soon to hook up their dos. There were social engagements to think about later in the season, such as Hubert and Dominique's engagement party and the harvest dance at the end of August.

One Saturday morning, as she lay dozing on a lounge chair on the patio, Fabienne's favorite spaniel, Trudee, brown and white with a long silky wavy coat, lying next to her, she felt raindrops on her face and opened her eyes to see Joshua standing over her.

He had a glass of water in his left hand, and the fingertips of his right hand were, suspiciously, wet.

Erica laughed as she rose to a sitting position. "I would have preferred to be awakened with a kiss."

Joshua squatted next to her. He was wearing his soccer uniform, and Erica's eyes immediately went to his muscular thighs. She smiled. He'd said sex was off-limits until she knew him intimately, but that didn't preclude an intimate perusal of him with her eyes.

"Come on, we'll be late for the game," he said.

"You don't check your messages regularly, do you?" Erica asked as she got to her feet and walked over to the fig tree. She leaned against it and regarded him with an amused expression.

"No, I didn't check my messages before coming for you, I was too damned eager to see you after going a whole week without you," he told her, his brows creased in a frown. His dark eyes expressed his confusion.

He went and stood in front of her. "Where is my kiss, by the way? We haven't been together in seven days, and I don't even get a hug? What's going on?"

Erica came forward and placed a chaste peck on his cheek. Joshua tried to turn his head so she would get his mouth instead, but she was too quick for him.

Eyes narrowed, Joshua said, "That isn't a kiss, *this* is a kiss." He roughly pulled her into his arms and his mouth hungrily devoured hers in a kiss so intense and sensual that Erica was weak-kneed when he finally let go of her.

She took a deep breath and smiled up at him. "The message said that Fabienne, Dominique, and I were going to Paris today. That we'd spend the night and be back in Beaune by tomorrow afternoon."

"But you *know* how I look forward to our weekends together," he said, disappointed.

"That's why I phoned you two days ago to explain that I needed a little time to get my hair done, and other things."

"Other things?"

"You don't want to know."

"Yes, I do."

"Waxing, plucking, clipping, tucking. You know, girl things."

Shaking his head, Joshua laughed. "You look fine to me."

"Yes, I know that, and it's going to *stay* that way!"

He sighed resignedly. "All right. You go get overhauled. I guess we'll have to win the game without you and Dominique cheering us on."

Erica hugged him. "I'm sorry, baby."

Joshua buried his nose in the side of her neck. She was wearing a light, flowery perfume that, when combined with her own scent, produced an enticing aroma that did crazy things to his libido.

Erica's body relaxed in his warm embrace, initially. Then she felt his breath on her neck, and her nipples immediately hardened. She put her hand on his chest with the intention of coaxing him away from her. Once her hand touched the hard muscles of his chest, though, she could only think of one thing: making love to him. His ban on sex had been hard to abide by these past six weeks. Especially when a mere touch sent her desire for him spiraling out of control!

Alone in the backyard, they stood holding one another, trying to resist the strong pull of mutual need. Nearly two months of pent-up desires, searching for release. Many, *many* years of holding each other in their hearts.

Unable to hold on any longer, Erica intently gazed into his eyes and said, "Make love to me, Joshua."

"And have you miss your hair appointment?" Joshua joked. While he had also been aroused by their embrace, he had not been on the same wavelength. He had promised himself that he would not make love to

Erica until she said the words *I love you.* Until then, he was committed to celibacy. No matter how blue certain parts of his anatomy turned out of sheer need.

Not cracking a smile, Erica shook him. "I mean it. I'll cancel my trip, and you'll miss the game. You'll take me back to your place and thoroughly ravish me."

"Sounds like a plan," Joshua said, still in a joking mood. "But we agreed—"

"*You* decided on that arrangement, Joshua Knight, I didn't!"

Regarding her with a straight face, he said, "What's gotten into you?"

"*I love you.* Are you so unobservant that you can't see that? I melt whenever you lay a hand on me. I can't keep my eyes off of you. I love the sound of your voice, the shape of your hands, the breadth of your shoulders."

Now he was serious. His breath had caught in his throat. He took a big gulp of air and slowly released it. "You can't be in love with me, you don't know me well enough."

"Why are you so hung up on time?" Erica shouted, then immediately lowered her voice. "You are the most anal man I've ever met."

"And you *love* me?"

Her eyes were fierce. "That's the thing about love, it covers a multitude of faults."

Dappled sunlight renders her eyes the color of brandy. That was what Joshua was thinking when she stormed off, leaving him standing in the shade of the fig tree.

He snapped out of it in time to look up and glimpse her retreating back as she rounded the corner of the house heading toward the path that led to the vineyards. The dog, Trudee, trotted after Erica, perhaps thinking this was a good opportunity for a walk.

Joshua was a few paces behind the dog. "Darling, wait, we need to talk."

"Talk about what?" Erica tossed over her shoulder. "I said I loved you, and you said, 'You can't love me. We haven't known each other long enough.' How long is 'long enough,' Joshua?"

"I don't know," he answered truthfully.

Erica spun around and faced him. "Aha! You don't *know*!"

Joshua went to her and grasped her by the shoulders. Holding her gaze, he said, "I adore you. What I feel for you surpasses romantic love. That's why I've got to know that you return my feelings before we make love, physically. I want everything to be perfect for you. I won't accept anything less."

It occurred to Erica, then, that Joshua wasn't being completely honest with her. His words rang true, but behind his eyes lurked some untold truth, something he wasn't ready for her to know about him. "What do you mean by perfect? I'm just a woman, Joshua, a woman asking you to love her. I don't want perfection. I want a flesh-and-blood man to hold me and reassure me that he'll be there when I need him. What makes you think you have to have perfection before we make love? If you're looking for perfection, you won't find it in me!"

"I want you to be certain about me. You should have no doubts whatsoever that I'm the man you want to be with before we go to see your parents," he said evenly.

"What have my parents got to do with anything? I'm twenty-seven. They don't have a say about whom I fall in love with."

Joshua's rein on his temper broke. "I don't want your parents thinking I'm not good enough for you!" he ground out impatiently.

Erica stared at him in disbelief. "If you knew them, you would never have said that."

Still angry, Joshua said, "Yeah, I'm sure they're wonderful people, but the fact remains that they had a reason for keeping us apart seventeen years ago."

"They were protecting *you* from *me* when they refused to let me go to your mother's funeral. They knew I probably would have done something to embarrass you and your family. Joshua, that's the only reason."

"No, Erica, they were afraid you would have become more attached to me than you already were if you had attended the funeral," he insisted.

"You can't blame them. They thought they were doing what was best for everyone. They told me to forget you because you were too old for me to be mooning over."

"And they were right. But that problem no longer exists. What does exist is the fact of where we each come from. You, from a privileged background and I, from an impoverished one. You can't understand what I've been through to get where I am today, Erica. You've never had to struggle. You've never wondered where your next meal was coming from, nor whether the electricity would be turned back on after it was turned off for nonpayment. Your parents could think I only want you because being with you somehow raises my social status."

"My parents would never think you're a social climber! Joshua, look at what you've achieved. You're the right-hand man of one of the premier vintners in Burgundy. How can you stand there and denigrate yourself?"

Joshua shook his head. "You don't get what I'm saying. I'm not putting myself down. I'm proud of who I am. I simply want *you* to be sure of how you feel about the man I've become. Because I'm sure there will be those who will doubt that we belong together."

"Nobody, and I mean *nobody*, tells me how to feel about someone. I make my own decisions. I've been making my own decisions about important things since I turned eighteen and went away to college."

She walked into the circle of his arms. Their eyes met

and held. "I love you. Nothing anyone can do, or say, will ever change that."

Joshua hugged her tightly. "I love you so much it hurts."

Erica laid her head on his chest. "Good, because I don't make love to anyone who doesn't love me back." She smiled up at him. "If *that* was your biggest fear, that my parents will think you're not good enough for me, then you can relax. They're going to love you."

Joshua released her. Glancing down at his watch, he said, "I missed the start of the game. Can you think of anything we can do for the rest of the afternoon?"

"God, *yes*!" Erica exclaimed as she grasped his hand in hers. "Just give me a couple of minutes to make my apologies to Fabienne and pack an overnight bag!"

Love in the afternoon.

Erica wanted to go straight to Joshua's house and make a beeline for his bedroom. However, Joshua had given the seduction some advance thought and instead took her to the farmers' market in Beaune.

Saturday mornings found the market packed with townspeople and country folk who only came to town once a week.

The market was a place where you could pick up fresh fruits and vegetables, fresh flowers, cheeses, and even a live rabbit if that was your gastronomic pleasure.

When they passed several men haggling over the price of a fat brown bunny, Erica cringed. She felt sorry for the doomed animal.

Seeing her expression, Joshua got her attention by pointing out the flower stall. "Look, baby, they've even got some lavender." He knew Erica loved the scent of the fragrant bluish purple plant. The plant he held up sat in a brightly colored pot and the clusters of light purple flowers were covered in dew.

Erica accepted the pot and brought it to her nose.

The odor was somehow richer than she'd ever imagined it would be. Before now she'd only smelled lavender in the form of soaps and sachet, never the real thing.

She smiled up at Joshua. How had he known she would appreciate the immensely sensual experience of smelling fresh lavender?

"We'll take this," Joshua told the stall owner. He pointed to some yellow roses whose buds had not opened yet. "We'll take a dozen of those too."

A few minutes later they were piling into the car with the flowers, some fresh bread, three kinds of local cheeses, garden greens, juicy ripe tomatoes, and a small salmon that Joshua was going to put on the grill.

Thunder rumbled in the distance as Joshua pulled the car into the driveway at the house. He'd had to stop at the gate and unlock it first. Then he'd pulled the car inside and locked the gate again. He didn't want any uninvited visitors today. No one capable of peeking in the windows.

He and Erica, he still in his soccer uniform and Erica in a pair of low-cut jeans and a sleeveless peach-colored silk blouse, worked in tandem in the kitchen, preparing a repast that would nourish them and provide the energy needed for what would transpire later.

Erica had taken off her sandals and stood barefoot at the sink, rinsing the garden greens and tomatoes for a salad. Joshua was seasoning the salmon before putting it on the grill on the stove. He liked to cook, and when he'd had the hundred-year-old house renovated, he'd insisted on a well-equipped kitchen.

Erica admired the confidence with which he handled the salmon. She knew cooks who were intimidated by fish. They either overcooked it or undercooked it. Having been around two professional chefs, her mother and her brother, she recognized when someone knew what he was doing in the kitchen. Joshua did.

"It's good to know I'm not going to go hungry with you as a lover," she said jokingly.

"I'm just making sure you'll have the stamina for what I have in mind," he said teasingly. His eyes possessively raked over her, leaving her feeling breathless with anticipation. "I don't want you giving out before I'm done with you."

Half an hour later they were sitting across from one another at a round table on the shaded patio. The yellow roses were in a vase in the center of the table. Erica had covered the table with a white linen tablecloth and set it with white ceramic dishes. Crystal wineglasses stood at the ready for the wine Joshua was uncorking.

He wore a determined expression as he pulled out the cork. Erica had read the label. It was a pinot noir from Etienne Roumier's private stock from 1978, the year she was born. Joshua poured the wine into the glasses and placed the bottle on the table.

Raising their glasses, they toasted each other.

"To 'Wendy,' who has grown into a beautiful woman," Joshua said affectionately.

"To 'Peter,' who waited for me," Erica returned, a mischievous glint in her eyes.

They each drank a mouthful of the wine.

Erica took a moment to savor the flavor. "Excellent vintage."

"It was a very good year," Joshua said.

Knowing he'd meant it was a good year because it was the year she was born, Erica rose, leaned across the table, and kissed him. When they came up for air and sat back down, neither of them was interested in the food any longer.

"You know," Joshua said, "salmon is excellent cold."

"Delicious," Erica concurred.

She was out of her chair and in his arms in under a second. "Joshua, Joshua, why'd you make me wait so long?" she breathed into his mouth. They kissed deeply, hungrily, as if it were a life-sustaining act.

Erica's body was taut with excitement. Tense and expectant and eagerly seeking a way to get closer to Joshua's.

Joshua's hands slid underneath her blouse, his fingers nimbly undoing the hooks and eyes on her bra. He sighed happily when the bra came apart in his hands.

Now his hands were cupping her full, firm breasts, and Erica was moaning softly, the sound like music to his ears. It was the first time he'd ever touched her so intimately. He had had erotic dreams about how her body would be, but they did not compare to the reality.

"I was a damned fool!" he said in reply to her earlier question.

Erica unbuttoned her blouse and simultaneously slipped out of it and the bra. They fell to the floor of the flagstone patio. Joshua buried his face between her breasts, relishing the softness, the fragrant appeal of her warm skin against his.

He gently grasped one of her breasts and bent to tongue the nipple.

When his warm tongue circled her nipple, Erica tensed, and then relaxed.

The insistent, pulsating sensation between her legs grew more urgent.

"Joshua, are you certain no one can see us?" she asked breathlessly, glancing behind them at the wall that enclosed the backyard.

Joshua reluctantly drew his mouth away from her breast and took her by the hand. "Better safe than sorry, huh?" He led her into the house.

Once they crossed the threshold, he swept her up into his arms.

Erica laughed. "What is this? Are you taking your last name literally now?"

"I'm *your* knight in shining armor. And don't you forget it," he said, smiling.

Erica wrapped her arms around his neck. "Whatever you say, my lord."

Chapter Nine

Joshua nudged the door open with his foot.

Erica smiled when she saw his utterly masculine bedroom. Sturdy furnishings made of maple by a gifted artisan from the past who took great care with each piece. The bed was huge and the headboard was meticulously carved. Erica could easily imagine it in the private chambers of Louis IV, or perhaps the bedroom of one of his courtesans, a woman kept for the sole pleasure of the king. It was certainly a bed to be shared.

The floor was hardwood and gleaming. The bed sat on a huge Persian rug woven in muted tones. The bedclothes were all snowy white and Joshua had folded the comforter, which was hunter green, out of the way, down to the foot of the bed in anticipation of this moment.

The blinds were slanted so that sunlight filtered in, putting the room in shadows.

On the nightstand was the potted lavender plant.

Joshua laid Erica on the bed and bent to kiss her again. She pulled him on top of her. He doffed his athletic shoes before putting his feet on the bed. "Now for the questions."

Erica's eyes were dreamy. "Don't worry, I'm healthy."

"Not that question. Of course you're healthy. So am I. Condoms are my best friends."

He smiled indulgently. "No, my questions deal with what you're comfortable with in the bedroom."

Erica had to think. She didn't have a lot of sexual experience. "I've only had two lovers, and to be honest, sex with them wasn't very memorable. Especially with my last boyfriend, who cared only about his own pleasure."

Joshua lay beside her on the bed and pulled her into his arms. He spoke softly next to her ear. "I'm sorry. I assumed that at twenty-seven, you would have had more lovers than that."

"I've always had a problem with casual sex. To me, the notion of going to bed with someone just to get off is totally inadequate. I want more. A connection with the man I make love to. I thought I had that with my last boyfriend. We'd known each other for four years. We met at UC Davis. He was a biologist and a few years older than I was. We dated for months before we became intimate. I was excited about our first time, but it was a big letdown. He gave absolutely nothing. He made love in a rush. He didn't know a thing about foreplay. And he wasn't interested in learning. When I told him I wasn't enjoying our time in bed, he was insulted. He never spoke to me again."

Joshua laughed. "Okay, then. You, my dear, are a clean slate." He was gently squeezing one of her nipples between his thumb and index finger as he spoke.

"Exactly," Erica said, her voice rife with passion. She sat up and met his gaze. "My suggestion to you is, *just do me.* I'm game for anything."

Joshua regarded her with a lascivious gleam in his eyes. His penis grew even harder in his shorts. He got to his feet. Erica went to get up too, but he gently pushed her back onto the bed and reached for the top button of her jeans, undoing it.

He pulled the low-cut jeans down over her hips. Erica wriggled a bit to help him. Joshua tossed the jeans onto a nearby armchair.

She had long, well-toned legs and thighs whose lines were wholly feminine. His eyes lowered to her crotch, and his hands went to her panties. He pulled them off her. Erica didn't flinch. Nor did she look away when, after he'd removed them, he drew them across his face, relishing the smell of her sex. She smiled, in fact. He had a little freak in him, a prospect that delighted her.

The panties went the way of the jeans.

"Open your legs, I want to look at you," Joshua said.

Erica obliged.

While he savored the erotic picture she made, spread-eagled on his bed, he was slowly removing his clothing. The shirt first, revealing his broad, muscular chest, pectorals clearly delineated, and biceps bulging with each movement of his arms. Erica's gaze lowered to his six-pack, then still farther as his hand slid inside his shorts and he began tugging at the waistband.

She held her breath just a little when he pulled his shorts and briefs down as one. His penis hung long and heavy in its semierect state. He kicked the clothing aside and approached the bed. Now he reached for Erica and she extended her hand to him. He pulled her up and into his embrace. His hands moved down her back to grab hold of her firm, ripe buttocks. "What a lovely behind you have, all nice and round, with enough to hang on to in a clinch."

Erica reached down and clasped his penis. She felt him throb in her hand. "This is nice to hang on to."

"It's even nicer when wet," he told her.

"Why don't we get it wet then?"

Okay, the game was over now. He could not wait any

longer to plunge into her. He kissed her roughly, his tongue plundering, demanding. Erica was breathing like an asthmatic in the middle of an attack when he let go of her to go get the condoms. On wobbly legs now, she held on to the side of the bed as she watched him rummage in the top drawer of the nightstand.

Breathing hard himself, and his hands shaking slightly, Joshua cursed when the foil wrapper proved more difficult to tear than usual. He wound up attempting to tear it open with his teeth. "Damn it to hell!"

Erica laughed and took the foil-wrapped condom, easily tore it open, and then commenced rolling it onto his fully erect penis. "I thought you might swear in French in the bedroom."

Joshua smiled and kissed her forehead tenderly. His penis moved in her hands.

Done, Erica smiled up at him. "Patience is a virtue."

Joshua growled, picked her up, and dropped her onto the bed butt-first. "Look who's talking about patience!" he said before straddling her.

He did slow down, though. He did not want to be accused of rushing through lovemaking as her former lover had done. He bent and kissed her between her breasts.

"I am not a gobbler. I enjoy my meals in order to derive the utmost pleasure from them." His tongue tasted her right nipple. Her skin smelled of the flowery scent that he liked so much. The taste on his tongue was sweet and a little salty, probably dried perspiration. However, his sense of smell and taste did not come close to adequately describing how having her nipple in his mouth made him feel. The act of suckling her touched off a domino effect of sensual pleasures. He felt it in his own nipples. He felt it in his penis, of course. But most of all, he felt it deep in his heart.

Touching Erica in intimate places made him divinely happy.

He had read somewhere that making love was the closest mankind could get to touching the Divine. Maybe it was true. He didn't know. All he knew was, Erica was his mate. She was the love of his life.

And he hadn't even entered her.

In the throes of passion, Erica had thrown her head back and simply gone with the tide of mounting sexual voluptuousness. As far as she was concerned, Joshua had already surpassed her past lovers.

And he hadn't even entered her.

Joshua sank to his knees, his tongue working its magic all the way down to Erica's belly button where he left a wet trail around it. Erica tensed when his hands parted her thighs. She could guess what he had in mind, but she wasn't at all sure of her ability to accept that form of pleasuring. She'd never received oral sex. She certainly had never given it.

Sensing her reticence, Joshua peered up at her. "I guess that's not something you're familiar with?"

She shook her head.

Joshua wondered where her past lovers had come from, a seminary? He knew some men of God who knew more about pleasuring a woman than her ex-lovers had apparently known.

"It's like this, sweetness," he patiently explained. "You close your eyes, open your legs, put your trust in me, and simply enjoy it."

Joshua rose and kissed her again until she felt like putty in his hands, and then he backed her toward the bed. When her legs came up against the bed, he pushed her down so that her legs hung over the side of the bed. "Now lie back and relax."

Erica tried her best. She lay back on the bed, put her feet up, and opened her legs.

Joshua knelt next to the bed, pulled her toward him, and placed a hand on either side of the inside of her thighs. Lowering his head, he started by kissing her inner thighs. He felt her quiver. "Look at me," he ordered her.

Erica held herself up on her elbows.

Joshua smiled at her. "Watch me. And don't abruptly close your legs. You could injure me for life."

Erica laughed softly. "Okay, I'll try to control myself."

Joshua licked the moist opening of her sex. Erica had to admit that formerly she had thought that only men were turned on by visual aids, but watching Joshua put his mouth on her was definitely liberating.

He delved deeper, and she moaned. His hands forced her legs open wider. Erica scooted closer to him. Seeing this as a go-ahead, Joshua increased his efforts. His tongue caressed the soft folds of her labia, teased her clitoris. Exulted in what made her a woman.

"Oh my God!" Erica cried.

Joshua smiled. He knew she'd get religion soon.

He could tell by how stiff her clitoris had grown against his tongue that she was nearing a climax. He slowed down, relishing the taste of her, feeding off of the evident enjoyment she was deriving from his manipulations.

Erica bucked when the orgasm hit her. Her back arched, raising her body off the bed, then she settled back down, feeling light and spent and wholly satisfied.

"For a novice," Joshua joked, "you're doing quite well."

Erica got up and hugged him she was so grateful. She kissed his face repeatedly.

Joshua rose with her in his arms. He was laughing, white teeth flashing. "I take it that was good for you." He kissed her lips, then directed her attention back to the bed. "Let's see how you like this. On your back, please."

Erica felt loose and relaxed and more sexually desirable than ever. She eagerly spread her legs and enjoyed the look of awe on Joshua's face as he knelt between her legs and placed his penis at the opening of her vagina.

He'd grown hard again, just looking at her wet, moist mound.

Erica arched her back, welcoming him inside her. She had a selfish thought as he drove home and her vaginal muscles contracted around him: she might actually have more than one orgasm for once in her life!

Joshua gathered her up in his arms. She'd taken all of him, and was still asking for more. He thrust, aching with intense pleasure with each push. Erica's hands were splayed on his back. He felt the rise and fall of her chest with each breath she took.

Her warmth suffused him. The side of her face was pressed to his chest and it was her feathery breaths on his chest, coupled with the deep penetration he'd achieved, that made him slip over the precipice.

He climaxed. It felt as if it had been aeons since his last orgasm.

But then, he'd never been with anyone who had given him more pleasure.

He shuddered with satisfaction.

When he peered into Erica's face he sensed that she had been looking at him the entire time. "I know," he said self-deprecatingly. "I look like an idiot when I come."

"You look gorgeous to me."

Joshua grinned, pulled her to her feet, and picked her up.

"Have you ever taken a bath with a man, my love?"

"No," Erica said, smiling shyly.

"Then today is your lucky day."

A few minutes later they were luxuriating in his big claw-footed tub with Nina Simone's voice serenading them on the CD player. Joshua was sitting with his back at the far end of the tub, and Erica was sitting between his legs, playfully sticking her big toe in the spigot.

Nina was singing "I Put a Spell on You," her deep, emotional instrument dipping and rising with impassioned flair.

"You're going to be very embarrassed if your toe gets stuck and I have to phone a medic to get you unstuck," Joshua warned.

Erica laughed at his overactive imagination, but removed her toe nonetheless.

"Joshua," she said indolently. "Why didn't you ever look me up? You knew where I was, didn't you?"

"Yes," he said, his tone guarded.

"Then why didn't you try to find me and talk to me? Don't you think that if I knew where to find you I would have come to you, just to see how you were?"

"Erica, I tried to put all of that behind me. I thought your parents behaved the way that they did because they didn't *want* us to grow closer than we already were. I focused on my career. I was driven. I tried not to think about what you were doing, or whom you were doing it with. But I told myself that if I ever came face-to-face with you again I would try to get to know you better, and I did."

"Did Hubert know?"

"No. I lived for the times Hubert would talk about you, but no, I never told him that I knew you and your family. Like I said, I was trying to put the past behind me."

"So our meeting was purely by chance?"

"Yes, it was. I knew Hubert was coming to the tasting, but he never mentioned he was bringing you. When he came up to me at the tasting and told me he'd brought a guest and then told me your name, I was floored. I thought of leaving, but I had to see you."

"That's so sad," Erica said. "You're sad." She turned to look into his eyes. "You left your happiness up to fate when it was within your power to change both our lives."

"I had no way of knowing you'd remember me, Erica.

I'm not the sort of man who who lives on pipe dreams. I had a goal: to earn enough money to buy a little winery in northern California. Only when I had something of my own would I come looking for you."

"Sad," Erica repeated, shaking her head. "You're one sad puppy! Proud, but sad."

At first, Joshua thought she was serious, but then a mischievous glint appeared in her brandy-colored eyes and he knew she was pulling his leg.

"I suppose you would have tracked me down here in Burgundy and forced me to remember you?"

"Damn straight I would have," she said with a laugh. "I would have seduced you within an inch of your life, Joshua Knight." Her tone turned wistful as she resumed her former position in the tub with her back to his chest. "When I was a freshman at UC Davis I ran into a guy whose name was Joshua Jackson. He was around your age. I wanted him to be you, but of course, he wasn't. He didn't have your dark, liquid eyes or your beautiful mouth. All he did for me was bring back painful childhood memories."

"You looked for me?" he asked softly. He gently kissed the side of her neck.

"I *hoped* for you," she told him.

Chapter Ten

Dominique arrived at the Etienne Roumier Winery offices bright and early one morning in August. Since her father had given her permission to delve into any aspect of the business, she had checked the wine in the barrels, gone over the financial records with the company's accountant, and today she was visiting the laboratory.

She'd visited once more than two years ago when Joshua had attempted to get her interested in her family's legacy. However, she'd been too stubborn to listen then.

"Good morning, Mademoiselle Roumier," said her father's assistant, Henri Dugat, as he walked toward her in the hallway.

Dominique grimaced. She knew Henri didn't want her there. He'd tattled on her to her father a few weeks ago when he'd caught her testing the wine in the barrels, and he had not been very forthcoming with information when she asked him a question, even though he knew she had her father's blessings to learn as much as she could about the winery.

She put on a pleasant face when he got closer.

"*Bonjour,* Monsieur." She never referred to him by his name, although he'd asked her to on numerous occasions in the past. She did not want to feel familiar with him. For some reason, being in his presence made her uneasy.

He looked to be around fifty, and was of medium height and weight. His brown hair was graying and he had a prominent widow's peak. Small brown eyes squinted at her from above a hooked nose. His lips formed a thin line when his mouth was closed.

Perhaps if he smiled more often his appearance might be more pleasing to the eye, Dominique thought. But he wore a sad expression all the time, as though he were contemplating his life so far, and found it wanting.

"You've been here every day for the past six weeks," he observed stiffly. "I suppose we're becoming quite boring to you by now."

"On the contrary," Dominique told him. "I'm thoroughly fascinated. I should have taken an interest long ago."

Henri seemed to draw himself up inside his dark business suit. "Yes, well, if I can be of any assistance please don't hesitate to ask." He turned abruptly. "Good day."

"Monsieur," Dominique said, dismissing him.

She was relieved to see his back.

Continuing down the hallway, she saw her father, leaning heavily upon his cane, going into his office. "*Pere,*" she called. "I missed you at breakfast. How are you today?"

Etienne turned with a warm smile on his face. He waited for Dominique to join him inside his office, then he closed the door behind them. Dominique kissed his cheek. He did not return her kiss. "I thought you would be spending more time making wedding plans rather than haunting these corridors," he said.

He went and sat behind his desk.

Dominique sat on one of the plush leather chairs in front of the desk and crossed her legs. She was wearing a navy blue skirt suit with a white blouse open at the neck.

"I've got plenty of time to plan for the wedding," she said lightly. "Joshua is showing me the lab today. I'm looking forward to it."

To her surprise, her father had offered no objections when she and Hubert had gone to him and told him they wished to wed. At first she'd cynically thought he didn't care whom she married as long as she married *someone* and gave him grandbabies. But as time wore on, she had decided he was genuinely happy for her and Hubert and he was willing to let bygones be bygones.

"Good, good," Etienne said. "But remember, Dominique, you're going to be a wife soon, and no husband wants his wife spending too much time away from home."

Dominique blanched. However, she tried to hide her dismay from her father. Had nothing she'd done the past six weeks registered with him? She looked up at him. Her eyes were glassy with unshed tears. "I had hoped to work after the wedding," she said softly.

Etienne sighed impatiently. "Work where, my dear?"

"Here."

"Darling, there will be a place for Hubert if he wishes to work with us, which I sincerely doubt. He has his own family's winery to see after. But you will be busy taking care of your husband, your home, and your children when they come along. I assure you, you will have your hands full. You won't have time to work here."

Dominique's nostrils flared in anger. "But Joshua has told you time and time again that he wants his own winery. He doesn't want to work for you forever."

"When Joshua takes it into his head to leave, there are many worthy men waiting to step into his shoes," Etienne said complacently.

Dominique rose unsteadily on her feet. She felt as if her head were about to explode, she was so enraged by her father's insensitivity to her needs. All her life, she had never been able to please him. She had made excellent grades at school. None of her girlfriends could compare to her in matters of comportment. Afraid of disappointing her father, or embarrassing him in public, she'd learned to carry on conversations with heads of state without missing a beat. She had millionaires eating out of her hand. Two of them had wanted to marry her.

But the only man's attention she wanted, that of her father, she could not get.

"You are a throwback to a forgotten era," she told him shakily. "You are too blind to see that I would be the best choice to lead this company. Simply because I was not born with a penis—"

"Dominique!" Etienne cried, shocked and appalled.

"Because I don't have a penis between my legs," Dominique reiterated loudly, "you stubbornly refuse to acknowledge me. You know what, Father? I think Christian didn't accidentally run into that tree, he ran into it on purpose just to get away from you!"

Etienne firmly placed both hands on his desk and pushed himself up. His face was thunderous with rage. "Get out of here, you guttersnipe, get out of here and don't come back. I will not have you disrespecting me in this manner!"

"I'm going," Dominique said. "And I won't be back. I should have moved away from here a long time ago. There is nothing for me here. Not even a father who loves me. I *have* no father!"

She turned and fled.

Just as she came barreling out of her father's office, a man slipped around the corner in time to prevent her from catching him eavesdropping at the door.

* * *

Hubert offered solace in his arms, but Dominique was inconsolable.

She had phoned him the minute she got into her car and asked him to meet her at a sidewalk café in Beaune. He had been working at the time, but got up from his desk and the sales figures that had commanded his attention all morning and went to meet her.

She sat now, eyes covered by dark glasses, imbibing her second glass of wine.

"He didn't object to our marriage, because he was all too happy to be rid of me," she told him, sniffling. She lifted her sunglasses to dab at her eyes.

Hubert had moved his chair close to hers so that he could put a comforting arm about her shoulders. He thought back to the advice he, Erica, and Joshua had given her that night in Paris more than two months ago. They had been wrong, and now Dominique was suffering because of it. Etienne Roumier was an unrepentant sexist. Dominique's efforts had been wasted on him.

"I am so sorry, Dominique. If I had known your father was this unyielding, I never would have advised you to put yourself through what you have the past few weeks."

Dominique removed her sunglasses and met his eyes. "It's not your fault," she said sincerely. "It's mine for ever putting my hope in his ability to change. But I'm not going to wear myself out trying to please him anymore."

The note of finality in her voice panicked Hubert. He didn't want her doing something desperate in an attempt to get back at her father. "Dominique, you need to try to calm down and think about what you're going to do next."

"I already know what I'm going to do," she said confidently. "I'm going back home to pack my things, and then I'm moving out of his house. Thank God my grandmother left me a trust fund. I don't need his money to live on. I should be able to find a nice little place to rent near here."

"You're not going to rent an apartment, darling," Hubert told her. "You're going to come live with my family."

"I couldn't," Dominique told him softly.

Hubert pressed his lips to her forehead. "Of course you can."

"But would your parents want me in the family now that I've probably been tossed out by the one and only Etienne Roumier?"

"Darling, we're probably the only family in Burgundy who does not care about your father's influence. You will be welcomed with open arms," Hubert said affectionately.

Dominique threw her arms around his neck and hugged him tightly. The tears began to flow for the second time that morning. But these were tears of happiness instead of anger and disappointment.

The next day, Erica was one of many workers harvesting grapes in the vast vineyards. They would clip the bunches and place them in baskets and the basketful of grapes would then be poured into a huge collection bin on wheels attached to a tractor.

The weather was beautiful, warm with clear blue skies with nary a rain cloud in sight. Erica had liberally applied sunscreen in order to ward off sunburn. As usual, the chatter in the vineyards was lively.

She caught snippets of the workers' conversations, mostly gossip about their neighbors, but she was more interested in what Sobran was saying to Hubert about Dominique.

"I know you wish to support her," he told Hubert. "But Etienne is her father, even if he *is* being a tyrant. She will eventually have to make up with him. What is she going to do, never set foot in his house again? That's ridiculous. You can't let bad blood be between members of a family. Etienne is not going to change. So, Dominique will have to. If she wants, she can work with you. *I* will be happy for another pair of hands. And your children will be Lafons, anyway. Once she marries you, *she* will be a Lafon. She had just as well call a truce with her father. Etienne won't be here forever. She does not want to have to forgive him on his deathbed."

Erica thought Sobran was probably being sympathetic toward Etienne because he, too, was a father. She did not understand his reasoning concerning Etienne's refusal to allow his only child to take a bigger part in running the family business, though. It was like Sobran was giving Etienne a slap on the wrist and sentencing Dominique to a life cut off from her birthright. But perhaps, Erica conceded, she was too emotional about the subject because she was a woman and stood to inherit her family's property one day too. She had no right to impose her opinions on people whose culture was so different from her own. Therefore, she only listened while Sobran spoke and didn't offer any comments.

That night, after dinner, as they were all on the patio listening to jazz, and sipping wine, someone knocked on the door.

Fabienne, wearing a cotton caftan in purple, and no shoes, went to answer it.

Erica was laughing at Hubert, who was singing along with Sarah Vaughn. "Good Lord, Dominique, can't you shut him up?"

"I can't," Dominique said, giggling herself. "I don't want to discourage him."

"Somebody needs to discourage him," Sobran said. "For the sake of my delicate ears."

Fabienne returned with Joshua in tow.

Erica had not been expecting him until the next night. He'd said he had to work.

One look at the grave expression on his face, though, told her he wasn't there for her. "*Bonsoir,*" Joshua greeted them all.

Erica got up and went to him. He briefly hugged her and kissed her on the cheek.

"Darling," he said for her ears only. To the rest of them, he said, "I'm sorry to interrupt your evening, but I didn't want to give Dominique the news over the phone."

Dominique sprang to her feet and went to Joshua. Erica went and sat down next to Fabienne, who reached over and grasped her hand.

"What is it?" Dominique asked Joshua, her eyes frantic with worry.

"This afternoon, one of the lab technicians discovered that some of the wine in the cellars had been salted."

"Who would do such a thing!" Sobran cried. He knew it to be an act of sabotage. A deliberate attempt to ruin a winemaker.

"Sobran, please let Joshua continue," Fabienne said quietly.

Sobran, who had gotten to his feet in his indignation, sat back down.

"Henri Dugat told your father that you were the last person to go into the cellars," Joshua told Dominique.

"I would never do such a thing!" Dominique exclaimed.

"Of course she wouldn't," Hubert said, defending her.

"Don't you all have cameras down there for security purposes?" Erica asked.

"Etienne is very old-fashioned when it comes to electronics. He prefers to hire men to guard the door at night. During the day, the door is locked. Only a few people have access to the cellars," Joshua informed them.

"Which included me," Dominique said regrettably.

She sighed sadly. "How can he think I would do something so evil? Even if I detested him, I would not do anything to tarnish his reputation!"

Hubert took her in his arms. "Don't worry. We'll get to the bottom of this." He looked at Joshua over her head. "Have you all called in the authorities, or will it be kept quiet for now?"

"Etienne would prefer to keep it quiet. So far, we've only found ten barrels that were contaminated. Enough to get his attention, but not enough to ruin him."

"Another reason why he believes I did it," Dominique said. "It was enough to spite him but not enough to affect him financially. He probably figures I would do it as a prank but would not carry it so far that I would wind up making Mother suffer along with him."

"Whoever did it knew about your argument with your father," Erica put in.

All eyes turned on her.

"Why do you say that?" Dominique asked.

"Well, the salted wine was discovered after the argument. If anyone wanted to cause a rift between you and your father, it was the perfect time to do it. You look guiltier now, Dominique. And your father is more liable to believe you're capable of doing such a thing since he thinks you want to get back at him for telling you you'll never work for him."

"She's right," Fabienne said. "It was a setup!"

"But why would anyone want to get rid of Dominique?" Hubert asked.

Joshua had a good idea, but he wasn't ready to tell them what he suspected. Instead, he said, "We all know Dominique didn't do it. The question is, who stands to gain if Dominique is no longer snooping? Sorry, Dominique, but to someone threatened by your presence at the winery, you were a snoop."

"No offense taken," Dominique told him. A determined glint came into her eyes. "If I were to guess who would want to set me up my first guess would be Henri Dugat."

"Why Henri?" Joshua wanted to know. "He's been your father's assistant for nearly twenty-five years. He's a glorified secretary with no hope of one day running the winery."

"No, but what happens to him when Father retires?" Dominique queried. "Will you hire him as *your* assistant?"

"No, I already have an assistant."

"Then Henri will retire too unless he finds a position elsewhere, and how many people are looking to hire someone in their late forties or early fifties? I don't know his exact age, but he's nearly as old as Father is. It won't be easy for him to get another job. What's more, Father is not known for being generous. You know what a tightwad he is, Joshua. Poor Henri may not get a nice severance package like some other companies give their departing employees."

"That's not it," Joshua said. "Your father may be a tightwad with his family, but he treats his employees well. If Henri has to retire he will get a nice annuity from the company. And Henri is not as old as you think he is. He's only forty-five."

"Then it's revenge, plain and simple, for some wrong done to him!" Dominique cried. "A personal vendetta."

"How do you figure that?" Joshua asked, once again being the devil's advocate.

"I don't know," Dominique admitted. "I'm grasping at straws!"

Everyone laughed, lightening the mood.

Erica sat, thinking. She'd only met Henri Dugat once, and that was when Joshua took her on a tour of the winery. However, he didn't strike her as a sinister person. Sad, perhaps, but not nefarious. He was brown and mousy, and seemed to fade into the background. That didn't mean he wasn't capable of doing what

Dominique accused him of. Sometimes it was the quiet ones you had to look out for.

Something occurred to her: "How much salt was put into the wine?" she asked Joshua.

Joshua turned to gaze at her, one eyebrow cocked. "Quite a lot. I'd guess about a pound in each barrel."

"Obviously administered using a wine thief," Erica said.

"Probably," Joshua said. "It would take a lot of effort to open a barrel by yourself, but doing it using a wine thief would be a cinch. All you would have to do is fill the tube and then pour it inside the hole where you would normally siphon off the wine."

"Well," Erica said, "what are the chances that whoever salted the wine bought the salt somewhere around here? Good, I would think. And there aren't that many places where you could buy that much salt."

"Our loaner has her thinking cap on, Sobran!" Fabienne said proudly.

"Too bad we've got to give her back at the end of the month," Sobran joked.

Chapter Eleven

Lucy and Ethel.

Although which of them was Lucy Ricardo and which was Ethel Mertz had Erica stumped. Both she and Dominique were behaving irresponsibly. In some instances she'd instigated their behavior, and in others it was Dominique who had dreamed up the scenarios.

For the past week they had been driving all over Beaune, armed with a photo of Henri Dugat and his mother that Dominique had taken about a year ago at a winery picnic to which all of the employees and their families had been invited, asking clerks at grocery stores and farm supply stores (it turned out they sold salt licks for cattle) if they recognized the man in the photo.

The reason they were behaving irresponsibly was that they hadn't told anyone what they were doing. Neither Joshua nor Hubert knew about their investigation. They had instinctively known the men would advise them not to go around asking questions about Henri.

Joshua assured them that Etienne considered the case closed on the incident. However, Dominique refused to be labeled a saboteur and not do anything about the insult.

She had knocked on Erica's bedroom door two nights after Joshua had brought them the news of the wine salting. It was after midnight, and Erica was sleeping. A light sleeper, she instantly awakened and went to the door. "Who is it?"

"Dominique!" Dominique whispered.

Erica opened the door and Dominique slipped inside. Erica laughed softly when she saw what Dominique was wearing, pink pajamas with feet.

Dominique glanced at her feet, then back at Erica standing there making fun of *her* when *she* was attired in a short bright yellow nightgown with the image of Garfield across her chest. "My feet get cold at night," she explained with a grin. "Besides, I think they're sexy."

"Yeah, I'm sure Hubert is going to love it when you come to bed in that getup," Erica said, walking over to turn on the lamp atop the nightstand. She sat on the bed with her legs folded under her. "Now, to what do I owe this late-night visit?"

Dominique sat in the big overstuffed chair next to the bed. Leaning forward, she said, "You've got to help me clear my name."

Erica yawned. "Joshua said your father was dropping it. We all know you didn't do it. Why do you need to clear your name?"

"To prove to my father that he was wrong about me!"

"He doesn't deserve your consideration," was Erica's opinion.

"I know that," Dominique said. "But people gossip. I don't care how much he says he's going to keep it quiet, it'll get out. This is a small town. And in small towns, people talk. I'm not going to be labeled a vandal for my children to grow up and hear tales of what a hell-raiser

I was, and what a horrible daughter I was to their grandfather. The real culprit has to be caught."

Erica took a few minutes to ponder what Dominique was asking. Her brain needed time to wake up properly. "How do you suppose we should go about clearing your name?"

"By doing what you suggested the other night: check at area shops to see if we can find out who recently purchased a large amount of salt."

"What makes you think anyone's going to talk to us?"

"Because we're two attractive women, and men are idiots when it comes to pretty women," Dominique said.

"And what if we run into a shopkeeper who's a woman?"

"Then we pay cash for information."

"I take it that there will be no men on this fact-finding mission. What are we going to tell Joshua and Hubert?" Erica wanted to know.

"Absolutely nothing!"

"Let the record show," Erica said, "that I think this is a screwball idea. But I'll do it anyway."

"Do you know this man?" Dominique asked, holding the photo of Henri Dugat and his mother under the nose of a young man in a small shop that sold foodstuffs. She gave him her prettiest smile, but he was busy looking toward the entrance where Erica stood.

"*Non, non,*" he said, disinterested. His dark eyes remained riveted on Erica.

Dominique sighed and returned to Erica. "He wants you," she said, handing Erica the photograph.

Erica reluctantly took the photograph and sashayed over to the clerk. She was wearing a short skirt and heels per Dominique's instructions, devised so that they would have the maximum eye appeal for their unwitting victims.

"*Bonjour,*" Erica said, looking him straight in the eye. She smiled apologetically. "Do you speak English?"

"*Oui, un peu,*" said the man whose dark brown hair was cut close and lay flat on his well-shaped head, reminding her of the drawings she'd seen of Julius Caesar in various history books. He smiled at her. "Yes, I speak . . ." and he indicated a small amount with his thumb and index finger millimeters apart.

"Good," Erica said. "My friend and I are looking for this man." She held the photo up so that he could peruse it. "He told us he was a photographer and would make us stars. But when we gave him money, he disappeared. The police won't do anything to help us find him. We're desperate. I'm an American. I can't buy a plane ticket to go home unless I get my money back."

"You are beautiful," he told her. "No one should treat you like that. Yes, I know him. He comes in here several times a week, sometimes with his mother, sometimes without her."

Erica hid her excitement. She looked relieved to hear he knew Henri Dugat, but not too relieved. "Are you sure it's him?" she asked. "Because the guy we're looking for said he wanted to pour salt over our naked bodies. He thought it would be artistic or something. I thought he was a pervert, if you know what I mean."

The man's eyes stretched in horror. "So that's what he wanted all that salt for! I had to place a special order to get so much, but he didn't mind paying for it. Fifty pounds of salt is a lot for a small establishment like this. I told him he should try a farm supply store where he could buy a huge block of salt. But he said it had to be granular."

"If I had a copy of that receipt, I'm sure the police would help us then," Erica said sweetly. She pleaded with him with her eyes.

"I'm sorry, but we can't give out that information."

He gave her a blatantly sensual look. "But if you would have a drink with me later, we could discuss it."

"Excuse me," said Erica.

She walked over to Dominique, who had heard their conversation and was barely able to contain her excitement. Erica saw it in her radiant eyes.

"I'm not going out with him to get further proof that Henri is the guilty party. Do you agree that this is enough evidence?"

"Yes!" Dominique said. "Let's go."

Erica turned and beamed at the clerk. "Thank you so much for your help. Good-bye!"

"But wait," the clerk called. "What about that drink?"

Erica held up the photo. "That's how it got started with him, too. I've learned my lesson about getting involved with you suave French guys."

"I'm not so suave," the man yelled. "I haven't had a date in six months!"

"Good luck," Erica yelled back, and she and Dominique were gone.

The clerk slammed his hand on the counter. "And she looked just like Beyonce!"

Erica drove while Dominique ranted all the way back to the Chateau Lafon.

"That rat! I knew he had done it, what did I tell you!"

Erica sighed. "Okay, so we know he did it, but why did he do it?"

"I don't care why he did it," Dominique said. "We have proof now, and the police can do with him what they will."

"Your father may not want the police involved."

"You're bringing down my high," Dominique complained.

"All I'm saying is, your father is the one who has to press charges, so he's the one who should be told what we found out before you go running to the police. You don't want to be embarrassed if he decides not to do anything about your accusations."

"*My* accusations? You heard the clerk identify him."

"He identified him to us, under the influence, I might add. Do you want to explain to Joshua and Hubert how we got the information? I don't! We have no way of knowing if the clerk will talk to the police. And if he talks to the police, he's going to tell them the story I told him, that we were two gullible women who got taken by a con artist."

Dominique was silent for a long time.

At last, she said, "You're right. We would have to go to my father first. But there's one problem, Erica. My father always thinks the worst of me. Look how easily he swept everything under the rug. That proves that he thought I was guilty. Without even questioning me, hearing what I had to say on the subject, he simply assumed I'd done it."

Erica had come to know and admire Dominique over the months they'd been friends. Therefore, she knew Dominique had devised another plan to get irrefutable proof that Henri Dugat was out to harm her father. Proof that even Etienne Roumier would have to respect.

"Okay," she said knowingly. "Let's have it. What do you propose we do next?"

"We go see his mother," Dominique told her, sounding very sure of herself.

Erica had to give her full concentration to a curve in the road. These hilly roads could be treacherous. "Why his mother?"

"Don't you think his mother would like to know what her son has been up to at work?"

"No," Erica stated emphatically. "The woman's old, her heart might not be able to take it."

"Then we need to watch his house."

"For what?"

"He may make more nocturnal visits to the winery. We could follow him and catch him red-handed. After all, if my father's keeping things quiet, Henri doesn't suspect anyone's on to him. He may not be finished exacting revenge."

Erica considered her request. "That makes more sense than terrorizing his mother. But how do we explain our nightly jaunts? It was hard enough to sound convincing when we lied and said we were shopping for your trousseau to cover for the time we spent canvassing area shops. But what godly reason would we have for going out every night?"

"Picking up men?" Dominique joked.

"That would go over big with Joshua," Erica said, laughing.

"I don't know," Dominique said, coming up with another scenario. "Perhaps the woman who is making my dress keeps strange hours and you are kind enough to accompany me to her shop since it's at night and women should not be out alone at night. Besides, Hubert will not object to my spending more time with you. He loves you like a sister, and in a sense, you and I will be sisters once he and I are married."

"It'll take a miracle to pull that off," said Erica.

"I know, but that's the best I can do right now." Dominique sounded apologetic.

"Let's give it a rest, shall we?" Erica suggested. "We did good for a week's worth of digging. I've got a date with Joshua tonight. That should relax me."

"Then you and he are lovers now," Dominique stated, not fishing, but genuinely happy for her and Joshua.

"Our first time was that day I didn't go to Paris with you and Fabienne."

"Ah yes." Dominique smiled at Erica. "He's a good man, your Joshua. I had a huge crush on him years ago, and flirted outrageously, but he always treated me like a little sister. I think he took being Christian's friend to heart."

"What was your brother like?"

Dominique closed her eyes for a moment, remembering Christian's handsome face.

"He was tall, almost six feet, and had olive skin like me, but his eyes were a startling green. He got those from my mother's side of the family. I inherited my father's brown eyes. And Christian also had the temperament of my mother's people. He was gentle and kind. My father tried his best to turn him into another Etienne, but Christian disappointed him. For one thing, he defied him by going to school in the States. That's where he met Joshua. One summer, he brought Joshua home with him. At first, I thought our father was going to be standoffish with Joshua, but Joshua was so charming he won my father over in no time. I think he impressed him with his knowledge of wine more than anything. Honestly, I've never seen anyone so driven. But his ambition doesn't threaten, so in a sense it's reassuring. It certainly was to my father, because when Christian died, he immediately invited Joshua to come here to work for him."

She paused to wipe away tears. "I guess you can see it's difficult for me to talk about Christian. I started out talking about him and ended up talking about Joshua. I think it's because Christian was one of the few people who loved me, and it still hurts so badly that I'll never see him again. Plus, Christian believed in me. He told me I could do anything."

"You *can* do anything," Erica said.

"Yes, I can," Dominique said. "Including make my father eat his words about me. He called me a guttersnipe."

"What the heck is a guttersnipe?"

"Somebody with a rough or vulgar manner," Dominique said, smiling. "On second thought, maybe I *am* a guttersnipe. I was raised by *him*, and he set the example."

"How often do you make it back home?" Erica asked Joshua as they dined at a bistro in Beaune. The restaurant was one of Joshua's favorites and he'd been going there for years. Set back from the street as it was, and with an unremarkable storefront, one could miss it altogether if not for its wonderful reputation, which garnered it a loyal clientele, some of whom came all the way from Paris. The house specialty was *poulet de Bresse farci aux asperges* (stuffed Bresse chicken with asparagus), which was what Erica and Joshua had ordered tonight.

The waiter carved the chicken at the table, and it was served with vegetables and a cream sauce. Made with dry Madeira, a wine fortified with brandy, the pan sauce, redolent with Madeira, was also drizzled over the chicken before eating.

"Maybe once a year," Joshua said as he wiped the corners of his mouth with a pristine white cloth napkin. His dark brown eyes looked almost black in the candlelight. "There isn't much of a reason to go home anymore. My dad died two years ago, and Joslynn and I don't see eye to eye."

Erica's brows arched with curiosity. "Oh, why is that?"

Joshua smiled at her. All he wanted to do was look at her in this light. She was wearing a white dress with a halter top. The expanse of brown arms, shoulders, neck, and cleavage was altogether too enticing, and he found himself eating too fast with a mind to getting out of the restaurant, back to his place and the bedroom as soon as possible. Now she wanted to have a serious conversation.

Of course, he could deny her nothing. "Because when I was eighteen, I went looking for my biological father, and she thought that was a betrayal of Dad. I talked it over with Dad before doing it, and he didn't have a problem with it, but Joslynn took it personally. We haven't had more than two words to say to each other when we meet at family gatherings since then."

Erica was gazing at him with a mixture of sympathy and keen interest. "Did you ever find your biological father?"

"I found his family. He'd died five or six years previously."

"I'm sorry," she said, her voice low and compassionate.

Joshua smiled. "Darling, I can't grieve for someone I never knew."

"You can grieve for what might have been."

"I don't think like that. I'm a forward-thinking person."

"Your coping mechanism."

"Possibly," Joshua said with a thoughtful look. "You can't change what's already been done. All I knew about my father was that he was a good athlete, and he was tall. Oh, Aunt Dee, my mother's sister, sometimes let certain salient points, like he cheated on Mom and that's why she left him, slip through. Aunt Dee is the person in the family whom everybody else has to remind that family business stays in the family. And that young ears should not be exposed to certain things. Needless to say, she's my favorite aunt. Thanks to her, I got a lead on where to start looking for my no-good daddy. That's what she called him. 'Why you wanna find 'yo no-good daddy?' she asked me. 'He ain't never done nothin' but cause your mother heartache.'"

"He helped make you," Erica told him. "And for that I'm truly grateful."

Joshua clasped her hand across the tiny table. He had started feeling melancholy, but she'd cheered him up with just a few well-chosen words. "You know what I love most about you?" His eyes glittered with mischief.

"What?" asked Erica. She glanced down at his strong hand holding hers. She loved his hands. Then her gaze returned to his beloved face whose lines and angles she knew so well from looking at him, undetected, every chance she got. Right now, her knight's noble nose was flared, his wide-spaced eyes beheld her with intense interest, his full-lipped mouth was in repose.

She watched him with bated breath, expecting him to say something profound.

Joshua's lips parted, and he said, "It's your breasts. You have magnificent breasts. The shape, the taste, the way they fill my hands, is enough to make a grown man cry."

Erica scowled. "You *will* be crying soon, my love, because you aren't going to even get a *glimpse* of these babies tonight in payback for that comment!"

Joshua's face fell. "Not one glimpse?"

"I thought you were going to say something like what you loved best about me was my quick wit, or my devotion to my friends and family. But no, you went for a typical male response. My breasts! That's like saying I love you for your *penis*."

Joshua frowned, wondering why she hadn't taken his comment for what it had been, a joke. But did a sister have to talk about a brother's penis? That wasn't playing fair. Penises had ears and would not come out to play if they felt they'd been belittled.

Seeing his face, Erica giggled delightedly. "Gotcha!" She reached for his hands and clasped them across the table. Giving him an unmistakably sensual once-over, she said, "I'm glad you think my breasts are magnificent. I feel the same way about every *inch* of you. Let's go home and explore each other further."

Joshua didn't have to be asked twice. He called the waiter. "*Garçon!*"

Chapter Twelve

While Erica and Joshua were en route to his house, in the gardens of the Chateau Lafon Dominique and Hubert were having a lovers' rendezvous. The night was mild, and there was a light breeze. The August new moon was bright in the sky, and a few clouds languidly drifted past it.

They were sitting on a stone bench, wrapped in each other's arms, their mouths pressed together in a longing-filled kiss. They drew apart, and Hubert murmured, "I missed you today. You and Erica were gone so long." He smoothed her silken hair behind her ear. "I've been wanting to kiss you all day."

Dominique tilted her head up, her kiss-stung lips full and moist, her doe eyes smoldering. "I missed you too, darling. Now kiss me again."

Hubert obliged.

Dominique smiled seductively. "And anyway, Erica and I won't be going out during the day anymore. We're done with the shopping for my trousseau."

"Wonderful," Hubert said, expressing relief. "That means you and I will get to spend more time together."

"More daylight hours," Dominique told him. She

sighed with regret. "The woman who is making my wedding gown wants me to come in for my fittings at night. Starting tomorrow night, I'll have to go out for a few hours. Erica has agreed to go with me."

"Erica doesn't have to go with you, I'll go with you!" Hubert said, sounding hurt that she hadn't asked him. "I never thought I'd say this, but I'm jealous of Erica."

"You can't go with me, Hubert. It's bad luck for the groom to see the bride in her dress before the wedding."

"That's nonsense," said Hubert. "You don't have a superstitious bone in your body."

"Okay, then I want another woman's opinion on how I look in it. You know Erica, she'll be brutally honest. All you would say is, 'You look beautiful.' I want an unbiased opinion." Dominique was amazed that all of these lies were spilling from her mouth. *If I don't get irrefutable proof against Henri Dugat soon,* she thought, *I might turn into a compulsive liar.*

Hubert nuzzled her fragrant neck. "I thought if we went out together, we'd be able to find some place where we could make love again."

Dominique had understandably told Hubert she would feel uncomfortable making love to him in his parents' house. It would be different if she were married to him, but she felt that if his parents heard her and Hubert down the hall in the throes of passion, they would never look at her the same. France might be a country with a reputation for condoning romantic trysts, but there were still codes of conduct you lived by.

She wanted him, too, and felt guilty for having to lie to him.

"Hubert, if I tell you something, will you promise me you won't get angry?"

Hubert removed his mouth from her neck and straightened. "I don't know, does it involve another man?"

Dominique laughed shortly and kissed his cheek. "No, silly! You're all the man I need."

"All right, tell me." He lovingly held her face between has hands while looking into her eyes. "I promise not to get angry."

"For the past week, Erica and I have not been buying things for my trousseau, we've been trying to link Henri Dugat to the wine salting."

Hubert dropped his hands to his lap. His eyes were still on her face though. "How?"

"By showing shopkeepers his photo and asking if they remembered him."

He placed his hands on his knees as though he were about to rise, lowered his gaze to the ground in front of him, and took a deep breath. He released it and turned his gaze on Dominique again. "Didn't it occur to you that doing something like that might be dangerous?" He did not raise his voice, for which he was very proud. He'd wanted to shout it at her.

"That's why I asked Erica to come with me. We could watch each other's backs."

Hubert sighed. "I can't believe Erica agreed to help you. She's the levelheaded one! Wait until I get my hands on her."

"You said you wouldn't get angry," Dominique reminded him, her tone accusatory.

"I'm not angry," Hubert denied. "It's just that I wish you'd come to me instead of going to Erica and endangering her right along with you. I thought you loved me, Dominique. You should be able to tell me anything."

"That's why I'm telling you now," she said softly. "Because I love you, and I didn't want to keep a secret from you." Her eyes shone with tears. "I'm sorry I didn't come to you, Hubert, but I thought you'd tell me not to do it, and I *had* to do it. My father took Henri Dugat's word without question. I haven't been in the cellars in over two weeks. I could not let it lie, as my father wanted to do. Erica and I found someone who identified Henri. He not only remembered him, he recalled that he'd specifically asked for granular salt. A block of salt would not do."

"What are you going to do with the information? Your father has decided not to pursue the matter."

"Only because he thinks I did it. If he knew it was Henri, he might change his mind. Henri did it. He had a reason for doing it. He may still have it in for my father. Did you ever think of that?"

"No," Hubert admitted. He pulled her close to his side. "Okay, your father should be told. And I'll go with you."

"Wait," Dominique told him. "There's more. . . ."

"So," Joshua said as he drove, "how are you and Dominique getting along? Are you driving each other crazy yet, shopping for wedding linens and things?"

"No, we haven't had any knock-down-drag-outs," Erica told him lightly, perhaps too lightly. "And what do you mean by 'yet'? Two women can get along without resorting to fighting, you know."

"I didn't mean anything by it," Joshua said. "I was just making conversation. The question is, why are you so nervous all of a sudden?"

"I'm not nervous."

"You just squeaked," he pointed out. "You only squeak when you're nervous or excited. Did my asking you about you and Dominique make you nervous? And if so, why? Come on, Erica, talk to me."

"There's nothing to talk about. We went to several shops today, and that's all. It was kind of boring, if you must know."

"Okay, fine, let's drop it," he said with an edge to his voice.

"Fine," Erica said, echoing his sentiments.

"But if you were doing something out of character, you would tell me, wouldn't you?"

"I thought you said we were going to drop it."

"That was before you took on that irritated tone," he said. "Why would my asking you about your day with Dominique make you irritated? I'm going to be straight with you, Erica. When I told Dominique that Etienne was dropping the matter, I didn't like the look on her face. She was furious. And then it occurred to me that if no one else was going to try to find out who had salted the wine, she might. I know if someone accused me of something, and I wasn't guilty, I'd be pissed off enough to try to find the culprit myself. Like I said, I saw Dominique's face, and if she's gone off on a wild-goose chase, I don't want her taking you along for the ride. That's all."

He pulled the car in front of the house and put it in park. Turning to face her, he added, "I don't want anything to happen to you."

"Do you think trying to find out who really salted the wine could be dangerous?" Erica was sincerely surprised by his comment.

"If it's someone who has it in for Etienne, and if he knows you and Dominique are on to him, yes, I think he might be dangerous when cornered."

It had not occurred to Erica that Henri Dugat, a man who looked like he wouldn't hurt a fly, might be dangerous. She frowned when she had another thought: what if Henri Dugat returned to the shop they'd been in asking questions? It could happen, the shopkeeper had said he was a frequent shopper there, and the shopkeeper, miffed at Erica for not having that drink with him, might have told him that they'd been asking questions about him. A brief description of her and Dominique would be all that Henri would need. He would definitely recognize Dominique. He'd known her practically all her life. He'd worked for her father for nearly twenty-five years!

A chill came over her. "We found proof that it *was* Henri who salted the wine."

"I'm listening," Joshua said evenly.

Erica told him everything. When she was done she felt horrible for having betrayed Dominique's trust. However, she also felt relieved. She'd hated keeping a secret from Joshua.

"You don't really think he's dangerous, do you?" she asked, upset now and talking too fast. "The shopkeeper *did* say he'd bought fifty pounds of salt. That means he hasn't used it all. That's the first thing I thought when the shopkeeper told us that. You said that only ten barrels had been salted, and your lab technicians had estimated only a pound of salt had been used per barrel. That means he probably has forty more pounds of salt left. Plenty to ruin more wine with."

"Breathe, baby," Joshua said quietly. "Let's go inside, and I'll tell you what I know so far. It isn't as bad as you're imagining."

Erica breathed.

Once she and Joshua were in the house, he took her wrap and hung it on the hall tree and placed his jacket there as well. He motioned to the living room. "Please, sit. I stumbled upon this information by accident only a few months ago, and it's been weighing heavily on my mind since then," he said as they went to the living room with its comfortable sofas and chairs. "I've got to tell someone who can keep a secret."

Erica sat on the couch and kicked off her shoes.

Joshua sat across from her in a chair and leaned forward, his big hands clasped together and dangling between his legs in a relaxed manner. "One night, not too long ago, I overheard Etienne and Henri in a heated argument. It was late, and I think they thought everyone had gone home for the day. I was finishing up some lab work, and they were right outside my door. 'I love you,' said Henri. 'But I won't wait on you forever.' At first I was in a state of disbelief. It sounded like the two of them were lovers. Then I heard Etienne say, 'You won't have to wait forever. I'm old. I'm going to retire soon, and then, son, the business will be yours to run as you see fit.'

"I'm such a Boy Scout," Joshua continued, "that I went to Etienne the next day and confessed that I'd overheard their conversation. I offered to leave because I knew the nature of the wine business in Burgundy. The son usually runs the business after the father steps down. But Etienne told me he needed me. He told me, point-blank, that he could not leave the business to Henri because Henri was illegitimate and if he left the business to Henri he would have to confess to being his father, and his wife, Berenice, would have proof of his infidelity and leave him."

"Taking half his fortune," Erica put in.

"Yes, at least," Joshua concurred.

"She probably already knows," Erica said. "The wife usually finds out one way or another. Henri is in his forties. Do you imagine that no one in all of Beaune has let it slip to Berenice that Etienne has an outside child?"

"You're right, she could know. But that isn't the point. The point is, when I went to Etienne after the wine-salting incident and told him that Henri had done it, we had him on tape—"

"But I thought you said you all didn't have cameras in the cellars."

"I never discuss Etienne Roumier business, especially the particulars, around the Lafons. They're the competition. Etienne had told me it was all right for them to know about the wine salting because it was to be believed that Dominique was to blame."

"He left her to twist in the wind!" At that moment, Erica liked Etienne even less than she already did. "She was right to try to find the guilty party on her own. I'm glad I helped her!"

"You won't be so glad if she stumbles upon the fact that Henri is her long-lost brother," Joshua guessed.

Erica pursed her lips. He was right. She imagined the news would devastate Dominique. "She really has a fire in her gut for him. She would like nothing better than to string him up by his balls."

"What puzzles me," Joshua said, "is why Etienne let Dominique take the blame. He must realize that she's not going to let it simply go away. I don't know what kind of game he's playing, but if Dominique keeps digging it's all going to blow up in his face."

"It *should* blow up in his elitist, sexist face!" Erica cried.

Joshua laughed. "You sound like an avenging angel."

He got up and joined her on the couch. Pulling her into his arms, he said, "This doesn't concern us, darling. I'm going to quit soon. I can't continue to put off my plans. I've purchased a hundred acres in northern California. The land's perfectly suited to grow pinot noir grapes. The house sits on a hill and it's in shambles, but I'm handy with a hammer and a saw. And I'm young. I can do anything." His eyes bored into hers. "If I have a good woman by my side."

Erica smiled slowly, the smile progressing across her features like the sun coming over the horizon until the day was alight with sunshine. So it was with her face. Her eyes were luminous with her love for him. "Sounds like paradise," she said.

Joshua's warm, firm lips claimed hers. Erica lay back on the sofa and he went with her, his mouth never leaving hers. Joshua hitched her dress up to her hips. "Does that mean you'll come live with me?"

"For always," Erica said. And they were kissing again, this time urgently, their bodies aching for the kind of closeness that their clothing prevented.

Joshua's talented hands undid the clasp at her neck that was holding her halter top together. She wasn't wearing a bra, a fact that Joshua noted with some satisfaction. Honey-brown breasts with dark chocolate areolas were welcomed into his hands. He bent his head and kissed both of them in turn. His eyes held hers. "Do me a favor, sweetness, and reach into my back pants pocket and get the condom."

As Erica retrieved the condom, she asked, "What part of northern California?"

He immediately knew she was asking where the land he'd bought was located.

"Healdsburg," he told her. "You won't be far from your folks."

"That's in the Russian River Valley. It's pretty up there," Erica said.

"Are you comfortable?" Joshua asked, more interested in her pleasure right now.

Erica's neck was against the arm of the sofa. "No, I would prefer the bed."

That's all she had to say.

Joshua bent and picked her up.

Erica wrapped her arms around his neck. "You lift me way too much."

"Let me lift you while I can. When I'm old and gray I won't have the pleasure."

In the bedroom, he set her on the floor and began removing her dress. "Nice dress, but how do you get in and out of it when you're alone?" The dress zipped low in the back. He couldn't imagine her arms reaching that far.

Erica demonstrated how she got out of it by first lowering the halter top and then twisting the dress around far enough so that she could easily reach the zipper and pull it downward.

"Aha!" said Joshua laughing softly. "I knew you ladies had some tricks up your sleeves. Thank God men have buttons and zippers in front where they're a snap to undo."

"Basically there's a running joke in the fashion industry that those who design the clothes are mostly men who don't particularly care for women. Hence, the reason why our clothes are more difficult to get in and out of. Now, why it should be that our clothes are also usually more expensive than yours, and dry cleaners charge us more to clean them than they charge you all, is beyond me!"

Joshua kissed her, rendering her speechless. "You talk too much when you're nervous."

Erica smiled at him. "I don't know if I'll ever find the prospect of making love to you a mundane, everyday event, Joshua Knight, so bear with me."

She handed him her dress. He tossed it onto the chair next to the bed.

She stood before him in only bikini panties. He made short work of removing them.

He made even shorter work of coming out of his clothes.

Erica glanced down and immediately backed up. "Whoa!"

He was fully erect and nearly sticking straight out. Joshua smiled. "He's been wanting to come out and play with you all night long."

Erica tore open the condom she'd had in her hand all this time. "So that's what I kept feeling under the table."

She stepped in front of him, placed the condom on the tip, and rolled it toward his flat belly. Joshua pressed her firmly to him. Her arms encircled his waist. He lifted her, she wrapped her legs around his waist, and he carried her to the bed in that position.

Slowly, he lowered her onto the mattress, going down with her.

Erica opened her legs to him. He plunged into her

welcoming softness. For them, the foreplay had begun at the start of the date; now was the time to consummate what they had been promising each other all evening.

There was no more talk, just kissing, licking, sucking, and moans of sheer pleasure.

Later, as Erica lay awake next to him in bed, she thought back to when he'd asked her to come live with him. Had it been a marriage proposal? Or had he literally meant what he'd said? She'd never lived with a man. Nor had she ever had a desire to.

But Joshua was different. She loved him. Had loved him since she was ten.

She closed her eyes, trying to will herself to go to sleep, to no avail.

The question nagged her: why hadn't he simply asked her to marry him, instead of asking her to live with him? Her thoughts surprised her. She'd never imagined she was old-fashioned, but maybe she was. Or perhaps it was the thought of telling her parents she was going to live with Joshua without the benefit of marriage that made her sick to her stomach. Chances were good her mother would understand. Her father, however, would have a fit and strangle Joshua, *and* her!

Chapter Thirteen

The next morning they showered together and had a quick breakfast of coffee, thick slices of fresh bread with butter and peach preserves, while sitting on the patio watching the sun rise. Both of them needed to be at work early. It was harvest time and all of the employees at the wineries in the Cote d' Or would be extremely busy.

Erica was wearing jeans, a sleeveless, pleated white blouse that buttoned down the front, and white athletic shoes. Joshua wore jeans, a black T-shirt, and black athletic shoes. He had not shaved that morning and his square-chinned face had a shadow.

Erica held her coffee cup in her hands, her eyes downcast, her expression thoughtful.

"Joshua, I need to have something clarified. Last night when you asked me to come live with you, was that your way of proposing to me? Or did you mean it just as you said it?"

She looked him in the eye.

She saw his struggle with what to say behind those expressive eyes of his. She instantly knew it had not been a marriage proposal, and she felt foolish for asking.

Honest as always, Joshua said, "I don't have anything to offer you except a broken-down house on a piece of property and a dream, Erica."

I'll take it, she thought. She would never say it though. Desperation wasn't a part of her repertoire. Not even for the man who'd been the focus of all her romantic fantasies for most of her life.

She took a sip of her coffee. "I understand."

His eyes raked over her face. "Do you really?" he asked gently.

Erica smiled for him. "Of course. I know how proud you are."

"It's not my pride I'm concerned with," he told her. "It's yours. The man you marry should have more to show for himself."

"The man I marry only has to love me."

"You say that now, but wait until the bills are late, the electricity's been turned off, and you can't afford groceries. Love is wonderful, Erica, but you can't live on it."

"There's no use discussing this," Erica said reasonably. "We're never going to see eye to eye on the subject. We're opposites when it comes to this sort of thing. You're by the book, and I'm all for taking a chance on life. Maybe because, as you've pointed out, I'm from a so-called privileged background and you're not." Her eyes turned steely. "Well, let me tell you something about my privileged background: my parents had to struggle to hang on to the land Dad inherited. There were times when we wondered where we'd get the money for food. When you showed up that summer, my parents were just coming back strong. I know to you it appeared as if we had it all, but I can remember the lean times. And I've never known my mother to sit down and let my father work himself to death for her and the kids. She pitched right in!"

"I didn't mean to suggest that you were spoiled—" Joshua tried to explain.

Erica cut him off with, "I know you didn't, but you did, anyway. Now, would you please take me home? We have a big day ahead of us, just as you all undoubtedly have a big day ahead of you at Domaine de Roumier."

"You're angry with me." Joshua sat gazing at her, obviously astonished by her reaction to his offer to live with him. "I suppose now your answer is no, you won't come live with me once I get the house in shape."

"No, I won't," Erica told him.

"You're just being stubborn. What's the difference between what we're doing now and your living with me in California? We're already lovers."

Erica smiled benignly. "If you don't know the answer to that, I'm not going to enlighten you."

"Don't pull that with me, Erica. I'm not a mind reader! I want to know exactly why you won't agree to living with me without marriage. Is it your folks? If so, I thought you said no one makes your decisions for you," Joshua reminded her irritably.

"I do care about how my parents would react to the news, but no, they're not the reason I won't live with you," Erica said calmly.

It was her calmness about their first real argument that incensed Joshua more than the argument itself. He was about to burst a vein, and she was smiling saintly at him as if none of this upset her whatsoever!

"The reason is, when you told me your asking me to come live with you last night had not been a proposal, and then you explained why you thought it was too soon to think of marriage, it occurred to me that you would always want everything to be perfect for us. You didn't want to make love to me until you were satisfied that I loved you. Now you don't want to get married until your finances are right and your house is fixed up, and I'm sure, if we ever did get married, you would have to wait for the perfect time to have children. I know that to most people, your request is not unreasonable. It's smart to be financially stable before getting married. And some people argue that it's sheer stupidity to bring a child into the world without financial security. Still, lots of kids manage to survive when born to parents who weren't exactly expecting them. And couples, my folks among them, manage to have very happy marriages even when they marry without one thin dime between them. I guess what I'm saying is, Joshua, until you have faith in somebody other than yourself, you won't know where I'm coming from."

"Life has taught me that depending on others is a losing proposition," Joshua told her. "I learned only to depend on myself for survival."

"Yes, I know," Erica said sadly. "And I suspect you now regret walking up to me at the tasting three months ago and saying hello, instead of continuing to pretend you didn't know me." Tears sat in her eyes.

His glimmered with them, but he blinked them away. "I could never regret that," he said, his voice catching.

Both of them knew it was over between them, but neither wanted to be the first to voice the words that would make it final.

Erica rose. "I'd better get my bag."

He placed his hand atop hers, keeping her there. "Erica." In her name was a prayer he hoped she'd answer.

Erica bent and kissed him. There was a tender yearning quality to it that had never been there before. "I hope you'll be happy in your house on the hill."

Joshua looked into her eyes and saw that she sincerely wished him happiness.

That was when his heart broke.

* * *

Most wines are made the same way, the grapes are harvested and delivered to a winery where the fruit is crushed in a mechanical press. In the not-too-distant past the fruit was crushed by stomping on it. The *must*, or juice, is then pumped into fermentation tanks. If white wine is being made, the grape skins are removed. If a rosé, a pale red wine, is the goal, the skins remain a short while before being removed. And if red wine is preferred, the skins remain in the fermentation tank for a longer period of time. Hence, it is the skin of the grapes that give wine its color.

Complete fermentation gives the vintner a dry wine; in order to make a sweet wine he has to interrupt the fermentation process. Following fermentation, the wine is aged.

Sobran had had a good year. His vines were healthy; his fruit was covered in *Botrytis cinera*, a beneficial type of mold that helps to make wine sweeter. He was set.

It was time to celebrate!

The Chateau Lafon was lit by Chinese lanterns strung in the front and in the back where the party was being held. Erica walked, alone, among the revelers smiling and stopping to chat awhile when she encountered one or more of her fellow vineyard workers.

The ladies wore summer dresses, and the men, on the whole, wore white shirts, either with ties or without, and dark pants and shoes. That seemed to be their uniform for semiformal occasions.

A string quartet played classical music, and waiters in white coats served guests who went to the laden buffet tables for the catered gourmet fare. Sobran and Fabienne had spared no expense. There was braised pigeon in cranberry sauce, foie gras Souvarov (potted goose liver with black truffles), grilled lamb chops, a variety of fresh local fruits and vegetables, rich desserts, and, of course, plenty of wine.

Erica was standing with Jean-Luc and Lisette Chave,

a young couple whom she'd met in the vineyards, laughing about when Lisette had told Jean-Luc she was pregnant with their first child, a recent development. Lisette was petite, pretty, and quite trim. Her stomach was just beginning to acquire a slight roundness.

"One night, I made dinner and put it on the table," Lisette said, gazing at her husband lovingly. "Jean-Luc went to get a bottle of wine, and when he sat down to pour it in our glasses, I put my hand over my glass, and said, 'None for me.' Then I just looked into his eyes, and he knew."

Jean-Luc held her close to his side. "Of course, when Lisette refuses wine, you know something's wrong!"

She elbowed him in the side.

"But we had been trying for over a year, it was our fondest wish, and it came true!" He sounded triumphant, as if becoming a father was the most coveted prize he could imagine.

"I'm so happy for you both!" Erica said excitedly. "Congratulations!"

Both of them spontaneously hugged her.

Erica was moved, quickly made her apologies, and walked away from them before they could see the tears in her eyes. While tears of joy were expected when a close friend announced the impending birth of a child, she didn't know Jean-Luc and Lisette Chave well enough to express such emotions, and it would make them feel uncomfortable to witness them.

Besides, Erica thought as she hurried around to the front of the house, *tonight is for joy, not sadness.* It had been two weeks since she'd last seen Joshua, and try as she might she couldn't shake the melancholia that had claimed her.

In the darkness, she leaned against the cool stone of the house's facade. Sometimes she wished she were a serious drinker, anything to make her forget. But while she could go get a bottle of wine, find a lonely place, and drink all of it, she knew she still wouldn't be adequately drunk, because wine had such a low percentage of alcohol in it. She might wake up with a whopper of a headache, though. And she didn't need pain on top of pain. What she needed was to be in Joshua's arms.

Thinking of him only made her weep more. She slowly sank to the grass, being mindful not to tear her sleeveless summer dress. It was white with purple orchids on it, and it molded itself to her figure like a glove. Though the material didn't look it, it was capable of stretching. It gave as she sat down and stretched her legs out before her.

This isn't like me, she thought. *Moping, crying at the drop of a hat. I should be back there dancing with every male who asks me.* Several unattached men had shyly approached her, but she'd politely declined.

She had gone looking for Hubert, who was always able to cheer her up, but had not been able to find him or Dominique anywhere.

Several miles away, Joshua was at a similar party, although this one was not set outside but was in the ballroom of the Roumiers' chateau. Guests were encouraged to dress to the nines, and a twelve-piece orchestra played standards.

He was bored out of his mind. If it were possible, he would have begged off, but it was tradition for the head of the company to be there to meet and greet the employees and thank them for their hard work.

Etienne had turned all duties over to him. Etienne had done only one thing this evening, he'd joined Joshua on the podium to welcome the guests. Then he and Berenice had taken seats at a large table where they were surrounded by old friends.

Joshua saw Henri Dugat at a table with his wife, two children, a girl and a boy, and his mother. They looked like they were enjoying themselves. As if this was a special night for them.

He passed the time visiting tables, chatting with employees, laughing with them, listening to their anecdotes about their work environment or "the old man," as they affectionately referred to Etienne. Many of them expressed their support of his being named Etienne's successor, for which he thanked them.

An hour into the evening, Joshua looked up and saw Dominique enter the ballroom. Etienne had not mentioned she might be coming. He thought they were still estranged. She was not dressed for a formal dance, however. She was wearing jeans, boots, and a leather jacket.

Sensing trouble, Joshua headed toward her. She spotted him and turned, in no rush so as not to draw attention to herself, away from him. Her eyes searched the room. When she saw Henri Dugat sitting at a table with his family, she made a beeline for him.

Joshua seriously thought of leaving the Roumiers' to their dysfunctional family drama. He should be at Chateau Lafon trying to win Erica back. He ached for her. These people had taken enough of his life. But he thought of Christian, who had been his best friend. He remembered how Christian had always protected Dominique from Etienne's cruelty, and tried to shield her from his domineering ways as much as he could. Since Christian wasn't there, he would act in his stead.

Dominique was seething by the time she reached the Dugat table.

Henri saw her approaching and grew tense, his eyes darting to the faces of his loved ones at the table, his wife, Nanette, looking radiant tonight in her good dress. She was so proud of what he had accomplished. She told him so practically every day. Their children, Philip and Anne, were actually behaving themselves. He had married late, in his midthirties, and they were seven and nine, respectively. To top it off, his mother was not bothered so much by her arthritis tonight. She was fairly glowing with pride.

"Look at you!" Dominique screeched when she was within earshot of him. "Sitting there pretending you haven't done anything wrong!"

Henri smiled nervously. "Are you talking to me, Mademoiselle Roumier?"

"You weasel! You know I'm talking to you," Dominique yelled at him.

Joshua arrived at that instance and grasped her by the arms from behind. "Come on, Dominique. You don't want to do this. Not here and now. Think of your mother."

"I'm doing this for my mother," Dominique said as she wriggled mightily in an attempt to break Joshua's grip on her. "Maybe it'll inspire her to stand up to my father once in a while."

"Dominique!"

All eyes turned to the entrance of the ballroom. Hubert ran inside, perspiring and breathing raggedly as if he'd been running for quite some time. Joshua breathed a sigh of relief at the sight of him. He made the mistake of loosening his hold on Dominique, who wrenched free of him and leaped on Henri, pummeling his face and body with her fists. The band stopped playing. Voices began murmuring in alarm.

Henri raised his arms defensively in an attempt to ward off her blows but did not try to fight back. His wife, children, and mother all cried out in shock and got out of their chairs in order to try to pry the madwoman off of their beloved Henri.

The other guests craned their necks, then began coming out of their chairs and crowding around the Dugat table. Joshua and Hubert rushed forward. Hubert grabbed the wildcat that Dominique had become around her waist and pulled. She firmly held on to Henri with one hand and hit him with the other. Joshua grabbed her legs and lifted them off the floor. There she was elevated, her legs in Joshua's arms and her torso in Hubert's. Still, she would not stop holding on to Henri and taking out her hurt and anger on him.

"Dominique!" cried a strident feminine voice.

The hum of human voices immediately ceased. Dominique continued to hit Henri.

Berenice Roumier parted the crowd around the table and walked up to it, where she stood next to Henri's mother. "Dominique, quit hitting your brother."

Dominique went still. She held on to Henri's tuxedo jacket with one hand, but she had dropped the one she'd been using to hit him, and it dangled at her side. She raised her eyes to her mother's face. Breathing hard, confused, she appeared to have been unaware of what had transpired around her while she'd been possessed by rage. She looked surprised to see more than fifty people standing around her.

She finally released her hold on Henri. Joshua and Hubert set her on her feet again.

"What did you say?" she asked her mother in a small voice.

Berenice spoke up clearly, as if she did not care who heard her. "I said Henri Dugat is your brother." Berenice was sixty years old. She was a small woman with salt-and-pepper hair, which she wore long and in an elaborate upswept style. Elegant suits usually adorned her slim body, and tonight was no different. She looked quite handsome.

She turned to Henri's mother. "I am sorry if I am embarrassing you, Madame. It is not my intention. But it's time that our children got to know each other."

Colette, the Dugat Matriarch, who had never been married, only smiled. "You are not embarrassing me, Madame. I wholeheartedly agree with you."

Now that Berenice had that settled, she went to Dominique, stood before her, and took both of her trembling hands into hers. "You have such passion, but it's directed at the wrong person. Henri hasn't done anything to you. He is an innocent." She smiled at Henri. "You are both hurting because of your father's behavior toward you. You, Dominique, because no matter how brilliant you were, your father never acknowledged your efforts. You, Henri, because he never acknowledged you at all. I'm old. And I'm fed up. With your combined strength you can defeat Etienne." She turned her gaze on Joshua. "No one has been more loyal than you, Joshua. I love you like a son, but your debt to Christian was paid a long time ago. You have dreams of your own, and time is not kind, it's gaining momentum as I speak. I hear you're in love. She's a lucky girl. Don't treat her shabbily." She looked pointedly at Colette, and everyone knew she was referring to Etienne's treatment of Colette many years ago.

However, for Joshua it had a more recent meaning. He thought of his asking Erica to live with him instead of marrying him. How could he have made such a blunder? You don't ask the woman you adore, the woman you cannot imagine living without to cohabit with you, you give her the respect she deserves and ask her to marry you. There is security in marriage that simply living with someone does not provide. Not only the legality of marriage, but the commitment it demonstrates to the world. When you sign your name on a marriage license, exchange vows and rings, you are saying to everybody: this is my wife, the love of my life, and I will stand by her come hell or high water.

"Thank you, Berenice, I love you, too, but I have some place else I should be," Joshua said in a rush. "Good night, everybody!"

He left them, but not before spotting Etienne trying to leave the ballroom unnoticed.

"Etienne!" Berenice called. "Why don't you join the discussion? I'm sure everyone would like to hear what you have to say for yourself."

Enthusiastic applause erupted.

Dominique smiled for the first time that night. Perhaps now her father would have to answer to a higher power: her mother.

Joshua started running once he was out of the house. If he made good time, he could be at the Chateau Lafon in under fifteen minutes.

At the Chateau Lafon, Erica was in the kitchen with Fabienne laughing at a story her "loaner" mom was telling her about Sobran's marriage proposal.

Fabienne was resplendent in a royal-blue caftan and slacks, her tiny feet in matching sandals, and her hair had been cut even shorter into a sleek style that accentuated her sharp features. She was standing next to the refrigerator and Erica was standing with her back to the French doors that led to the patio where the party was in full swing.

"He picked me up on his motorbike and we were headed to a café, the same one where we'd met two years earlier. I knew something was up because he had on a jacket and it was a warm night. Sobran never wears a jacket unless it's cold out. Summertime, he's usually in his shirtsleeves. I'm on back of the bike, with my arms wrapped around his waist, and he is so nervous he isn't watching where he's going and runs over a pothole. We take a spill. Neither of us is badly injured, but my left knee has a gash in it and it's bleeding. He panics. I mean, the man loses it on the side of the road. The bike won't start, and it starts to rain. We run under a nearby tree to try to miss the worst of the storm. He pulls me into his arms and says, 'This must be the most miserable date you've ever been on. You'll never marry me now.' He then takes the ring from his pocket and shows it to me. It must have been the tiniest diamond

I'd ever seen in my life, but, of course, I adored it on sight." Fabienne laughed.

"And we lived happily ever after," Sobran announced as he came into the room.

"Haven't I told you it isn't nice to eavesdrop?" Fabienne said, going to hug him.

"Yes," said Sobran. "But I hear such delicious things when I do."

Chapter Fourteen

"Erica, come dance with me," Jean-Marc said as he playfully pulled Erica toward the patio door. "You haven't danced with me all night."

"Go dance with Sophie," Erica said, dragging her feet. "She didn't seem at all amused when you joked that you and I were getting married someday!"

Jean-Marc flashed his devastating smile. "Sophie's dancing with someone else right now. She won't mind."

"Go," Fabienne encouraged her, waving her and Jean-Marc out of the kitchen.

Erica relented, and Jean-Marc pulled her through the doorway, across the patio, and into the vast yard where a dance floor had been erected.

When Sobran knew she was out of earshot, he regarded his wife, his eyes flashing with anger. "If I ever see Joshua again, I'm going to punch him in the face."

"You will not!" Fabienne said with a laugh. She went into his arms. "Lovers have spats. Those two are not done with each other."

"You told me she said it's over."

"Her mouth might have said it, but I don't think her

heart is finished with him yet. She's lovesick. The poor child misses him with every fiber of her being."

Sobran sighed. "Okay, my love, you know the human heart much better than I do."

Fabienne tiptoed and gently kissed his lips. "I know yours pretty well."

"Do you, Goose Egg?" Sobran said, giving her a wicked look. "What am I thinking now, eh?"

He pinched her bottom.

Fabienne muffled a scream and took off in the direction of the living room, Sobran on her heels. "Stay away from me, you horny goat!"

Sobran laughed delightedly. "No, my love, we've got a yard full of guests who can look after themselves for an hour or so, and there's no one in the house but us. This is the perfect time for *l'amour.*"

"We just made love last month!" Fabienne joked. "You're insatiable."

Sobran gave a villainous chuckle as he rounded the corner, only a couple of feet behind her. "Man does not live by wine alone," he said, massacring the Bible verse with his witticism.

Fabienne had made it to the staircase, just off the foyer. As she put her foot on the first step, someone used the brass knocker at the front door.

Both of them stopped in their tracks.

"If that's a guest," Fabienne said, "they're very late."

"I'll get it," Sobran said. "You go on up and put on that new negligee I bought you."

"Okay, but be nice," Fabienne said, knowing how impatient he could be when anybody stood between him and *l'amour.*

"I'll be nice, go, go." Sobran shooed her. He was already impatient. He was over sixty and it wasn't every day he felt as randy as he did right now. A beautiful woman waiting for him upstairs, and he had to attend to a tardy guest!

He opened the door, saw who it was, and immediately closed it again. "Go away!"

Joshua had assumed he wouldn't be welcomed, but this was ridiculous. Exactly what had Erica told them about their breakup?

He didn't have time to consider the possibilities though. "Please, Monsieur Lafon—"

"Oh, drop the formalities, Joshua, we've known one another long enough for us to call each other by our Christian names." He, however, did not open the door. "You hurt her, and you promised me you wouldn't."

"It's a bit more complicated than that," Joshua told him. "I didn't leave her, she left *me*!"

"I'm sure she had a perfectly good reason," Sobran said confidently. "What did you do, cheat on her?"

"Absolutely not!"

"Did you hit her?"

"I would never!"

"Then, what *did* you do?"

"Sobran, you're getting a little personal."

Sobran opened the door and glared at him. At least four inches shorter than Joshua and thirty pounds lighter, he nevertheless puffed up his chest and tried his best to look imposing. He stepped back, allowing Joshua entrance, raised his fists, and began dancing on the balls of his feet like a boxer.

Joshua stood there in his tuxedo with a puzzled expression on his face.

"I've never had a daughter, so this may be the only time I get to defend a daughter's honor. *En garde*!"

"Isn't that a term used in fencing?" Joshua asked.

"Whatever! Defend yourself," Sobran told him, and threw a punch at his face.

Joshua ducked in time. Frowning, he swiftly moved forward and grabbed Sobran from behind, pinning his arms at his sides. "What is wrong with everybody tonight? First Dominique jumps on Henri, and now you want to beat me up. I didn't notice there was a full moon on the drive over."

Fabienne ran down the stairs wearing a thick white terry cloth bathrobe. "What is going on here?"

Joshua let go of Sobran and put a little distance between the two of them.

Sobran smiled sheepishly at his wife. "I told you if I saw him again, I'd punch him in the face."

Fabienne continued down the steps. "Good evening, Joshua," she said graciously.

Joshua greeted her. "Madame Lafon." He warily eyed Sobran.

"I take it you're here to see Erica. She's in the back with the rest of the guests." She pointed toward the kitchen. "The door leading to the backyard is right through there. You can't miss it."

"Thank you," Joshua said, and walked backward until he was certain Sobran wasn't going to try anything, then he turned around and hurried in the direction Fabienne had indicated.

Fabienne went and grabbed Sobran by the nose, pinching it until it stung.

"Ouch!"

"I told you not to interfere!"

Sobran gingerly rubbed his nose. "I questioned him and he wouldn't tell me why they argued, so I had to defend her honor."

"Erica doesn't need you to defend her honor, you fool. She's perfectly capable of defending her own honor." She laughed. "Come on upstairs before you get into more trouble."

Sobran liked the sound of that. His brief skirmish with Joshua had invigorated him. He felt like he could make love all night long.

Fabienne ran back upstairs.

He followed her example, but had to slow down to

catch his breath by the time he reached the landing. Maybe he would be satisfied with making love for *half* the night instead of all night long.

Joshua's eyes had to adjust to the dim lighting when he stepped into the backyard that was illuminated only by Chinese lanterns strung in a square formation around the perimeter and electric lights hanging over the buffet tables. The guest tables had fat candles in holders sitting in their centers.

Earlier, the evening's musical entertainment had been provided by a string quartet, but going into the third hour of the party, the string quartet had to leave. Jean-Marc and a couple of friends had pumped music into the backyard via an expensive sound system. On the CD player now was Prince's latest offering, *Musicology*.

Many of the older couples had called it a night. The younger guests partied on. Joshua spotted Erica on the dance floor executing moves with Jean-Marc that he found way too intimate only because he wished she were doing them with him. His stomach muscles constricted painfully as he watched her hips sway seductively, every inch of her erotic eye candy. Jealousy, dark and covetous, seized him.

She and Jean-Marc were grinning at each other as if no one else in the world existed except them. Maybe there was more to Jean-Marc's assertion that he was going to marry Erica someday. Joshua walked closer.

That dress she had on was hitting every curve of her delectable body. Someone should have told her it was wholly inappropriate for the provinces. The other women there didn't look nearly as dangerous in their frocks.

He walked onto the dance floor and tapped Jean-Marc on the shoulder just as a slow song began.

Jean-Marc turned around, a smile on his bearded face. His eyes widened in surprise. "Joshua! Erica, look who's here."

"May I cut in?" Joshua asked, unsure of the reception he would get from Erica.

Jean-Marc's brows rose questioningly at Erica.

"It's okay," she said softly. "Thanks, Jean-Marc."

He smiled at her and turned to leave. Joshua stepped forward and pulled Erica into his arms. Both of them were rigid at first, and then he felt her relax, with a sigh, against him. He breathed in her essence. The tension he'd felt upon seeing her dancing with Jean-Marc dissipated.

Erica broke the silence with, "I thought you would be at your own party tonight."

"After Dominique crashed the party, tried to kill Henri with her bare hands in front of everybody, and Berenice told the entire room that Henri was Etienne's illegitimate son, there seemed no point in staying. So I decided to crash your party."

Erica was listening to him, but the riotous effect his showing up had had on her equilibrium was commanding most of her attention. She felt like weeping again she was so happy to see him.

Only her pride kept her from dissolving into tears.

She tilted her chin up, meeting his eyes. "So, Berenice *did* know all along. I suppose Etienne will have to face the music now."

"Whatever happens," Joshua told her, devouring her with his eyes, "I'm leaving."

"How soon?"

"I'm hoping Etienne will come to his senses and turn the business over to Henri and Dominique without a fight, but even if he doesn't I'm gone in a matter of weeks."

"I see," she said. She glanced down, her heart thudding. "And then?"

"And then I'll be moving to Healdsburg and beginning repairs on the house."

"Oh?" She raised her eyes to his.

"It's a rotten way to spend a honeymoon, but I'll make it up to you with a trip anywhere in the world after our first sale."

Erica's face broke into a wide grin. It could take new winery owners five years or more to make their first sale, but she didn't care. Her eyes glimmered. "Yes!"

Laughing, Joshua picked her up and hugged her tightly. The dancers around them moved aside, giving them room to exult in the moment. "We're engaged!" Joshua shouted in answer to their questioning looks.

They kissed to the sound of applause and calls of "*félicitations*" and "*bonne chance*."

Upstairs, Sobran and Fabienne went to a window and peered down at the kissing couple. "I guess they've made up," Fabienne said.

"That, or he's removing something from her eye," Sobran joked. "Back to bed, Madame Lafon."

Downstairs, on the dance floor, Erica and Joshua finally came up for air.

"Let's get out of here," Erica whispered. She suddenly felt self-conscious being the center of attention.

Joshua was more than happy to take her some place secluded, some place where he could kiss her the way he wanted to. He took her hand and they stepped off the raised platform of the dance floor and made their way through the other guests, saying, "Thank you," as they went because people were still congratulating them.

Jean-Marc, with Sophie in the crook of his arm, waylaid them. "Hey, not so fast," he said, smiling. "Can I at least wish you happiness before you go?"

"Thank you, Jean-Marc," Erica said, laughing softly.

Jean-Marc kissed her cheeks. "Maybe this getting engaged stuff is in the air."

Sophie, who had been his steady girlfriend for more than five years, looked doubtful.

"He's immune," she said.

To which the four of them burst out laughing.

"Congratulations," she said, and she briefly hugged Erica.

"Thank you," said Erica, straightening. "Good night, you two."

She and Joshua continued on their way.

"Your place?" Erica asked.

"Do you have to be any place tomorrow?"

"No, you?"

"No. Why don't you run upstairs and get a couple changes of clothing? Don't forget your swimsuit." His house was within walking distance of a large river that the locals used for swimming.

Erica left him in the foyer while she went upstairs to pack.

When she returned, Hubert and Dominique were coming through the front door.

"I thought you would be at your father's house for some time," Erica heard Joshua say as she approached them.

Dominique laughed shortly. "You should have seen him," she began, her velvety brown eyes dancing. "He blustered for a good ten minutes, calling Mother a traitor, Henri and me good-for-nothing parasites, and then he told everybody to get out of his house. Oh, he's going to have a lot to confess the next time he sees a priest!"

"I see you're no worse for the wear," Erica said. "In fact, I haven't seen you this lighthearted in weeks."

"I know," said Dominique. "Tonight was a revelation. It was cathartic. I feel as if a heavy weight has been lifted from my shoulders. I have a brother. I apologized to Henri for attacking him. He looked at me in such a way that I knew he'd forgiven me. We're somewhat alike, he and I. Life is going to be interesting the next few days."

"Darling," Hubert said, gazing lovingly at her. "Life is always interesting with you around."

"I do keep you on your toes," Dominique said jovially.

"You certainly did tonight," Hubert said. He went on to explain his words. "She and I were supposed to be going to the Chateau Roumier for her to pick up an article of clothing she said she'd left there and wanted to wear to *our* party here tonight. Instead, she jumps out of the car and runs inside, hoping to get a head start on me, which she did, and she goes into the ballroom and jumps on Henri. I was winded by the time I caught up with her, too late, I might add, and tried to pry her off him with the aid of . . ." and then he rolled his eyes in Joshua's direction.

"By the way, where were you going in such a rush?" Dominique asked Joshua. She smiled at Erica. "As if I have to ask. Are you two back together?"

"And engaged," Joshua said, supplying the happy news.

Dominique screamed and hugged Erica.

"Dominique, Dominique," Erica pleaded. The tiny woman was stronger than she looked, and was squeezing her too tightly.

Dominique released her. There were tears in her eyes. "I'm so happy for you."

"She was miserable without you," Hubert told Joshua. "I'm glad I didn't have to resort to packing her up and leaving her on your doorstep."

"That would've worked," Joshua said, and gave Erica such a sensual perusal that she blushed to the tips of her ears.

"That amounts to kidnapping," Erica said, narrowing her eyes at him.

"Sounds romantic," Dominique said, pointedly glancing up at Hubert.

"Well, good night, dear friends," Hubert said. "Dominique and I just came back to tell my folks we're off to Paris for the weekend. Do you two want to come?"

"No, thanks, we have plans," Joshua spoke up.

He pulled Erica close beside him. She clutched her overnight bag in one hand and her purse in the other. "We were headed out, too."

She and Joshua gave them one last wave as they left.

Outside, the air was warm with a gentle southerly breeze. Hand in hand, they walked to the Mercedes, which was parked out where tall, spindly trees lined the half-mile road that led to the chateau. Many of the other guests had parked there too, and it looked like a parking lot. Since Joshua had been among the last to arrive, his car was farther down than the others. The stars were out and helped light their way.

Now that she had him alone, Erica asked, "What happened? Why did you change your mind about waiting to get married?"

Joshua gently squeezed her hand. "I didn't want to turn out like Etienne."

Erica was even more puzzled than she'd initially been. "A man who tried to control all of those around him and wound up sad and estranged from the people who could have loved him in his old age?"

"No, ruled by the almighty dollar, instead of the human heart."

"Please explain."

"When I discovered Etienne's secret and went to him and told him I knew, he told me a story. He said he could have married Henri's mother, Colette. But she was poor, and he came from money. He met her many years before he met Berenice. He made his decision. And because he chose money over love, he went on to make more than *his* life unhappy. He kept his secret from Berenice, from anyone important in his life. He led a double life for years. To Berenice he was a devoted husband. To Dominique and Christian, he was the provider. He admits he loved Christian more. After all, he would carry on his name. He loved Dominique too, in his way. He wanted the best for her, which in his eyes meant a good marriage. He also made certain Henri and Colette were taken care of. They were his backstreet family. Until the backstreet decided to come out of hiding and one day Henri walked into his office. He was twenty-two years old, and he asked him for his inheritance. Etienne convinced him to come work for him as his assistant, telling him he would one day turn the business over to him. He lied to Henri, of course, because he also had Christian, his favorite child, whom he was really going to leave the business to. Christian, however, got himself killed, and instead of preparing Henri to take over, he hired me."

He sighed heavily. "Do you see how one bad choice led to so many others?"

"Yes, I do," Erica said.

Joshua stopped walking and turned to cup her face in his hands. "I knew deep down, when I asked you to come live with me, that you would not agree to it. Yes, it was said in the heat of the moment, but when I think back I have to admit, I knew. I think something in me just didn't believe you could truly love me. That I was worthy of your love. You were right about me. I have a hard time trusting anyone with my heart. It's been broken too many times. Not by women, whom I never let myself get close enough to in order to get hurt by, but by life in general. I learned to focus on hard work. And in working hard, I had the perfect excuse for excluding anything emotional from my life."

He remembered how he'd kept his distance from Lucy. "My last relationship? I never learned one personal thing about her. We went into the relationship with no expectations. The last time I saw her, she'd met someone else and broke it off with me, saying she never saw me anyway, which was the truth. You were the first woman to tell me about myself and have the strength of will to stick by your guns."

"It broke my heart to tell you that you didn't know how to trust," Erica told him, her tone soft, regretful.

"But you told me anyway, because you love me."

"Yes." She let her bags fall to the lawn.

Joshua pulled her into his arms. "I can't change overnight, but I promise to work on it. Sometimes, you might have to give me another good, swift kick in the ass to remind me I'm supposed to be working on it."

"Will do," Erica said happily as she rose up on her toes to meet his mouth in a deep, soulful kiss.

"God, it's good to be home," Erica said as she lay back against Joshua's broad chest in the big bathtub in his house. Joshua's hands were cupping her breasts, his thumbs and index fingers rubbing her nipples between them.

They had not made love yet, choosing to prolong the sweet agony they were experiencing being so close, naked, their bodies acutely attuned to each other. The rules were, they could touch, they could kiss, they could work themselves into a frenzy, but no intercourse until the desire was so strong that neither of them could stand it any longer.

Erica had been amazed when Joshua had suggested they try this, but she knew he liked to push her to the limit where sexual desire was concerned. He'd been a good teacher, and she'd been an eager student. She was always safe in his hands.

Now his hands were moving downward, along her smooth sides, made slick by the soapy water, to caress her flaring hips, onward until they rested on her inner thighs.

Erica sighed deep in her throat and arched her back. Joshua bent his head and licked the side of her neck as his right hand found the spot he'd been searching for. He made long, lazy strokes with his index finger up and down the soft folds of her labia, gently massaging her clitoris. Meanwhile, his mouth found her earlobe and he suckled.

Erica gave short gasps of pleasure, practically panting with the want of release. It was when she began wiggling, thrusting against his hand, that he promptly withdrew. Erica sighed. "You're driving me crazy."

"That's my goal, sweetness. The water's getting cold. Let's get out and I'll towel you dry."

Erica carefully moved forward in the tub so as not to step on anything important. She got to her feet, stepped out of the tub, and looked back to watch him get out. His dark, muscular body glistened, hard pectorals, thigh muscles, and biceps flexing as he pulled himself up. The important thing that she'd not wanted to step on was semierect and lay heavily between his legs.

Her female center began throbbing in earnest.

Joshua picked up a thick white towel. "C'mere, baby girl," he said, his eyes alight with latent sexual hunger.

That look made Erica tremble inside.

She went and stood in front of him.

"Spread your legs," Joshua said, his voice thick. She probably had no idea that her soft feminine curves—slender limbs, full breasts, and rounded hips—were what men craved most. Mass media made women believe that a thin body was what men desired, but what man wanted to cuddle up to cold, sharp angles when he could have a woman in his arms whose body welcomed him with softness and warmth?

Erica's body was perfect in his estimation. In fact, he longed to see her when she was carrying his child. He knew she'd be breathtakingly beautiful.

He sponged her dry with the towel, dabbing instead

of wiping, taking his time and enjoying the sound of her short breaths, and gasps, when he'd pause from time to time to kiss her here or there. To lick her clavicle or gently bite her on the behind.

Erica could not believe this man, torturing her like this. His hands, his mouth, his tongue, and his teeth teased every inch of her. Heightening her already high level of arousal. When he'd gently bitten her on the ass, she'd almost had her first orgasm of the night it had been such a delicious surprise.

She watched him as he slowly circled her like some predatory beast looking for just the right tender spot to sink his teeth into. His dark eyes, almost black, entranced her and filled her with sense of vulnerability: she didn't know what he would do next. And power: as the object of his desire, she was the one who had put that look in his eyes. She'd never felt powerful with any other man. He'd brought it out of her.

Which gave her an idea.

She took the towel from him, draped it around his neck, and pulled him down for a brief kiss. Turning her head and breaking off the kiss, she said, "Let's flip the switch. I get to do anything to you and you can't touch me at all."

Joshua frowned at the mere suggestion of such a thing. *Not touch her!* Then he thought of all the possibilities for pleasure inherent in the arrangement, and flashed her a grin. "You can have your way with me, darlin'."

"All right," Erica said, wiping his body down with the towel. "First let's rid of any excess moisture, then I want you to lie facedown on the bed for me."

After he was lying on the bed, Erica said, "I'll be right back, I have to get something from my bag."

She'd left her bag in his bedroom closet.

She strolled in there, naked, humming, contemplating all of the fantasies she'd wanted to enact with him. Tonight, she planned to fulfill one of them.

"What are you getting?" Joshua called from the bedroom.

"Nervous?" she asked with a chuckle.

"A little."

"Good, it'll heighten the suspense. But don't worry, babe, it isn't something that will permanently paint your penis *blue* or anything."

Joshua laughed. "I haven't fallen in love with someone who's a secret dominatrix, have I?"

"You're much too inquisitive. Just relax and enjoy," Erica said as she pulled a bottle of peppermint body oil from her overnight bag. All natural, it was perfectly safe for human consumption. She remembered how she'd smiled when she picked it up in a shop in Beaune and read the label.

"I'm back," she announced, returning to the bedroom. She stood a moment and admired the symmetry of his long, muscular body stretched out on the bed, his back, shoulders, buttocks, and leg muscles in repose but beautiful to behold nonetheless.

She went to the nearby bureau, opened the bottle of oil, and poured a bit into her palm, then set the bottle on the bureau's top and rubbed her palms together to heat the oil before applying it to his warm skin.

He was following her instructions, lying on his stomach, his head resting on his folded arms. Erica went to the bed, straddled his waist, and began massaging the oil into his back, beginning at the top and slowly working her way down to his waist.

Joshua enjoyed the feel of her warm thighs when she mounted him, and especially the heat between her legs. Already semierect, his penis grew harder with just those actions; however, when her hands touched him and began to rhythmically work the muscles in his back he could not stifle a moan of sheer ecstasy.

The aroma from the oil when warmed by his body heat was rich and sensual. It wafted upward, assailing Erica's nostrils as she kneaded his muscles. Momentarily, she got up and went to get more oil, then she massaged the length of him until he was putty in her hands.

She ended at his feet. "Okay, turn over now," she ordered him.

Joshua obliged.

Erica swallowed hard. Her plans for seduction were going better than she'd ever imagined.

Lying on his back, with his hands clasped behind his head, Joshua smiled at her reaction. "I take it you've never given a man a massage before."

"No, I haven't," Erica told him. "I see there are certain side effects."

"Yeah, you could say that."

She was busy unwrapping a condom. She tossed the foil wrapper onto the nightstand and went to him. "I want you to close your eyes."

Joshua did so. He inhaled deeply and exhaled, preparing himself for anything. He could still see her in his mind's eye: her luscious body, skin fresh from a bath, hair slightly limp from the steam in the bathroom, lips swollen from his kisses, eyes full of mischief and passion.

He felt her kneel on the bed. Immediately detected her body heat. She came closer and bent over him. Then she licked the side of his neck, her tongue warm and wet and firm. She moved upward. He thought she was going to put her tongue in his ear, but she didn't. Instead, she said, "Damn, you taste good."

She straddled him again, and he tensed a little in expectation of next feeling her hands on his shaft in order to put the condom on him. What he felt was her breath on his stomach, then her mouth, then her tongue, and she was moving down. Now her hand wrapped itself around his penis. It felt so good to him that he throbbed in her hand.

Erica let go of him when she felt him throb. Joshua thought she'd lost her nerve. He was almost relieved, because she was an innocent and he didn't want her first oral experience to be unpleasant. If it was, she might never attempt it again. However, she surprised him again, because the next thing he felt was her hot mouth over his shaft, then her sweet tongue circling the tip slowly and with torturous deliberation.

He broke his promise and opened his eyes.

He nearly came when he saw her mouth on him. Those juicy lips encircling him, and her eyes, when they met his, so full of love.

"Oh God," he cried, helpless to resist her, but well aware that if he allowed her to go any further, he wouldn't be any good to her for at least twenty minutes. And there were still things he wanted to do to her before he climaxed.

"Baby, hold up," he said softly.

Erica paused, her mouth releasing him, her lips sliding slowly off of him.

He closed his eyes tight against the sight of her beautiful lips, now wet and glistening, opening to remove him from her soft mouth.

Looking at her again, he sat up and pulled her into his arms. Lying back on the bed, he took her with him. He kissed her, relishing the salty taste of her mouth, remembering the pleasure she'd so unselfishly given him. Erica's body molded itself to his. Her nipples rubbed against his hard chest, feeling somewhat abraded but stimulated simultaneously. She felt his hard penis at the opening of her vagina, and she naturally pushed. He was inside her, and as the kiss deepened, so did his thrusts until they were caught up in the delectable hedonism of the moment. Lost, both of them.

Her hands found his, they clasped together, and that was when she came to her senses enough to realize she still had the lubricated condom in the palm of her left hand. Joshua also felt the latex condom on the palm of his hand, but try as he might, he could not pull out of her now. For one thing, she was on top, and pushing her away from him was out of the question, so in the heat of passion, he left the decision up to her.

Erica rode him slowly, her head thrown back, her breasts thrust forward. Joshua's hands were fondling her breasts, alternately rubbing the nipples with his palms and pinching them with his fingers just enough to heighten her arousal.

He was all the way inside her, and Erica's cries of satisfaction were making him even harder. Completion felt close, so close.

Erica, too, was nearing orgasm, but she wanted him on top for the penultimate moment.

She bent and kissed his mouth. "Put my feet in the air."

Joshua groaned loudly with pent-up tension and flipped her onto her back. He rammed himself into her, heeding her demands of "deeper, deeper." Pushing her legs higher, her feet in the air as she'd requested, and her behind nearly in the air as well, he came with a roar.

A heartbeat later, with her fist pressed to her mouth, Erica smothered a scream.

Still in her, Joshua gently gathered her to his chest. His hot breath was on her neck.

"Oh, baby, I'm sorry."

Erica had let the condom fall to the bed, and now it was under her butt. She reached underneath her and pulled it out. Holding it up, she said, "It's not your fault, I had the darn thing in the palm of my hand and forgot all about it."

She smiled at him. "I just got over my period. You're not supposed to be as fertile just after your period."

Joshua nuzzled her neck. "If you are, you'll just have to marry me sooner."

Chapter Fifteen

Erica and Joshua spent the next two days, Saturday and Sunday, strolling the squares of Beaune and visiting the area churches whose architecture Erica wanted to explore more closely. They did the sightseeing Joshua had promised her when they'd first met in Paris, but to which neither of them had time to devote because of work.

The nearby towns of Pommard, Volnay, Meursault, and Puligny-Montrachet all got their attention, if only for a few hours. Erica so loved the fourteenth-century church in the vineyard town of Volnay, with its views of the Burgundy plain and Mont Blanc, that they threw a blanket down in the square outside the church and had a picnic. From the number of tourists they saw, on foot and on bikes, it was a popular site.

"What do you miss most about home?" Erica asked Joshua as she brought a wineglass half filled with pinot noir to her lips.

"Basketball," said Joshua without hesitation. "Watching it on TV and playing it."

"But you're such a great soccer player," Erica teased. "You look so cute in your shorts."

"I'm not putting down soccer, it's a good game. Very competitive and it gets your heart pumping. But when you grow up playing basketball, it's hard to get it out of your system. And I think I also miss the behind-the-scenes things that used to happen on the court when you're playing with friends or the guys in the neighborhood."

"Like?" Erica asked.

"The challenges, the threats, the outright insults from your opponents. 'You play like my grandma. No, my grandma is even faster than you!' or 'What's that I smell? Hey, Josh, put your arms down, man!' and 'Looka here, y'all, he finally made a basket, call ESPN!' Things like that. Then there'd always be some guy who took the insults personally and a fight would break out."

"Good times, huh?" Erica asked, smiling at him. "I'm telling you now, my brothers cheat in basketball. And they're hustlers. They've been playing together for so long, neither of them can get anything over on the other one, so they lie in wait for suckers who don't know them, and take them for everything they have. It's a matter of honor with them. Kill or be killed, that's their motto. My mother says she weaned them too soon."

Joshua laughed. "That's what I remember most about your mother, she had a great sense of humor. She would have everybody cracking up, usually about something your dad had done."

"Ah yes," Erica said. "The misadventures of Eric Bryant. My mom could write a book on him. The man has injured himself on the farm in every conceivable way. He's been thrown by a horse; got his foot caught in the winepress, how that happened, I'll never know; and been butted by a goat. Now, the goat business was probably my fault and I take full responsibility. A neighbor's goat had kids and she offered me one and I begged my parents until they said yes. That goat was so ornery no one would go near it, including me. We finally gave it to another neighbor who wanted it to keep her grass mown. I hope it didn't end up on somebody's barbecue grill."

"Barbecued goat?" Joshua said, laughing. "I've lived in France for more than a decade, and I've never eaten goat meat. Pigeon, snails, rabbit, beef tripe, yes. I've even had the testicles of a lamb. . . ."

"What did they taste like?" Erica wanted to know.

"Chicken," Joshua told her matter-of-factly.

She burst out laughing. "God must have really loved the chicken since he made so many things that taste like it."

In Glen Ellen, California, the Bryants were a week behind the Lafons in their harvest. Eric still got excited every August. Today, he was walking between the rows of vines, observing the work of the pickers, giving advice where needed, sometimes demonstrating the proper way the grape bunches should be removed from the vine, other times commending the workers.

It was hot today, nearly ninety, and for some reason he didn't feel like his old robust self. For one thing, he should not be this fatigued. He was used to long days in the vineyards.

Tall, and in good physical condition from weight lifting every other day and working hard at his job, Eric prided himself on the fact that his waist was still the same size, thirty-eight, as it had been the day he married Simone. Simone couldn't say that, but then *he* hadn't given birth to three children!

He smiled, just thinking about her. Several years his junior, that woman kept him on his toes. She might be a tad thicker around the waist than she had been on their wedding day, but she definitely knew how to use what God gave her. Last night had been like a fine wine: sweet on the tongue at first, graduating to fleshy with some spice, and ending with a memorable aftertaste. That's how it had been between them. She'd made him feel as if they were lovers who were just getting to know each other, when they'd made love countless times during their marriage.

Eric envisioned her sweet face, smiling at him when he left the house this morning.

Suddenly, a sharp pain squeezed his chest. He tried to draw a breath and found it difficult to do so. He figured he'd been out in the sun without a hat for too long.

Simone had always warned him that "the bear" would catch him if he didn't watch out.

Must the woman be right all the time? The ground, a gravelly soil, a mixture of decomposed granite and loess, could be rocky in some spots. Luckily, he fell face-first into a soft patch.

Thanks to the fast thinking of his foreman, Claude Leroux, a Haitian-American with a thirst for knowledge who'd taken CPR at the local YMCA when it was offered for free, Eric was awake by the time the paramedics arrived and took him off the back of the farm's pickup truck. Simone was there, bending over him, fear and hope in her expression. "Don't you die on me. You owe me a Winnebago!" she said fiercely.

The paramedics tried to talk her into following them, but she insisted on riding in the back of the ambulance with him. Eric kept his eyes on her, his compass. With her there, he knew he'd never get lost.

"He's gonna make it," one of the paramedics, a kid with red hair and pale blue eyes, said. He smiled at Simone. "Ma'am, since you're here, maybe you could tell me a little about his health. Has he ever had any problems with his heart?"

"No, never."

"How old is he?"

"Sixty-five."

"He looks great for sixty-five!"

Simone laughed. Eric always said that. He'd flex his biceps and say, "Ain't you glad you got pulled by an old man like me?"

Watching her, Eric knew exactly what she was laughing at. That's how well he knew her. When he got his energy back, he'd make her pay for such impudence!

He laughed too and ended up coughing. After his coughing bout, he thought the pressure in his chest had eased up a bit.

Simone looked concerned to see him laughing and coughing.

"That's a good sign," the paramedic told her.

She peered closer at the name tag on his shirt. Farsighted, she'd forgotten her glasses. *Tim Braugher*, it read. "Thank you, Mr. Braugher, I'm glad to hear that."

Tim smiled as he checked Eric's blood pressure. It was elevated but not so high as to require immediate medication. "The thing is, muscle men, like your husband, sometimes forget to exercise the most important muscle of all, the heart. Even our governor had a problem with his heart, and we all thought he was the healthiest man alive."

Simone sometimes had to pinch herself to make sure she wasn't dreaming whenever she focused on the fact that Arnold Schwarzenegger was now the governor of California.

Eric laughed again. "Don't talk politics while I'm dying."

Simone gave him a stern look. "You be quiet and concentrate on *living*."

"Yes, Mr. Bryant," Tim said. "You just rest while your wife fills me in." He continued his questioning. "Does Mr. Bryant take Viagra?"

"Not that I know of," said Simone. "Now you can talk."

"No, don't need it," said Eric.

Tim smiled at that assertion. "Have you been engaged in any strenuous activities within the last twenty-four hours?"

"She had her way with me last night," Eric said.

"Surely sex isn't a strenuous activity between a couple who is as old as we are," Simone said, looking at Tim for elucidation.

"That depends," said Tim. "If his heart was already on the verge of sending him a signal, then that might have pushed him over the top."

Eric laughed. "It's the *only* way to go!"

"Can't you give him something to knock him out?" asked Simone seriously.

Tim laughed. "You two are a riot."

Jason Bryant was walking up the steps of the courthouse in Bakersfield, California, in order to file for a continuance in the case of his newest client, a divorced man accused of stalking his soon-to-be ex-wife, when his cell phone rang. A divorce attorney for the past eight years, he was rapidly growing tired of all the drama associated with divorce: husbands who insist on controlling their wives. Wives who lie and say their husbands hit them in order to sway the case in their favor. Jason thought there were enough genuine cases of abuse out there without these women adding to the amount of paperwork already clogging the system.

He was just tired of all of it, and his tone of voice, when he answered the phone, clearly denoted that he was irritated. "Hello!"

"Jason, what's the matter with you?" asked his brother, Franklyn.

"Sorry, man, I didn't mean to take it out on you. I've just had a rotten day, that's all."

"Well, I'm sorry too, but I'm only going to add to it. Mom phoned me a few minutes ago. Dad's in the hospital in Glen Ellen. He had a heart attack."

"What!"

"Calm down, Mom says it isn't serious. He's doing a lot better. Preliminary exams show a minor myocardial infarction, the doctor said. It can be treated without surgery."

"He's tough," Jason said. Sweat had broken out on his forehead, though, and he'd had to sit down on the top step at the courthouse, his briefcase between his legs, and his cell phone held to his ear with his right hand.

"Yeah, he's tough," Franklyn agreed. "But I'm heading up there anyway. You wanna phone Erica?"

"You know I don't want to phone Erica, she'll show out."

"Jason, it's your turn. I phoned her when Mom had the cancer scare."

"You cheater!" Jason said. "That doesn't count. When you phoned, Mom had already gotten the news that the lump was benign. Dad's not out of the woods yet. She's going to get hysterical."

"You can handle her, you're a divorce lawyer, you're used to hysterical women."

"Wait till I see you, bro," Jason warned.

"I'm scared," Franklyn assured him. "But I'm more afraid of her than I am of you. Bye. See you in Glen Ellen."

Jason growled in frustration and hung up the phone.

An attractive woman, passing him on the steps, heard him. She paused.

"Bad news, tiger?"

Jason perked right up. Rising to his full six feet, he regarded her with interest. She had beautiful café au lait skin, her dark brown hair was in long locks, and she was wearing an expensive blue skirt suit with black pumps. He glanced down. Nice gams. In fact, she had nice *everything*, as far as he could tell.

"My day just got better," said Jason.

She smiled even broader. Her light brown eyes raked over his broad shoulders and flat belly. She liked how his suit hung on him, and wondered how he looked out of it. Moistening her full lips, she said, "Mari Eastman."

"Jason Bryant."

"The divorce lawyer?" Her eyes sparkled with delight.

Jason was glad she'd heard of him. That saved time. "Yeah, that's right."

She had her card out of her purse in a flash. "I've heard good things about you. I'm getting a divorce. Maybe we can go somewhere and discuss your representing me."

Jason blew air between his lips. What a letdown! "Thanks, but I've already got my hands full. I can recommend a colleague . . ."

She sidled closer, eyeing him with sensual intensity. "I can make it worth your while."

Jason, who rarely turned down an offer like that, accepted her card. "I'll call you."

She smiled confidently and continued on her way. "I know you will," she tossed over her shoulder.

Jason's smile told her he couldn't wait. However, a couple of minutes later, as he waited for the elevator in the lobby, he tossed her card into a nearby waste receptacle.

Calling her was just asking for trouble, and lately he wanted to simplify his life, not add to its burdensome complexity.

The cell phone seemed to be burning a hole in his pocket. He knew it was guilt, because he had no plans for phoning Erica right away. He'd go and file for the continuance, then when he got home tonight, and had had a cold beer, he'd phone her. Franklyn had said their dad was going to be fine. He told himself he was delaying Erica's anguish, when in reality he knew he was being a wuss. He hated being the one to bring his baby sister bad news. He and Franklyn had always protected her from harm.

He had joked with Franklyn about Erica "showing out" when he phoned her. But the real reason he and Franklyn each tried to force the other to break bad news to Erica was that neither of them wanted to witness her pain. She was five years younger than he, and eight years younger than Franklyn. When she was a child, they kept her from hurting herself. She'd been a rough-and-tumble tomboy, on their heels, doing everything they did for fear they'd label her a sissy. When she was a teen, they'd turned into bodyguards, not allowing any boy with sex on his mind near her. Now that she was an adult they knew they couldn't police every date she had, so they watched from a distance, hoping and praying she'd make the right choices in men. And they lent a ready ear whenever she wanted a shoulder to cry on.

Adulthood was more difficult for them both because now they couldn't, as a united front, go to each guy she dated and threaten him with bodily harm if he should hurt her. Jason wished it were that easy. No, now they had to stand aside and watch her stumble through life, sampling it, experiencing everything by way of trial and error just like every other human being.

Calling her and telling her their dad had suffered a heart attack would be painful to him because he wouldn't be there to comfort her after he'd told her. She would be in anguish, and he would be powerless to alleviate it.

So, he did something he rarely ever did: he procrastinated.

Finally, all of the medical personnel had left the room, leaving Eric and Simone alone. He was awake, but groggy. They'd given him aspirin and a battery of tests that had left him even more tired than he was when he had arrived. On the plus side, the attending physician had told them that his heart was still in relatively good shape, and he'd probably live to be a very old man if he cut out the steaks he loved, the butter he slathered on his toast, and took up aerobics.

"Aerobics," Eric said as he reached for Simone's hand.

She clasped his hand, leaned over him, and kissed his cheek. He had a five o'clock shadow, and the bristles tickled her lips. "Walking, biking, jogging, anything that gets your heart pumping, and gives your lungs a workout."

"You mean like that walking you do every day?"

"That'll do it."

Eric scrunched up his nose. Normally, his skin was the color of roasted almonds, but today it was sallow. He had dark brown eyes, a long, almost aquiline nose, high cheekbones, a full, wide mouth given to smiling, and a square chin with a dimple in its center. Franklyn had his chin. Erica had his eyes. Jason had his skin tone.

He was thinking about his children now.

"I guess you were out there phoning the kids when you left the room for a few minutes," he said.

"I phoned Franklyn," Simone told him. "He'll tell Jason and Erica."

"Why do we have to bother Erica? All she'll do is panic. She'll be panicking all the way home."

"You know she'll pitch a fit once she finds out we called the boys and didn't call her. Stop coddling her. She can handle this."

"I know, I just don't want her to worry."

"You can't save her from worry," Simone said gently. "It won't be your job to protect her from worry soon, anyway. She's getting married, remember?"

"How can I forget?" Eric asked. "Joshua Jenkins, of all people. That boy worried me from the moment I met him. He was too intense. He asked too many questions."

He ran a hand over his curly white hair. Cut to about half an inch from the scalp, it was matted now and slightly damp from perspiration. "I never thought we'd see that boy again and here he's turned up seventeen years later and gotten himself engaged to our daughter!"

"You don't sound too pleased about it," Simone said with a smile.

Eric sighed. "It doesn't matter whether I'm pleased about it or not. She's in love with him, and we trust her judgment."

"The doctor said no stress for a while," Simone reminded him.

"I'm only stressed when I bottle things up," Eric said. "So I'm going to say it and get it over with: she's only known him three months. How does she know she loves him?"

"I only knew you six weeks," Simone said.

"That was different. We were living in a different time then. It was safer to take a fella at his word. These days a woman can't be too careful."

Simone laughed softly. "I'm going to tell you what Erica told me. She says she never forgot him. He was always in the back of her mind, his image making her judge every man she met by his standards, and they never measured up. Let's face it, Eric, darling, our daughter has known Joshua a lot longer than three months."

"I guess there's no stopping the wedding, huh?"

"Like I told Franklyn, the only thing that stands between Erica and Joshua is Erica and Joshua. Let's pray that they hang on to their love and let nothing come between them." She laughed again. "I thought Franklyn or Jason would get married first."

"Our boys aren't finished sowing their wild oats," Eric said with a smile.

"Franklyn never had any wild oats to sow, and Jason is about sowed out, I think."

They both laughed.

Then Simone fluffed up his pillow, making sure he was comfortable. "I'm going to get me a cup of coffee, will you be all right for a few minutes?"

"I'll be more than all right if you'd sneak me a burger in here," Eric said shamelessly.

Simone gave him a sharp look. "If you ask me for another burger, after the scare you gave me today, I'm gonna kill you myself!" Her accent lapsed into the Louisiana patois she'd grown up using. Whenever she did that, Eric knew she was good and mad.

"All right, dearest. Don't put no hex on me!"

Simone laughed as she left the room. "A burger, indeed! You're gonna be living on tofu for the next few months."

Eric frowned. He'd rather be dead.

Chapter Sixteen

Berenice met them at the door of her home. She smiled warmly and stepped aside, "Welcome, Erica, Fabienne."

She kissed Erica's cheeks, then Fabienne's. "Dominique insisted on cooking for us today. She's in the kitchen."

Dominique had moved back home. Her mother had convinced her that her father wanted her to be there so that they could plan her wedding as a family. She went on to tell her that some things would be changing. Etienne was signing the business over to her and Henri. Dominique, surprisingly, no longer had any interest in following in her father's footsteps, but she asked to be consulted on important issues that concerned the business since she, along with Henri, stood to inherit it one day. Henri told her he welcomed her input.

Today, the women, Erica and Fabienne, and Dominique and Berenice, were lunching together as a sort of going-away party for Erica. She only had seven more days before she was to return to the States.

Fabienne and Berenice clasped hands as they followed Erica to the kitchen.

"It's to the right, Erica," Berenice instructed. She

smiled at Fabienne. "I so regret all the years I couldn't invite you to my home. We'll make up for lost time."

Fabienne squeezed her hand. "Yes."

Erica could not help craning her neck to take in the twelve-foot-high doorways and intricately carved molding. The chateau had marble floors throughout, extremely large rooms with large-scale sculptures, opulent chairs upholstered with Aubusson tapestries, on Aubusson carpets. Flowers filled the rooms, which were all designed on a grand scale. Erica had not seen anything like it since she visited some of the mansions in San Francisco. Beautiful homes with well-tended gardens in Pacific Heights, or near the bay. She realized that some of the builders of those homes had borrowed architectural ideas from the French.

"Erica!" Dominique cried, coming around the counter, her hands covered with flour.

The two women hugged, Dominique keeping her hands away from Erica's lovely pale pink blouse. Erica laughed. "You're cooking, huh? Should I be afraid, or very, *very* afraid?"

Dominique laughed. "I'll have you know I studied at the Cordon Bleu."

"For a whole week," her mother put in, "before she threw raw eggs at the pastry chef and got booted out."

"Yes, well, I learned a lot in that week, and I've taught myself a lot more since then," Dominique said good-naturedly.

Berenice went to pat her on the back. "Yes, you have, dear."

Soon, they were seated around a table on the large patio off the kitchen. The weather was pleasant, in the high seventies, and the garden around them was abundantly green and boasted new blooms on the flowering plants. It had rained last night, and the fresh smell of healthy vegetation was in the air.

Dominique had prepared fresh sole with hollandaise

sauce, asparagus, red potatoes, and for dessert a dense chocolate cake. The ladies were all dressed in varying pastel shades. Erica in a pale pink cotton peasant blouse with blue jeans. Dominique in a yellow dress. Fabienne in a sky-blue sleeveless pantsuit whose top buttoned down the front. And Berenice in a lavender sleeveless cotton blouse over a pair of white slacks.

Erica had to give Dominique her props when she tasted the sole. The fish was so delicate it came apart on her tongue, and the sauce was a lovely complement to it.

She looked at Dominique with admiration in her eyes. "This is delicious, girl. You *can* cook!"

"I told you!" Dominique said, thoroughly pleased.

Erica thought back to when they'd met, and how antagonistic Dominique had been toward her. Several weeks of getting to know each other had certainly worked wonders!

"I'm going to miss you," Dominique told her, suddenly turning serious. "Can't you stay until after the wedding?"

"I wish I could, but our winery is in the middle of the harvest too, and I have to be there to help out. They're doing the picking this week. Next week, we'll start the fermentation process," Erica explained. She smiled at her. "Besides, California is only a plane ride away. You all will have to come visit us."

Dominique grinned, remembering how she'd been the first to pick out the fact that Joshua was attracted to Erica. "I was right about Joshua's interest in you from the beginning. I knew he'd never looked at anyone the way he was looking at you that night."

"And I knew Hubert was in love with *you* the moment I saw you two together," Erica told her, smiling smugly. "Poor Hubert didn't know what to do since you wouldn't give him the time of day."

"But we're definitely on the right track now," Dominique crowed. "Both engaged to men we adore. Life is good!"

They gave each other enthusiastic high fives across the table.

"What do these two babies know about love?" Berenice scoffed, looking at Fabienne for support. "You have to live with a man for thirty years, at least, before you know anything about love and sacrifice."

"And you never really know them," Fabienne agreed wholeheartedly.

"You think you know them," Berenice said. "Then, one day, you're in a shop and a woman walks up to you and asks, 'Are you Madame Roumier?' You look at her, trying to place her, but realize you don't know her. 'Yes,' you reply. 'I just wanted to get a good look at you,' she says, then she walks out of the shop, her hand firmly clasping the hand of a small boy who has your husband's face."

"Oh, *Maman*!" Dominique cried, going to hug her mother.

Berenice had tears in her eyes. She returned her daughter's hug with fervor. "Darling, I know you won't end up like me. Hubert is a good man. I want you to cherish him. And realize, every day, what you could have wound up with."

"Here's to true love," Fabienne cried, holding her wineglass aloft.

Everyone picked up their glasses and toasted.

"Now, to you, my loaner daughter," Fabienne said to Erica. "I hope you don't mind, but I shared your and Joshua's story with Berenice. How you two met as children and were reunited here in France. We were both enchanted by your tale. In fact, we wanted to commemorate it with a gift to you."

Berenice, in anticipation of this moment, pulled aside the tablecloth where she was sitting and reached under the table to retrieve a large white rectangular box tied with a thick red ribbon.

She handed the box to Erica. "For you and your Joshua."

Erica was overwhelmed. She accepted the box, which was heavy, but when she pressed down on it, it yielded as if there was something soft in it.

"Open it!" Dominique cried impatiently.

"I thought I'd wait until after the wedding," Erica began.

"No, open it now," Fabienne insisted. "I can't wait that long to see your reaction."

Erica laughed. "Oh, okay."

She set the box on the tabletop after Dominique had been kind enough to move aside dishes and glassware, then she carefully loosened the ribbon, slipped it off, and opened the box. White tissue paper concealed what was within.

When she pulled the tissue paper aside, revealed was a thick white, crocheted throw. Done in butter-soft cotton thread, it was big enough for a queen-size bed, and in its center was the image of two lovers kissing.

"It's for the wedding bed," Berenice told her.

"Yes," Fabienne added. "The couple depicted on it is Tristram and Isolde from a medieval romance. The Germans and the British have their versions of it, the British tying the lovers to Arthurian legend. But the story goes like this: Tristram went to Ireland to bring Isolde back to Cornwall for his uncle to marry, but somewhere along the way the couple unwittingly drank a potion that made them fall in love. Like most romances, it was a tragic story, but for you and Joshua, we intend this to bring you luck. You're two lovers reunited, and nothing will tear you apart."

Erica was touched. She fingered the throw, admiring its fine workmanship. The softness of it. Smiling at all three ladies, she said, "It's gorgeous, and I can't wait to share it with Joshua!"

She got up and hugged each woman in turn. Tears were in her eyes when she sat down again.

"Now, stop that!" Fabienne ordered her. But she was busy wiping away tears of her own. "I swear, is this a party or what?"

"It's a party," Dominique said, and got out of her chair to switch on a nearby CD player. Strains of Ray Charles singing "(Night Time Is) The Right Time" filled the air.

Dominique pulled Erica up to dance with her.

"Next time we get together, we're gonna invite the men," Erica joked.

Of course, Dominique wanted to lead.

To the side, Fabienne bowed to Berenice. "May I have this dance?"

"I thought you'd never ask!" Berenice said and fell into a two-step with her.

Etienne came outside at that instance, saw them dancing together, didn't say a word, and went back inside. *Crazy women*, he thought acerbically.

All of the women had seen him.

"He never was much of a dancer," said Berenice.

To which everyone laughed heartily and let Ray Charles carry them away on a soulful wave of joy in a manner only he could accomplish.

When Fabienne and Erica got back home, they each retired to their rooms for a short siesta before going downstairs to start preparing the evening meal. The men of the house were gone to Montrachet to discuss the sale of the excess grapes, those not needed for their own wine-making purposes, to a winery there. Sobran had had a very good harvest.

Erica lay, stretched out on the bed, her shoes off, thinking. As was the norm lately, her mind was on Joshua. She hadn't seen him in the past forty-eight hours. He was in Paris, giving Henri a crash course on sales. That meant introducing him to their French distributor and taking him to some of the fine restaurants that bought their wines in bulk. A lot of Joshua's job entailed customer service. He was naturally charming, which went a long way in sales. Erica hoped Henri, who had led a rather provincial life according to Dominique, wouldn't be intimidated by the faster pace of Paris.

She fell asleep, wondering what Joshua was doing at that moment.

In an instant, it seemed, she was awakened by the sound of the phone ringing in another part of the house. She closed her eyes again and immediately went back under. Once again, she was interrupted, this time by several frantic knocks on her door. She yawned, sat up, swung her legs off the bed, and got to her feet. "Come in, it's open."

Fabienne entered the room, her brown eyes full of concern. "*Mon petite,* Jason is on the phone. I connected it to your extension."

Erica wondered why Fabienne looked so worried over a phone call from her brother.

"Is something wrong, Fabienne?"

Fabienne walked over and picked up the receiver of the phone that sat on Erica's nightstand. "Please, just talk to Jason."

Erica took the receiver and sat down on the edge of the bed.

"I'll leave you alone," Fabienne said and quietly left the room.

"Hi, Jason?"

Her brother immediately started talking fast. "Everything's all right, Erica. I could hear the concern in Fabienne's voice, so I can guess how her face looked when she went to get you. It's Dad. He had a small heart attack."

"A *small* heart attack?" Erica cried. "There's no such thing as a *small* heart attack!"

She held the receiver away from her and stared at it as if she could translate her consternation through the phone lines.

"He's fine," Jason was saying while she held the phone at bay. "He's been in the hospital two days and already has the nursing staff wrapped around his finger."

Erica put the phone back to her ear when he was in the middle of saying, "Two days."

"Two days!" she yelled. "My daddy has been in the hospital for two days and nobody phoned me?"

"I'm phoning you now," Jason reminded her patiently. "Mom and Dad didn't want you to be worried. He's going to be fine. They say there's no need for you to rush home. Everything's being taken care of. Franklyn's already there, and I'm heading up in a few hours."

"I'm leaving right away," Erica said, rising. She looked around her bedroom. A neat person by nature, she didn't have to run around gathering up her belongings. She could pack in under half an hour. "I can probably make the five o'clock train to Paris. My ticket is open-ended. I'll get the next plane to the States."

Jason sighed. "Erica, did you hear anything I said?"

"Not after you said Dad had a heart attack," Erica told him truthfully. Her focus had been on those words the moment they came out of his mouth.

"Call me once you get back on U.S. soil, and let me know when and where you'll be arriving," Jason said, resigned to the fact that she was coming home. "I'll come pick you up."

"No need," Erica told him. "I can rent a car at the airport and drive home."

"I know you can, but I prefer to come and get you."

"Is there something else you're not telling me, Jason?"

"Now, why would you think that? I'm just trying to be a good brother."

"Not that you're not a good brother all the time, but you tend to try to hide things from me that you think will upset me. All of the men in the family do it. I wish you all would stop that! And another thing, if you ever wait two days to phone me when Mom or Dad is sick, the next time I see you, I'm going to whip your butt!"

Jason laughed. "Yes, ma'am."

"Good-bye, sweetie. I've got to pack."

"Bye. And, Erica?"

"Yes?"

"I really am sorry I didn't phone you yesterday. We'll try our best to stop treating you like the baby of the family. But it won't be easy."

If he told her the reason he hadn't phoned her yesterday was that he'd fallen asleep on the couch after a long, hard day, and a beer to relax him, she'd *really* get on his case.

"I know, and I love you for it, but I'm a woman now, not a child."

"Yeah, but you'll always be my baby sister."

"Boy, please. I'm twenty-seven, getting ready to get married and, in due time, give birth. You've got to snap out of it!"

"Married and a baby, huh? Knight works fast."

"His name's Joshua, and don't you and Franklyn give him a hard time when you meet him!"

"He's got you running interference for him?"

"He doesn't need me to run interference for him. He's perfectly capable of defending himself against anything you or Franklyn can cook up," Erica confidently told him. She knew what he was trying to do. He was taking her mind off their father, attempting to make her laugh before she hung up. Her brothers were so transparent. She was aware of the frustration they experienced whenever she was upset and they couldn't do anything to comfort her. Behind their gruff exteriors, they were both sensitive souls.

"I guess he told you Franklyn and I told him to stop spending so much time with you back then," Jason said, shocking her.

Erica's voice was calmer than she actually felt. "No, he didn't. This is the first I've heard of it. Let's see, you were, what? About fifteen? And Franklyn was eighteen. Joshua was seventeen. Three teenaged boys. Exactly what did you say to him?"

"It was unnatural," Jason said in his and Franklyn's defense. "We told him you had a crush on him, and he was old enough to know better than to encourage a little kid like you."

"He didn't do anything wrong," Erica said, her voice tight. "I was the pest, following him around like a puppy. All he did was be kind to me."

"Well, we didn't want it to escalate. Something could have happened." Joshua sounded so reasonable that Erica did not marvel at the fact that he was an excellent lawyer and had won so many cases for his clients.

"I'm not going to have this conversation," she said. "Nothing happened between me and Joshua back then. I can understand your and Franklyn's need to state your concerns. But you should have come to me first. Don't you think I would have told you if there were something inappropriate going on?"

"Kids don't always know what's inappropriate and what isn't."

"He never laid a hand on me."

"No, but you were always throwing yourself into his arms."

Erica thought back. So that was why Joshua had asked her to stop hugging him. Her brothers had talked to him. He'd told her that his mother had mentioned that it would be best not to be alone with her. His mother was simply protecting her son. She'd probably known boys from Joshua's background who'd been accused of raping the boss's daughter. Erica could understand why she'd had a talk with Joshua.

"Well, he didn't mention it to me," Erica reiterated. "Probably because it doesn't matter to him. He knew you were my brothers and only trying to protect me."

Jason was silent for a moment. "I can respect that."

"You were just covering your butt in case he *had* mentioned it, and you thought I would be angry," Erica guessed.

Jason laughed. "You know me well."

Erica laughed too. "I love you, Jason!"

Now that he'd gotten his laugh out of her, he could get off the phone. "Thanks, baby girl. I'll see you soon. Bye."

"Bye."

Smiling, Erica hung up the phone and immediately went to her closet to get her big suitcase from the top shelf.

Chapter Seventeen

Joshua glanced at his watch. Daniel Chapel, their French distributor, was a born storyteller. It seemed to Joshua that the man hadn't taken a breath in over an hour. He was telling Henri the history of his twenty-year association with his father's winery.

Henri, polite to a fault, had not interrupted him once.

However, Joshua, not nearly as polite, could not wait any longer to make his exit. He had a very important appointment in exactly fifteen minutes. It would take him that long to get where he needed to go.

All three men wore business suits, Joshua in blue, Henri in gray, and Daniel in charcoal. They were dining at Alain Ducasse at 59 Avenue Raymond-Poincare. Many fine restaurants closed their doors in the summer months, especially the month of August, due to the fact that well-to-do Parisians spent the summer in the country. Alain Ducasse, instead, closed for the month of July.

Joshua cleared his throat as he got to his feet. "Daniel, so sorry to cut in, but I have another appointment. I'm going to have to leave you and Henri."

Daniel rose too and offered Joshua his hand. Five-eleven to Joshua's six-two, he looked up at him. "Of course, Joshua, it has been a pleasure doing business with you over the years. If you're ever in Paris, please phone me so we can have a drink together."

"I will," Joshua assured him with a smile.

His gaze went to Henri. "The best of luck with everything, Henri."

Henri had risen in anticipation of Joshua's farewell. He vigorously shook Joshua's hand. "You have been very gracious, and I thank you."

"I'm more than pleased to see you where you deserve to be," Joshua told him, and meant it. He inclined his head respectfully. "Au revoir."

"Au revoir," Henri said, his plain face a mask of smiles.

Joshua left them. When he turned his back on them, he could not help grinning. He was free! Loosening his tie, he pushed the door of the restaurant open and stepped onto the busy Paris street.

Immediately, his ears were assaulted by the sound of traffic. The air was warm and muggy, and above him the sky was gray. He longed to be back in Beaune. He, like Henri, did not care for the city.

Most of all, he wanted to hold Erica in his arms.

Erica. She was the reason he had to get across town.

He stepped close to the street and let out a shrill whistle. A passing cab heard him and pulled to the curb. Climbing inside, Joshua gave him the address of an exclusive jewelry store. He sat back on the seat. Two weeks ago he'd proposed to Erica on the spur of the moment. He wished he'd had the foresight to buy the ring before proposing, but when he'd expressed that sentiment, Erica had told him she didn't need an expensive ring to know he was serious about her.

He smiled now. She might not need a ring, but she deserved one. Something classic, tasteful, exquisitely beautiful, and well crafted. A friend of his told him about Jospin Jewelers. He'd phoned them and told them what he wanted: a tension-set two-carat diamond ring in eighteen-karat gold. The tension-set diamond ring looked like a work of art. The diamond seemed to be suspended between pincers. He'd expressed concern that the diamond might be lost from such a precarious-looking setting, but Monsieur Jospin had assured him that no one in the forty years since the tension set had been developed had reported losing a diamond. Joshua knew the unusual beauty of the ring would please Erica. She liked unusual things. She'd picked him, hadn't she?

An hour later, he was leaving the jewelry store with the ring in his pocket when his cell phone rang. He hailed a taxi with one hand while flipping open his cell phone with the other.

"Joshua Knight."

"Hi, sweetie."

He couldn't help smiling. "Erica," he said, his voice husky.

Erica was in her bedroom sitting on her suitcase while Fabienne clicked it shut and locked it. Fabienne smiled at her after she'd finished. "We always leave with more than we came with, don't we? I'll give you some privacy."

"Thanks, I'm going to miss you, Fabienne," Erica said with a smile.

"I'm going to miss you, too, darling," Fabiene told her sincerely.

She left the room, closing the door behind her.

Joshua had heard their conversation. "You're going somewhere?"

"My brother Jason phoned a few minutes ago. My dad had a heart attack. They say he's going to be fine, but I've got to go home, Joshua."

"Of course you do," he said. "You're not going to be satisfied that he's really going to be all right until you see him with your own eyes."

Erica sighed with longing. "See? That's why I love you so much."

"I love you too, baby."

A cab pulled up to the curb next to him. "My ride's here. Keep talking. What time will you be arriving at the train station here in Paris?"

While he got into the taxi, scrunching up his long legs because it was a small taxi, she told him what time her train would arrive at the station and what time her flight would leave the city.

"I'll meet you at the train station. We have six hours before your flight out. You can stay with me at my hotel until it's time, then I'll take you to the airport."

'That would be perfect," Erica said, so grateful to him she felt on the verge of tears.

"Darling, try not to worry. If your brother says your father is going to be fine, *believe* him."

"I'm trying."

"I can hear your emotions in your voice."

"It's still too soon to look at it from an impersonal perspective. Until today, I always thought my dad was invincible. Now I have to face the facts: he's sixty-five years old, and he's not going to be here forever. That was like cold water being thrown in my face. It's scary."

"I understand," Joshua told her. "But look on the bright side: you don't have to face losing your father. He's going to be all right. My mother had a saying that has stayed with me all these years. She used to say, 'Don't borrow trouble. What you have is sufficient for the day.' "

"Isn't *that* the truth!" Erica exclaimed, laughing softly. She looked at the clock on the nightstand. "I've got to go. I'll be giving Hubert his cell phone, so I won't be able to reach you en route to Paris."

"I'll be waiting at the station," Joshua promised.

"Okay, handsome. Love you much."

"Love you more."

"Let's not fight," Erica joked.

"I'd win."

They laughed and rang off.

Fabienne hugged Erica as if she would never let her go. Sobran also held on to her for a fairly long time, though, being male, he did not have tears in his eyes when he let go of her. He stoically blinked them back.

Jean-Marc kissed her gently on the forehead. "Take care of yourself, little sister. And give your family our best. Tell Eric that he and Simone are expected here on their vacation next year. And not to disappoint us. The Lafons don't take kindly to disappointment, we might all have to come to California to collect them."

"Yes," said Sobran. "Also tell him that he owes me a chess game. He won the last time we played. I demand a rematch!"

Erica waved good-bye to them as she, Hubert, and Dominique sped off in the Jaguar.

Erica and Dominique had tears in their eyes.

Hubert glanced at Dominique sitting beside him, and at Erica, sitting in the backseat, via the rearview mirror. "Please don't cry all the way to Dijon. You two act like we're never going to see each other again. We're the next generation of Lafons and Bryants, don't you see that? Just like Eric and Simone are good friends with my parents, you, Erica and Joshua, and Dominique and I will be friends for a lifetime. So quit it, now! Besides, you're going to stain my leather seats."

Erica and Dominique laughed, but ended up crying harder, as emotions sometimes make you do.

"I give up," Hubert said after a while. "Cry all you want."

* * *

Joshua was ten minutes early. He wanted to be there the moment Erica disembarked from the train. Afraid he'd lose the ring, or be mugged, he'd left it in the hotel safe. While at the hotel, he'd taken the time to change out of his suit into a pair of jeans and a white T-shirt. He looked like countless other young Parisian males, all wearing jeans and T-shirts.

He saw Erica before she saw him. She'd hired a porter and the man had her luggage on a hand truck. They were heading toward the exit and the taxi stand outside the station.

Joshua approached her from the side. She was looking directly ahead, her eyes riveted on the entrance, possibly hoping to spot him.

"Hey, beautiful!" he called across the station.

Erica turned at the sound of his voice. "Joshua!"

She hastily asked the porter to wait for her there, and then she ran and leaped into his open arms. Anyone looking on would have thought they hadn't seen each other in years.

Joshua lifted her in the air. They kissed.

Setting her back down, he said, "Come on, I hired a car for us."

"You didn't have to do that," Erica protested.

"I know, but I wanted to. It'll save us time, and time is a commodity we're short on."

He put his arm about her waist. "Let's go. We're staying at the Hotel Montalembert. It has a nice restaurant, so we don't have to go out for dinner."

Erica allowed him to lead her to the waiting car. He tipped the porter and handed her in. Once they were seated in the roomy backseat, he pulled her into his arms.

The driver pulled away from the curb.

"Has it only been two days since I saw you last? It feels like it's been much longer," he said as he held her close.

Erica relaxed in his arms. She laid her head on his shoulder, closed her eyes. To be in his strong arms, inhaling the heady aroma of his cologne mingled with the natural male scent of him, was pure bliss.

"I would just like to sit in a tub with you and forget about everything except you."

"Whatever you want tonight, my love, you'll get."

"I just want you."

"Done. I'm yours."

They rode the rest of the way to the hotel in silence, allowing their hands and mouths to speak for them.

At the Hotel Montalembert, a doorman greeted them and whistled for a bellboy, who came and collected Erica's luggage.

Soon, they were in Joshua's suite, and alone.

Erica immediately sat on the couch and began taking off her athletic shoes. Joshua bent before her. "Let me do that."

Erica smiled in wonder and obliged him.

He removed her shoes and socks and took the time to massage both her feet. Looking up at her from his bent-knee position, he said, "Is there anything else Mademoiselle would like me to do for her?"

Erica's brows arched with interest. "I'm a little tired. You could finish removing my clothes and then draw me a bath."

Joshua's eyes went to her luscious lips. He wanted to taste them again. He wanted to taste every inch of her, but first he had to dispense with that pink peasant blouse and those well-worn blue jeans. What sort of lingerie she was wearing, he was soon to find out.

He rose and pulled her to her feet. Moving close to her, he bent his head and sniffed her neck. She smelled of jasmine. Probably the body lotion she liked using. Erica saw his nostrils flare, felt his warm breath on her skin. A delicious slow burn began to spread outward from the pit of her stomach.

Joshua went behind her and pulled up her blouse. Erica raised her arms. Once he had the blouse off, he saw the lacy white bra she had on. Her nipples were visible through the sheer material. He tossed the blouse onto a nearby chair and cupped her breasts. Erica leaned back, the full length of her body flush with his. She sighed with pleasure.

Joshua bent and placed a kiss on the side of her neck. "Babe, I just thought of something I need to get from downstairs. You go ahead and get undressed, get into the tub, and I'll be right back."

Disappointed, Erica turned in his arms and regarded him with wide eyes. She didn't protest. After all, he was in Paris on business and was probably taking valuable time away from it in order to give her a proper send-off.

Joshua saw her state of mind in her eyes though. He smiled, his wide mouth turning up at the corners, his dark eyes laughing. "I'll only be five minutes, tops."

"All right," Erica said, holding a pout at bay.

He gave her a quick kiss on the lips and left.

Erica, standing in the middle of the suite, barefoot, her hair mussed from Joshua running his hands through it, her lips still tingling from his kisses, finally got a good look around her.

No Old World–inspired decorating for this fine hotel. Chic furnishings and details surrounded her, from modern natural-colored velvet-covered couches and chairs, to curvy white-lacquered tables with pale gold plush carpeting underneath. She looked down and lifted her right foot. It had left a deep indentation in the thick carpet.

She walked down the hallway to the bedroom. The bed was king-size. She sat on it. Firm mattress, but not too firm. She got up and went to the adjacent bathroom.

She sort of missed Joshua's big claw-footed tub, but this one would do. It was a sunken tub, long, wide, and with enough depth to easily accommodate both of them. She went over to it, engaged the stopper, and turned on the hot and cold water, more hot than cold. Several bottles of bath salts and bath oils lined the built-in shelf next to the tub. She picked up a bottle with white bath salts in it and read the label: *White Orchids*. She didn't know what white orchids smelled like or if, indeed, they had an odor in nature. Perhaps this was a fragrance a perfume manufacturer had invented and marketed. Opening the lid, she sniffed. It was a clean, fresh smell that reminded her of white roses because their scent was not overpowering either, but delicate and sensual. She poured some in the streaming water.

Humming "Feeling Good" by Nina Simone, she began peeling off her clothes, folding them neatly and placing them in a pile on the toilet seat. When she was nude, she stood before the full-length mirror on the wall next to the door. Five feet seven, and approximately 140 pounds, she had a flat stomach and a waist that was small but not waspish. She turned to the side. Did she see cellulite? She rolled her eyes. Was she turning too critical now that she actually had a lover who took time to make her body sing? No way. Her body was beautiful. Joshua made her feel beautiful even if she wasn't model thin and picture perfect. He liked her big behind, and marveled at her legs and thighs, which were her best features in her estimation. They'd been shaped from long walks, hard work on the farm, and running. Sometimes the impulse to run struck her and she'd do it for months on end, and then, as suddenly, it would leave her and she wouldn't run again for a long time. But running felt like flying to her. She loved the rush of the wind past her ears and the notion that she was parting the air with her face, nose-first, as she ran. The only thing remotely similar to it was horseback riding.

From the sound of the water filling the tub, she

guessed it was full enough. She went to it, saw that it was half-full, and turned off both faucets. The smell wafting off it was divine.

She ran her hand through it to test the temperature, discovered it was just right, and stepped into the tub. Sitting, she languidly reached for a thick bath towel sitting on a low shelf next to the tub, rolled it up, leaned back, and placed it beneath her neck.

Joshua found her in that position, with her eyes closed, when he walked into the bathroom, carrying a tray with a bottle of champagne and two flutes on it.

He set the tray on a lower shelf of the étagère that held the linen and quietly began undressing.

Chapter Eighteen

"You're not sleeping," Joshua said, his deep voice a caress.

Erica opened her eyes to his dazzling male beauty. He didn't have a stitch on. As always, her breath caught, and she sent up a prayer of thanks. *Lord, you are so good to me!*

Long muscular limbs, not bulky but so well proportioned she was hard pressed to find any kind of flaw in those arms, legs, and thighs. His thighs, especially, were finely sculpted from running and playing soccer. No wonder she couldn't keep her eyes off him when he was on the soccer field.

She put an elbow on the edge of the tub, cupped her chin in her palm, and eyed him with bold admiration. A sensual smile curled her full lips. "Turn around."

Joshua turned around. His behind had those indentations on the sides that only men who worked out prodigiously acquired over time.

"I am in awe of your butt!"

Having fun, Joshua made his gluteus maximus muscles jump.

Erica laughed. "You're so *talented*."

Laughing softly, Joshua faced her. "Show's over. Let's get down to business, shall we?" He went and poured champagne into the two flutes. His body hid what he was doing, so Erica didn't see him take her ring off the tray and slip it into her glass.

He went to her and handed her a glass. She accepted it and moved forward in the tub so he could join her. He handed her his glass to hold as well, then carefully climbed in behind her. Erica leaned forward while holding the glasses aloft.

After he was seated, he reached for his wineglass and offered a toast. "To the future. May it sparkle like diamonds."

Erica was lovingly looking back at him, so she didn't notice the ring sitting on the bottom of the flute, sparkling amongst the champagne bubbles.

It was only when she took a sip that she saw the ring. Gravity made it tip over in the glass, and with its movement she heard a soft tinkle. It was the sound of the gold ring hitting the side of the crystal glass that made her look closely.

"Oh my God!" Her mouth fell open in surprise.

She stared at the ring in the glass, then back at Joshua.

"What is that in your glass?" Joshua asked as if he didn't know.

Hands trembling, she fished the ring out of the glass and held it up, turning it this way and that way. "It's gorgeous!" She twisted in the tub and threw her arms around Joshua's neck. "Watch the merchandise," he said, laughing. Meaning his privates.

He was still laughing in delight when Erica kissed him. They were both laughing. Erica calmed down long enough to slide the ring onto her finger. Sitting back against him in the tub, she held her hand up, admiring the symbol of their love.

"How did you pick such a wonderful ring? I love the

setting. The diamond catches the light no matter how you turn it."

"I picked something with your personality," Joshua told her.

Erica fell farther into his embrace. "Oh?"

"Yes," he said. "It's classy, sexy, and slightly dangerous. The dangerous part comes in because the way the diamond is positioned makes it look like you could lose it."

"It does," Erica agreed. "It looks like those two prongs coming together are pressing the diamond between them and, at any moment, the diamond is going to come spiraling out and into the air."

"But the jeweler told me that in the more than forty years the technique has been used, no one has reported a lost diamond. I got it insured, just in case."

She kissed his lips. "You're so practical." She kissed his cheek. "Thank you."

"My pleasure," Joshua assured her with a grin. His big hands were on her waist, turning her around to face him. "Now, give me some serious loving, woman. It's been forty-eight hours since I had you in my arms, and we haven't any time to waste!"

Erica smiled against his mouth. He was so right. She had a plane to catch in under five hours, and then they would be apart for she didn't know *how* long.

She broke off the kiss and looked into his eyes. "How long is it going to take you to come to me in California?"

"I don't know, baby, I'm hoping not more than two weeks."

"Two weeks!"

"You make it sound like two years."

Her hands were clasped behind his neck, his hands were on the sides of her waist, and her body was turned in such a way that her breasts were squashed against his hard chest.

"Two weeks without my Joshua fix is gonna *feel* like two years!" she said petulantly.

"I'm free of Etienne Roumier and his winery. Now all I need to do is put the house up for sale, liquidate some assets, and sell the car. I'm thinking of buying either an SUV or a pickup. I don't know how long the legal work will take, and I'd prefer to get it all straightened out while I'm here. I don't plan on making a trip back any time soon."

"You'll be an American again."

"I never gave up my citizenship."

"I know. I meant you'll actually be living on American soil again."

She felt his hard penis throb against her hip. "Okay, I'm getting up, I'm getting up!" she said as if he were sending her a message to get a move on. They had some serious loving to do before he had to take her to the airport.

"I didn't say a word," Joshua joked. "But I agree with him. I'm hungry for you too."

Erica got up, her wet golden brown body a delectable sight. Joshua greedily took in every delicious inch of her. She stood there while he rose as well, his eyes moving up from her knees, lingering on the dark, shiny thatch of hair between her thighs. Onward to her belly button, her heavy breasts, their nipples erect, the gentle curve of her neck, a chin with a beauty mark that he found obsessively kissable, a mouth he didn't think he'd ever tire of, that haughty nose, and finally her wide-spaced, cognac-colored eyes that made him feel slightly drunk with need whenever she gave him a sultry stare.

Erica reached down and let the water out of the tub. "Maybe we ought to rinse off. I don't know what's in these bath salts. They may not be edible like that peppermint oil I used last time."

Joshua got harder just thinking about her hands

massaging the oil into his skin, and what she'd done to him when she made him close his eyes.

He tried to redirect his thoughts. If he didn't, he wouldn't last very long tonight.

The shower head attachment was behind Erica, so he did the honors. Besides, he'd used the shower before and knew exactly how it worked. He rinsed Erica, then rinsed himself off. By the time he'd finished rinsing them, the water had drained out of the tub, and they got out.

In their eagerness, they each grabbed a towel and dried themselves.

Neither of them diverted their eyes from each other, but thoroughly enjoyed watching the normal, but altogether erotic, act of someone you loved toweling himself dry.

Joshua dropped his towel to the floor and took hers. "You're dry enough."

He dropped it next to the other towel and pulled her into his arms. He never knew loving somebody could make you this crazy with lust. No stranger to lust, he'd known his fair share of women, but this was an all-consuming kind of lust that made him feel vulnerable and exposed.

He looked intensely into her eyes. "I've never trusted anyone with my heart before."

Erica got a lump in her throat. "Don't worry, I'll keep it safe and sound."

He kissed her then. A kiss filled with fragile, raw need. A kiss full of passion and longing. Finally, a kiss full of hope and surrender. He was hers.

She answered with wholehearted acceptance. She tottered on the brink of doubt. Could she give this formidable man what he needed from her? Suddenly, a stillness came over her and she no longer felt unsure of herself. His trust in her quenched some parched part of her soul that had never been showered with the waters of true love. She knew with every cell of her body that he was meant for her, and her alone.

She wanted to take the tall, rangy boy that he had been in her arms and reassure him that she'd loved him then and she'd never stopped loving him.

She took one of his big hands in hers and placed it over her heart. "What I am, heart, soul, flesh, will always belong to you, Joshua."

He picked her up and carried her to the bed, where their loving was fierce and immediate, neither of them saying a word. They were too full to speak. When Joshua felt her release was imminent, he did not give her surcease, but he gave her more, always more. She let out a deep sigh and trembled in his arms. He rolled his shoulders and increased his efforts. She climaxed again before he finally let himself go, and succumbed to the sweet pleasure she had given him.

They lay in bed, his arms holding her close to him, the sheet pulled over their bodies.

"Two weeks is far too long," Erica said quietly.

He laughed softly and nuzzled her neck.

Jason needed something to do. He'd been at the hospital for two hours now. His father was sitting up in bed, no longer on oxygen or anything else. In fact the old man looked like his former robust self. Only, that hospital gown had to go, or needed a new design. His dad had gotten up to go to the bathroom and mooned them all.

While he was still in the bathroom, Joshua turned to his mother, who had recently returned from home and a well-deserved nap in her own bed, and said, "Mom, give me an assignment. Anything. I can't stand hospitals. Never could."

He didn't have to tell Simone he couldn't abide hospitals. She'd been there the day his opinion of them had changed. It was the day Franklyn had gotten kicked by the horse Jason was riding. The boys had been cutting the fool, as usual, and the way Simone had heard it, Jason had dared Franklyn to jump from the barn's overhang onto the back of the mare. Franklyn had jumped, missed, spooked the horse, and while he was on the ground, the horse had stomped on him. Jason could do nothing but watch in horror as his brother was being stomped to death.

Afterward, Franklyn had been limp and bloody. Jason thought he was dead.

Franklyn sustained two broken ribs, a black eye, a cut lip, and his left leg was broken in two places. He'd walked with a limp ever since. Jason blamed himself for the accident. Franklyn didn't, but in Jason's opinion Franklyn's forgiveness didn't absolve him. He didn't think he'd ever forgive himself.

Simone looked at him now and said, "You can go pick up a couple of books the doctor recommended to your father."

"We have a bookstore now?" Jason asked. He was woefully ignorant about the new businesses that had sprung up in Glen Ellen since he'd lived away from home these past twelve years. First he'd gone to college at California State, and then when he'd finished law school, he'd been hired by a law firm in Bakersfield. Today he was a full partner. Simone was proud of him, even though she and Eric bemoaned the fact that their middle child seemed not to take romantic relationships seriously. It was one beautiful woman after another. And the women appeared to be interchangeable Barbie-doll types with little going on upstairs, but with killer bodies. As much as she wished he would settle down, she didn't want him bringing home an empty-headed beauty queen. "Sweetheart, we have two or three bookstores now. But I want you to patronize the African-American-owned bookstore on Arnold Drive, not too far from the Glen Ellen Inn."

She got up to get her purse. Rummaging inside, she withdrew a slip of paper and handed it to him. She also went into her wallet for two twenty-dollar bills. Offering them to him, she said, "They shouldn't cost more than this."

Jason smiled at her. "Mom, I'm a lawyer, I can afford to buy my dad a couple of books."

Simone put her money away. "All right, big-shot lawyer."

She watched him go, unaware that she'd just set him up. She hoped he'd take the bait, but you never knew about men. Sometimes they were pretty dense about recognizing a good woman when they saw one.

She sat on the couch and put her feet up on a nearby chair. "Eric, have you fallen in?"

"No, just taking my time," her husband answered from behind the closed bathroom door.

A few minutes later, Jason was pulling into the parking lot of Aminatu's Daughters, the bookstore his mother had sent him to. He got out of his shiny black BMW and locked the door. The day was bright and clear, not a cloud in the sky, and the temperature was in the mideighties. He loved days like this. They *usually* lifted his spirits. Maybe it was the name of the store that gave him a foreboding feeling. Aminatu's Daughters.

It sounded downright militant feminist. He hoped it wasn't run by a group of man-hating lesbians. Not that he had anything against them. It was just that they made him nervous. Anybody who found men dispensable made him nervous.

He had a coworker who was a lesbian. He'd known her for seven years. One day, out of the blue, she took him to lunch and asked him to donate some of his sperm in order to impregnate her partner. He might be a modern man, but he felt proprietary about his sperm. To say nothing of being the father of a child raised by two mothers who didn't want him to be a part of the kid's life.

He always said, to each his own. But he drew the line at random parenting. When he did become a father, he wanted to be there for his children every single day.

He pulled the door of the store open and stepped inside. The air was cool and the Afrocentric decor was somewhat soothing. On one side of the large space was a lunch counter, behind which were several coffee machines, including an espresso machine.

His mother hadn't told him that the place was a coffeehouse *and* a bookstore. Customers sat at the tables on the coffeehouse side chatting or reading books. Several patrons on the bookstore side were browsing the shelves. The sections were clearly marked. He had no trouble finding the health section.

His attention, though, was drawn to a tall woman with black braids nearly to her nicely rounded butt, and he stood watching her for a few moments, wondering who she was. Glen Ellen was a small town, and even though he hadn't lived there in a while, he figured he should know her. She had skin the color of bittersweet chocolate. It was smooth and unblemished, and her teeth flashed white when she threw back her lovely head and laughed heartily at something the guy she was with had said.

Joshua tore his eyes away from her before she caught him staring, and continued toward the back of the store where the self-help and health books section was located.

He kept taking quick peeks at her throughout his search for the books on his mother's list though. The guy she was with was wearing a business suit. A brother with a sharp fade and an easy, confident way about him.

Jason felt he was at a distinct disadvantage if she liked guys in suits. He was wearing a Cal State T-shirt, jeans that had seen better days, and a pair of athletic shoes that had also been worn to submission. No, if it was a sharp-dressed man she liked, he wasn't in the running today.

He found the books and started walking toward the checkout counter. It was at that moment that the beauty and the suit parted company and she began walking across the store. Jason paused. She would cross his path any minute now.

When she got within three feet of him, he said, "Excuse me, but can you tell me where the men's room is?"

It was trite, but that's all he could come up with on such short notice.

Her eyes, the color of a summer sunset, focused on his face, and he could have sworn she looked startled for a second before she recovered and said, "It's right next to the children's section." She pointed to the sign that denoted the children's section. It was bright yellow and shaped like a duck. He couldn't miss it.

"Thanks," he said. He thrust his hand out. "By the way, I'm Jason Bryant. I was raised here and thought I knew every African-American in a twenty-mile radius. But I don't think you and I have met."

Her eyes narrowed. Something in them grew cold and distant, as if she were shutting off her emotions, protecting them perhaps. He was good at reading people. He'd had a lot of practice as a lawyer, and he knew this woman didn't like what she saw in him.

"No, we certainly don't know each other," she said, her voice tight. "Excuse me."

She left him standing there with his books in his hand, and his heart in his throat.

Jason Bryant wasn't used to rejection. He was able to

charm the most recalcitrant judges. To woo juries who were dead set against his clients, to bring them around to seeing things his way. Yet, this tall, shapely Nubian beauty had turned her nose up at him and shown him her back.

He was puzzled. And a little upset.

When he got back to the hospital and gave the books to his mother, she asked pleasantly, "What did you think of Aminatu's Daughters?"

"Nice store," he said truthfully.

"Did you meet the owner, Sara Minton?"

Jason knew that name. He racked his brain. An image came to him of a chubby girl with glasses, standing helplessly at her locker while three or four big, rough football players made pig noises and taunted her unmercifully while he stood there and did nothing to stop them. That shy, overweight girl had had skin just like the beautiful diva who'd given him the cold shoulder a few minutes ago. She had also been cute back then, but unbearably awkward and unsure of herself.

Jason felt like a heel. "Yes," he answered his mother. "I met her."

"She named the store after an African queen," his mother went on to say. "I don't know if you remember Sara, but she was two grades behind you in school. I know her parents. Good people. Sara left here after she graduated, but she returned about two years ago to look after her ailing mother. Her dad's still working his farm, but Janie, her mother, isn't faring too well. Sara's their only child. She was doing very well in New York City as an advertising executive. Bought the store with cash, her mother said. Her mother loves to brag about that child. But what mother doesn't like to brag when the child deserves it? She was married, but her husband died in a tragic car accident five years ago. I don't think she's let herself get close to anyone since then."

Jason heard his mother's voice as if she were speaking to him from a distance. He was so preoccupied on how he could apologize to Sara Minton without appearing to have been part of the gang who had terrorized her throughout high school. It was true, he had not called her names, but hadn't done anything to prevent the abuse either. He castigated himself for not taking a stand in her defense back then.

He was glad when his cell phone vibrated. Hospital regulations required cell phone users to turn off their ringers, and if they needed to use them, to go to a designated area. He looked regrettably at his mom.

"I need to answer this, Mom. It could be Erica."

He swiftly left the room.

Indeed, it was Erica phoning from LaGuardia Airport in New York City. "Hi, Jase. How is Dad doing?"

"He's up and about," he told her. "They should be letting him go home either this afternoon or tomorrow morning. How was your flight?"

"Smooth," Erica said with a yawn.

"You didn't sleep on the plane, huh?"

"I did, a little, but I kept waking up, looking at my engagement ring," Erica said, laughing.

Jason laughed too. "You're really gone on the guy."

"Yes," said Erica. "You, too, could be this happy if only you'd let down your guard."

"As a matter of fact, Mom just tried to set me up with Sara Minton."

"You could do a lot worse. Sara's a phenomenal woman."

"Not you, too!"

"I was too young to have gone to school with Sara," Erica said. "I met her when she came back home. But I'm telling you, she's smart, poised, smart, beautiful, smart, and did I say she's smart?"

Jason laughed. "Yes, you did."

"We'll talk more when you pick me up. Gotta go!" Erica told him happily. "See you soon."

Jason groaned. "Please don't bend my ear about Sara Minton all the way from San Francisco!"

Erica only laughed and hung up on him.

Jason closed his cell phone and sat down at one of the umbrella-topped tables on the patio adjacent to the hospital's cafeteria. Diners were free to eat inside or take their trays outside to the patio. He noticed several more cell phone users occupying tables, and other folks taking cigarette breaks. Very few were actually eating a meal outside, because the day was warm and diners preferred eating their meals in air-conditioned comfort.

He flipped open his cell phone again. He needed to tell Franklyn their sister would be arriving at San Francisco International tomorrow morning. Franklyn had had to go back to work. He was both owner and head chef at The Vineyard.

Knowing Franklyn, even if he could not afford to spend the day with Erica upon her arrival, he'd still like the opportunity to come out to the airport and give his baby sister a hug after a three-month separation.

The phone rang in the kitchen of The Vineyard. Elise Gilbert, who was walking past the ringing phone, stopped to answer it. "Hello, kitchen," she said.

Jason wondered who the woman with the deep, sultry voice was. Could it be the mysterious Elise that Franklyn was so taken with? "Hi, I'm Jason, Franklyn's brother. Is he there?"

"I'm afraid not. The greengrocer forgot to deliver fresh endive today and Franklyn had to make a run."

"Oh," said Jason. "I'm sorry I missed him. Would you ask him to phone me when he gets back?"

"Sure, Mr. Bryant."

"Call me Jason. And you are?"

"Elise. I'm the pastry chef."

Jason paused for a second, thinking. "That's right. Franklyn says you're very talented."

"He does?"

Jason didn't know why that news should come as a surprise to her. But he supposed his too-shy brother also got tongue-tied when he wanted to give the lady a compliment on her skills as a chef. He really had to give his big brother a few pointers on how to talk to the babes. But then, he'd been shot down himself recently. Maybe he needed a refresher course.

"Yes, he does," he assured Elise. "And that's high praise coming from Franklyn, who is somewhat of a perfectionist, if you haven't already found that out."

"I have," Elise said, laughing. "I like that about him."

Good news for Franklyn, Jason thought, pleased for his brother. "Well, it's been nice chatting with you, Elise. You take care."

"You too," said Elise.

Jason was smiling when he hung up. "Go on, Franklyn. She sounds very tempting."

A few minutes later, Elise was icing a huge tray of petits fours when Franklyn came through the back door balancing a small wooden crate of endives on his powerful shoulders. She sighed quietly. That man was entirely too gorgeous to be a chef. He had the sexiest brown eyes. She melted every time he looked her way. If only he weren't her boss, she'd grab him and turn him every which way but loose!

She let him put the crate down before approaching him. "Ah, Franklyn, your brother phoned. He wants you to call him."

For a split second, Elise thought she saw longing in Franklyn's eyes when they settled on her face. Then, in a flash, it wasn't there anymore, and he was regarding her in the manner he always did, with mild interest, if that. "Thanks, Elise. I'll call him right away."

They each returned to their tasks. Elise felt utterly deflated. Hope had claimed her when Jason told her Franklyn had been talking to him about her. It had made her think that perhaps it meant that Franklyn had a personal interest in her. With one good look into his eyes, however, her hopes had flown.

Chapter Nineteen

Erica didn't know how much she'd missed her brothers until she walked down the ramp after deplaning and strolled through the doorway that led to the waiting area of the carrier she'd used. Sitting so that they could spot her as soon as possible, her brothers rose at once and went to her.

Jason wore khakis and a pale blue cotton shirt open at the collar. The shirt was neatly tucked in, and a brown belt encircled his waist. On his feet were his favorite pair of brown oxfords. He was casual, but not too casual. Frank, on the other hand, wore jeans and a black T-shirt. On his feet were a black pair of work shoes. The kind with thick soles and steel toes. Accidents happened in a busy kitchen.

She knew, by his attire alone, that he was working that day.

"Frank!" she cried, running toward them with her purse on her shoulder and her carry-on bag in her hand. "Jase!"

She hugged each of them in turn.

"You look good, short stuff," Frank said affectionately. He frowned and reached up to muss her hair. "Who told you you could cut your hair?"

"I did!" Erica said, laughing. For some reason they thought she needed their permission to cut her hair.

"Well, you look good in spite of it," Jason told her, a stern expression on his clean-shaven face. They walked over to the carousel and collected Erica's luggage.

"I think it suits you," Frank said as they hurried through the terminal, Jason leading the way. Since it was morning, his limp wasn't as pronounced. As the day wore on, and he grew fatigued, it usually became more noticeable.

"In fact," he said, observing her confident swagger, "I'd say love agrees with you."

Erica beamed at him and showed him her ring.

"Nice!" he said admiringly. "He's not cheap."

"No," said Erica. "He's kind and generous, and handsome and perfect!"

Jason, who had stopped to take a look at the ring, laughed at her assertion. "Yeah, she's definitely in love. I could have that appraised for you if you like."

Erica ignored his offer as they continued across the terminal. Jason was always the cynical one who thought somebody was always trying to pull the wool over his eyes.

"How is Dad today?" Erica asked.

"He's at home pestering Mom for real bacon," Jason told her. "She bought him meatless bacon. I tasted it. It has the consistency of shoe leather, and tastes like dog biscuits."

"You ought to know," Franklyn quipped.

It was a running joke in their family that Jason would eat anything on a dare. Among the things he'd eaten when they were kids were dog biscuits, rabbit grass, a weed that grew in the fields adjacent to the house, and assorted insects.

"Don't kid him, Frank," Erica said in his defense. "Jason hasn't eaten a caterpillar since he was fifteen."

The siblings separated in the parking lot, Franklyn going to his car and Jason and Erica going to Jason's.

When Erica hugged Franklyn again in parting, she whispered in his ear, "Love *is* all it's cracked up to be. Go get some!"

She kissed his cheek.

"If only it were that easy," he said with a contemplative expression on his dear face. She saw their father in his face. Of all of the Bryant siblings, he resembled their father the most. He had the same toasted-almond–colored skin and dark brown hair. He'd gotten his mother's dark brown eyes though. He was also the same height as Eric, whereas Jason was a couple of inches shorter.

Franklyn and Jason did that quick hug thing that men do. Bumping shoulders and a slap on the back.

Erica waved to Franklyn as she and Jason walked in the opposite direction.

When they were out of earshot, Jason said, "No, he hasn't asked Elise out *yet.*"

Erica didn't even comment on the fact that he'd known what she wanted to know now that Franklyn wasn't present. "Why not?" she asked plaintively.

"Because he's a chump," Jason said. "Our brother is a chump, plain and simple."

Erica would have punched him in the arm for saying that about her beloved Franklyn, but her hands were full of luggage. "*You're* the chump!"

"Am not!"

"You are if you don't try to get to know Sara Minton better. Mom's right about her. She's special."

They arrived at his BMW, and he used the key to open the trunk. Sliding her luggage inside, he said, "You can get in here with the luggage if you're planning to talk about Sara all the way to Glen Ellen."

Erica clamped her mouth shut.

Once they were seated in the car, though, she said, "What do you have to lose? Just go by her place and get a look at her. You don't even have to walk up to her and introduce yourself. Simply walk inside as if you're a customer and observe her for a few minutes."

Jason was concentrating on backing the car out of the space in the parking garage without scraping the paint off of his pride and joy. He blew air between his lips once he began driving around the circular path leading to the street below. "Can I count on you to keep this between the two of us?" he asked.

Erica sat up straighter in her seat. "Of course."

"Mom sent me to Sara's bookstore/coffeehouse to pick up a couple of books for Dad. I met Sara. It *wasn't* a joyous reunion."

"You already know Sara?" To Erica's knowledge he had never mentioned knowing Sara Minton.

"She was two grades behind me in school. When I was on the football team, I used to hang out with some guys who poked fun at her."

"In what way?"

"They made obnoxious noises and called her a pig."

"Did you ever—"

"No!" he vehemently denied, an angry expression marring his handsome features.

"Then you spoke up for her," Erica guessed.

"No," he said regretfully.

Erica was quiet for a minute or so. She couldn't believe her brother had stood by and let bullies insult an innocent girl. But she couldn't judge him, either, because he'd been young, and everybody makes mistakes. What she wanted to know was what he was going to do about it.

"I take it Sara remembered you when you two saw each other again?"

"From the look in her eyes, I'd be willing to bet she *vividly* remembered me," Jason said, his voice flat.

"There's only one thing you can do, if you're interested in pursuing any kind of relationship with her," his little sister said firmly. "You've got to tell her how much you regret not coming to her defense back then. It's the only way."

"I know that," Jason said quietly. "Even if we never have anything else to do with each other, I owe her that much. You should have seen the expression in her eyes, Erica. I never realized how that kind of treatment affected kids. How it stays with you and follows you into adulthood."

"*You* were never picked on," Erica said almost accusingly. "You were popular with the guys, and especially with the girls. I bet you can't remember a bad day in high school, can you?"

"I really can't," Jason admitted. "Does that make me a bad guy?"

"No," Erica told him. "It makes you a guy at a disadvantage when it comes to dealing with a woman who *was* mistreated, that's all. It's going to be hard for you to understand why she won't want to listen to you, let alone go out with you."

"You think it's going to be that tough?"

"Definitely."

Jason smoothly drove in and out of the morning traffic. "Why should she let something that happened sixteen years ago affect her life today?"

"She probably doesn't let it affect her on a daily basis," Erica said logically. "It's only when she's reminded of it, as she was when you walked into her store, that it bothers her. From what I hear about her, she's been very successful in advertising. Had a good marriage. Her husband was killed."

"Yeah, Mom told me. That's sad. In fact, she had a sad aspect in her eyes before she recognized me, and they turned absolutely icy."

"I'm sure seeing you again was a shock to her system.

But what I'm trying to say, Jase, is that a woman like Sara, who has had to build a defense around her heart in order to not get hurt by life, picks and chooses whom and what to let into her life. She won't be happy to allow you near her for fear you haven't changed, even if she *is* totally different. Why should she subject herself to *you*?"

"Thanks, sis. You make me sound like an infectious disease!"

"You are as far as Sara Minton is concerned," Erica said, laughing.

"I'm glad you're getting a good laugh out of this, because I don't find it funny at all."

"It's funny because you've never had to work to attract a woman. All you had to do was crook your finger at a woman and she came running into your arms. But Sara's going to be different. I dare you to ask her out!"

Jason laughed. "I'm not that boy who used to eat anything on a dare, you know. I'm a ruthless, sophisticated divorce attorney."

"Who still can't stand to be dared to do anything!"

"That, too."

"Then you'll do it?"

"What can she do to me? We're not in high school any longer."

Erica sat back on her seat and smiled. *He's toast,* she thought. *Sara is going to eat him alive!*

"Come here and give your dying daddy a hug," Eric said when Erica walked into his "sick room." In her opinion, it was unlike any room where a convalescing patient who was in dire need of rest might be found. He was still conducting business.

Propped up in bed on pillows, wearing pajamas, her father had his laptop computer on a roll-away bed tray in front of him. Erica went to him and hugged him. He squeezed her tightly, his strength seemingly not reduced at all.

She kissed his forehead and smoothed his wavy gray hair back. Looking into his eyes, she asked, "What's the big idea, falling out in the field like a common greenhorn?"

Before her father could answer, she turned and smiled at the three men gathered around his bed. His foreman, Claude Leroux, a short, wiry man in his early forties, sitting in a straight-back chair closest to the bed. Lucien Davis, a neighbor and a good friend, his brown eyes twinkling with humor. And Marcus McCutcheon, a vintner from the next county who bought fruit from them every harvest. "Good afternoon, gentlemen," she said pleasantly in a blanket greeting.

"Good to see you again, Miss Bryant," said Marcus, clutching his wide-brimmed cowboy hat in a big hand.

"It's about time you got here, Erica. Maybe you can talk some sense into your father," Lucien said. "He's talking about going ahead with the barbecue next Saturday night. We're trying to convince him to postpone it."

Every year, following the harvest, the area vintners got together to throw one big party. It was the Bryants' turn to host the party this year.

Eric looked at his daughter for backup. "Your mother and I already have everything organized for the event. We've hired the band, the caterers, and the pyrotechnics team. Everything's set. We see no reason to postpone the festivities."

Erica saw in his determined expression that he wasn't going to back down.

She smiled at the three men, but directed her question to the most important of them, in her estimation. Their foreman, Claude Leroux. "Claude, how are things going?"

"Running smoothly, Erica," Claude assured her with an easy smile.

That's all Erica needed to hear. Claude was indispensable to the family. He was wonderful with the pickers, thorough in his work practices, and a confirmed family man who wanted only the best for his family. He had found it with the Bryant Winery.

He was paid well for his hard work and genuinely appreciated by his employer. The combination made him a contented man.

He smiled as he elaborated. "We had some very reliable workers this year. The harvest went on without a hitch. The winepresses are going to be groaning."

Erica returned his smile. That meant there were very few inferior grapes that had to be thrown out this year.

"Good news for you, Mr. McCutcheon," she said. He got first pick of the excess fruit that the Bryants did not need to fulfill their wine-making goals.

Her comment elicited a smile from the usually taciturn vintner. "That depends on the price," he astutely observed.

Eric's right brow rose. "I had a heart attack, I didn't sustain brain damage. The price is ten percent higher this year. Those grapes are of the highest quality."

Marcus McCutcheon's forehead furrowed in a frown as he calculated the cost. Truth was, the grapes he'd bought from the Bryants last year had been under market price. A 10 percent hike was very reasonable.

He got up and stuck his hand out to Eric. "Deal!"

He and Eric shook.

Afterward, McCutcheon put his hat on and said his farewells. "Gentlemen, Miss Bryant. It's been a pleasure."

When he left, Lucien Davis said, "That settles business with him, but what about the barbecue, Eric? Will you see reason and postpone it until later? What is a party without your presence?"

"A damned sight less lively," Eric joked. "But I'm

going to be there. I just won't be able to dance all of you into the ground like I did last year."

Everyone laughed.

Lucien rose, went and shook hands with Eric, then placed a hand on his shoulder. "Okay, you old cowboy, do as you wish. Andrea and I will be here to help close the place down."

He smiled at Erica. "Welcome home, honey."

"Thank you," she said. "It's good to be home."

Lucien left then, shaking his head and smiling all the way out the door.

Claude got to his feet. "Well, I have things to do. Glad to have you back, Erica."

"Tell Rosaura and the kids hello for me," she said with affection. Claude and his family lived on the property in a three-bedroom house, a half mile away. Erica had gotten to know his wife, Rosaura, and their children, Claude Jr. and Katrina, very well over the years.

"I will," he promised, and left the room.

Alone with her father now, Erica went and sat next to him on the bed. She glanced down at the computer screen. Instead of looking at the winery's books, as she'd assumed he was doing, he had been playing solitaire. She snuggled close to him, and he put his arm around her.

"Don't ever scare me like that again," she said as she laid her head on his shoulder.

"It sneaked up on me, sweetheart. Otherwise, I wouldn't have eaten dirt like I did."

Erica laughed softly. He made a joke out of everything.

"Now," he said, changing the subject. "What is this I hear about you marrying Joshua Jenkins?"

"Knight."

"Joshua Jenkins, Joshua Knight, same difference," her father said seriously. "He's the boy who took improper advantage of you when you were ten."

Erica leaned away from him, forcing him to take his arm from around her. "He did no such thing!"

"The very act of his allowing you to get attached to him, a boy who was nearly a man, was improper," Eric reasoned.

"I don't see where I gave him any choice since it was I who stalked *him*!" Erica exclaimed. "And think about it, Daddy. He didn't know you. Maybe he thought you'd fire his dad, or something, if he weren't nice to me."

Eric considered this. He had judged Joshua's behavior based on his feelings as Erica's father, not as his father's employer. She might have a point. "So he was a gentleman?"

"To the max. I was the only one who had romantic dreams about one day growing up and marrying him. He treated me like a kid sister."

She showed him her ring. "Luckily, I'm not the only one, today, who has romantic notions."

Eric held her hand, looking at the ring. "Wasn't that expensive? I mean, what are you two going to live on, now that he's spent all his money on a bauble like that?"

Erica laughed. "Daddy, Joshua is a very practical man. He wouldn't blow all his money on a ring. At the most, he'd spend a month's salary, like any sensible man. He just earns a good salary."

"Working for Etienne Roumier?"

"He no longer works for the Roumier winery. He's going into business for himself right here in northern California."

This piqued Eric's interest. "Oh, really?"

"Yes," Erica informed him proudly. "He's already bought some land in the Russian River Valley. Over in Healdsburg."

"Remote, but not a bad spot," Eric said.

Erica nodded. "It has a house on it, but Joshua says it's in need of repair. We're young, though, and aren't afraid of hard work."

"Wait a minute," said Eric. "Do you mean to tell me you're getting married right away?"

"Yes, the sooner the better," Erica told him happily.

"Won't that interfere with your work here?"

"Dad, I'm the enologist. I mix different varieties to come up with the best taste for our wines. That's not something that requires living on the premises. You take care of the business side, and I'll come from Healdsburg to do my job. It'll work out."

"But what about the day-to-day *physical* running of the winery?" Eric asked.

"You have a wonderful man in Claude," Erica reminded him.

"Claude isn't a Bryant." Eric pursed his lips. "I'm not making myself clear." He touched her chin and tilted it up so that they were looking directly into each other's eyes. "Your mother and I are retiring. We're leaving in a couple of months. As soon as I get my strength back and we can buy a Winnebago."

"What?" asked Erica incredulously.

"This mild heart attack forced me to take stock of my life," Eric explained. "Your mother and I have been talking about seeing more of the country, and this is the time to do it. Sure, the doctor says I'll probably live a long time, but who knows? Your mother deserves to have her husband to herself for a change."

"But—" Erica started to protest.

"Be quiet and let me finish," said her father. "My mother and father left me this land. I married your mother and, together, we made a pretty good living off of it. We earned 1.5 million dollars last year. That ain't bad. But your mother and I have managed to invest over the years, and we're set for life. Aside from the business. The business is your legacy, and your brothers'. We're leaving it to you three. What you decide to do with it will be up to you. Whether you want to live here with Joshua and raise a family in this big house—"

"The house too?" Erica cried. She couldn't imagine her parents living anywhere else. Possibly because it was the only place they'd ever lived as a couple. The thought threw her into a panic.

"Your mother and I will live nearby. We've picked out a sweet spot on the north ridge where we'll build a small house. Nothing fancy. We don't need this big house. We've been rattling around in it for years!"

Erica put her hands to her temples and massaged them, trying to take in everything her father was saying. "I'm having a hard time registering all of this. It's going to be strange waking up in this house, going downstairs, and not seeing you and Mom in the kitchen."

Her father smiled at her. "You'll get used to it, honey. That's life. One day, you'll be leaving the business to one or more of your children."

"Have you told Franklyn and Jason what you and Mom plan to do?"

"Yes, we told them when they visited me in the hospital."

"Neither of them mentioned it to me!"

"I asked them not to."

"Figures," said Erica. She tried to smile at her father to show she supported his decision, but it came out as a grimace. "I suppose it's selfish of me to want you and Mom to continue as you have been doing all these years."

"I understand your feelings," Eric said. "It's a comfort to you for things never to change. But life changes, whether you want it to or not. You either go with the flow or get swept off your feet by it. Your mother and I plan to drift on a lazy river for the rest of our days."

Chapter Twenty

Erica went back downstairs to the kitchen where she'd left her mother and Jason when she went upstairs to say hello to her father. They were where she'd left them, at the kitchen table looking at the many photos she'd taken, or had had taken, while she was in Burgundy.

The kitchen was huge with redbrick-colored tile on the floor, solid pine cabinets with glass faces, and professional-size appliances. Simone had insisted on double ovens because she often cooked for crowds. This year would be the first time the family had hosted the harvest barbecue without preparing the food themselves. Eric had convinced her that it was too much work.

Erica joined them at the table.

Her mother held up a photo for her to see. It was of her and Joshua at the fourteenth-century church in the town of Volnay. Joshua had asked a passing tourist to snap their photo while they stood in front of a fountain in the square. "He turned out well. He was almost as tall as he is now the last time I saw him. Same smile. He's got his mother's eyes. You did good, sweetheart."

Erica took the photo and sighed with longing. She

missed Joshua. She raised her gaze to her mother's face. Simone was laughing at her with her eyes. "I miss him so much." Trying to shake her loneliness for him, she said, "How do you know he has his mother's eyes?"

"I took pictures at all of the harvest parties. The Jenkinses came to the party that summer. I have pictures of the entire family. I dug them out after you phoned and told me you had run into Joshua again."

"That's great! I'd like to see them."

"Of course," her mother said, sounding pleased. "They're in a keepsake box on the second shelf of the third bookshelf from the door in the family room."

Erica immediately rose and went looking for the photos.

Seeking his mother's wisdom, Jason took the opportunity to tell his mother about his,past experiences with Sara, and how he'd been more interested in maintaining his status as a football hero rather than doing the right thing and putting a stop to the ridiculing of Sara.

Simone sat looking into his eyes for a few minutes before responding. She saw the remorse in their depths, and the nurturing part of her wanted to soothe him. But the part of her makeup as a mother that believed telling the truth to your child benefited him more than mollycoddling him said, "I've never known you to be cruel, Jason. And I know you didn't shout obscenities at the child, but you didn't do anything to stop it either."

"You're disappointed in me," he said, feeling like a misbehaving schoolboy.

Simone smiled and shook her head in the positive. "You're so right. I am. But I'd be even more disappointed if you didn't apologize to that girl. I know it's been a long time coming, but restitution still tastes sweet in the mouth of the person who was wronged.

You helped take something away from her: her self-confidence. It's time you did your part in giving it back to her. I know it might not seem important . . ."

"No, no, I think it's important," Jason assured her. "The only thing is, I don't think she's going to believe I'm sincere."

"Make her believe," Simone told him as if it were a fait accompli. She had the utmost faith in her son.

"Well," Jason said as he pushed his chair back and got to his feet, "it's going to have to wait awhile. I've got a case going to trial and piles of paperwork on my desk. I need to get back to Bakersfield."

Simone rose too and hugged him.

"I'll go upstairs and say good-bye to Dad," Jason said after she'd released him.

Smiling, Simone watched his retreating back.

Her daughter was engaged to be married. Her middle son was making an effort to put more meaning in his life by pursuing a woman of substance. Now, if only her eldest son would work up the nerve to give Elise a ray of hope, she'd be batting a thousand. She knew all Elise needed was a signal from Franklyn that he was interested in her and she'd do the rest. Lettie Burrows, her spy at The Vineyard, had told her as much. But Elise wouldn't make the first move. She loved her job. She'd told Lettie that she lived to go to work every day. She'd tried to make it sound as if she loved her job because of the pay, the environment, and the people she worked with, but Franklyn had come into the room while she was talking, and Lettie said her eyes had lit up as if Denzel Washington had suddenly graced them with his presence. *Franklyn, Franklyn,* thought Simone. *Come on, boy, make a move. I want all three of my children settled by the time your father and I roll on down the road in our customized motor home!*

At that moment, in San Francisco, Franklyn was up to his elbows in late lunch orders. The Vineyard specialized in French cuisine, but bare-bones recipes that country folk in the provinces used, not the sophisticated cuisine of Parisians. Right now, he had a quail breast sautéing in butter under fire before he shoved the whole pan into the oven to finish cooking. He had two other main courses cooking as well. That's how his day went, juggling entrees with dexterity. It was a rhythm he was used to.

He liked the energy of the kitchen. Waiters, chefs, all moving fast, talking at the same time, arguing, cursing, laughing, telling lies and secrets. Gossiping about the patrons out front waiting on their food. They had a loyal clientele, so his people got to know them pretty well. They got to know what foods they liked and disliked.

Sometimes the waitresses reminded patrons of allergies when they ordered a certain food. "Ma'am, I'll be sure Franklyn doesn't cook that in peanut oil. I know you're allergic to peanuts."

Franklyn was grateful he had such a great staff, many of whom had been with him from the start when he'd struggled to stay open. Restaurants failed all the time. He knew how lucky he was.

He kept glancing at Elise, who was mixing some wonderful concoction at her workstation. As his pastry chef she had a certain amount of freedom. She could come in and work her own hours, just so long as she completed a designated amount of sweets for his customers every week. Unlike his role, for which he had to be present the entire time the restaurant was open to the public, Elise was free to leave when her quota was filled.

He knew she also used his facilities to prepare other delicacies that she sold to other restaurants. That was okay with him. He knew how hard it was for a pastry chef to get a foothold in this business. He hoped she was gaining new customers by selling her wares to other eateries.

He glanced up at the clock on the wall. It was nearly two. They usually slowed down around two, and then things picked back up around dinnertime. They closed their doors at ten. He didn't have a bar, he sold only wine, beer, and soft drinks with meals. He'd known since he first had the idea of owning a restaurant that he wanted it to be a place where hardworking families could bring their children. He loved kids.

Lettie Burrows, an African-American woman in her late forties, sidled up to him and said, "Cindi's in the bathroom throwing up again."

Franklyn checked the quail in the oven. He glanced down at Lettie, who was barely five feet tall. "Is she going to be able to finish her shift?"

"I don't think so, it's pretty bad."

Franklyn thought a moment. Without Cindi, they were going to have to hustle, but they'd done it before. "You might have to go out and charm the natives while I take over your duties," he joked.

Lettie could have kissed him he was so understanding. She smiled at him. "I'll go tell her to go home then. And I promise not to yell at the customers."

"Not even if some horny guy pinches you?"

"I won't yell at him," Lettie said. "I'll just slug him and keep moving."

Franklyn laughed.

Lettie left the room, going through the double swing doors.

Elise, who had heard their conversation, walked up to Franklyn. "Franklyn, if you want me to, I can take over for Cindi. I'm just about finished for the day."

Their eyes met, and Elise blushed in spite of her mental note to stay cool under his scrutiny. He smiled at her. "That's sweet of you, Elise, but I know you probably have some place else to be."

Elise smiled ruefully. "I wouldn't have offered if I had some place else to be. If you want me, just say the word."

" 'The word,' " Franklyn joked.

Elise laughed, her tone delightfully pleasing to his ears.

She slowly backed away. "Okay, I'll just finish what I'm doing and then change into a spare uniform."

"Thanks, Elise."

They turned their backs to each other, returning to what they'd been doing.

Elise closed her eyes and gave a deep sigh. Maybe after tonight, Franklyn would see her as a woman. The waitress uniforms were reminiscent of a French maid's outfit, although the skirt wasn't as short, and not as much cleavage was shown. She'd never worn a dress to work, and if there was one thing she knew about her body, which wasn't perfect, it was that she had a great pair of legs. She biked nearly every day, and she walked the hilly streets of San Francisco just as regularly.

Hours later, however, she once again saw her hopes dashed. They'd been so busy she knew Franklyn had not noticed her legs or anything else about her.

It was nine forty-five, and only two couples remained in the dining room lingering over coffee and dessert. She sighed inwardly when she put their checks on their tables. They were definitely going to be getting more love tonight than she was.

She did not regret volunteering to take over for Cindi, though. She'd gotten the chance to observe Franklyn in his environment longer, and her opinion of him had only improved because of it. He was so calm and collected under pressure. Unlike her ex-husband, Derrick, who was volatile when faced with setbacks and often took his anger out on her. She had told herself, after their divorce, that she would never trust her heart with another man. That was before she walked into The Vineyard and met Franklyn.

She remembered once, in her early days of working here, when she would prepare cherries flambé at the tables, and one guy, showing off for his fellow fraternity brothers, had had the audacity to remark on the curve of her butt and tell her what he wanted to do to her. She'd gone off on him! Because he thought the customer was always right, he'd demanded to see the manager. The manager was Franklyn, who came from the kitchen, heard the customer's grievance, took one look at Elise's crumpled face, and told the men to leave his establishment and never come back.

They did as they were asked because not only did the manager/chef have the build of a linebacker, he also had backup from two burly male waiters and Lettie Burrows, who'd come from the kitchen carrying a knife as big and mean-looking as a machete.

After they were gone, Franklyn had simply smiled at her and said, "You don't have to put up with behavior like that here, Elise." He'd looked around him until his eyes settled on a table with an elderly couple at it. "Why don't you give that flambé to the Winstons? I happen to know they both have a sweet tooth or two between them."

"Sure do!" Mary Winston said, her brown face crinkling in a grin.

To which everyone in the dining room laughed.

From that day forward, Elise felt secure at The Vineyard. It had been a long time since she'd felt safe anywhere.

The stragglers had gone, and the staff split into two crews, one to clean the dining room and the other to clean the kitchen. By eleven, they were done and everyone was saying their good nights.

Elise had changed back into her own clothes and collected her bag. Just as she placed her hand on the front doorknob, Franklyn called, "Elise!"

She turned, hope clutching at her tired-of-hoping heart. "Yes, Franklyn?"

"You're not riding that bike home in the dark, are you?"

She smiled at him. "It's how I get around."

"No," he said with finality. "You usually leave here in time to get home before dark. I'd feel better if you'd let me take you home. There's plenty of room for your bike in the bed of my truck." He owned a pickup truck that came in handy when he had to transport produce from his favorite greengrocers around the city.

"O-okay," Elise said slowly, trying to keep the excitement out of her voice.

Neither of them heard Lettie Burrows utter, "Hallelujah!" as she left just before them.

Erica had a separate phone line in her bedroom. When the phone rang at six o'clock in the morning, she knew it was Joshua. She also knew that it was three A.M. in France.

She opened her eyes, rolled over in bed, and grabbed the receiver without glancing at the caller ID readout. "I miss you so much," she said, her voice husky from sleep.

"Until I met you, I slept like a baby. Now here I am lying awake," he said, his voice so sensual it immediately got an answering response in the pit of her stomach. "I got your e-mail, but they're so impersonal. I wanted to hear your voice. Hear you breathing."

Erica sighed with pleasure as she rolled onto her stomach in bed. She was wearing his pajama top and nothing else. He'd kept the bottoms. "You got my e-mail, then you know about the photos Mom has had all these years, and I never knew about them. In one, you're standing between your mother and father with your arms crossed over your chest, looking every bit like Peter Pan for all the world. It's that cocky expression you have on your face. No wonder I was enchanted by you."

"Enchanted, huh?"

"Totally." She laughed softly. "What are you wearing?"

"Nothing. What are you wearing?" he countered.

"Your pajama top."

"Take it off."

Even though she knew he had no way of knowing whether or not she would do his bidding, Erica removed the top. Her curtains were closed, and the only light in the room came from the dimmed lamp on the nightstand.

"Okay," she told him. "It's off."

In Beaune, Joshua was lying in bed in the dark. He had the window open because it was warm tonight, and no one could see in anyway, because his bedroom window faced the walled garden. He could hear the cicadas outside. He'd read somewhere that it was only the males who made that sometimes irritating sound. They were probably lonely for their women too.

"Good," he told her. "Now lie on your back."

Erica rolled over onto her back. "Done."

"Now I want you to gently touch the side of your face going down, feeling your breath on your hand as you move it across your mouth and then down to your neck."

Erica ran her hand over her face, feeling her breath on her palm. She imagined it was Joshua touching her.

In Beaune, Joshua was mirroring her movements.

"Stop at your breasts," he said. He closed his eyes. He had hardened at the thought of running his hands over her beautiful breasts.

He heard Erica's breath catch in her throat, and knew she was feeling the same way he was. "Touch both of your breasts for me, darling."

Erica was amazed by her body's reaction to his coaching. Her nipples were hard. Her female center moistening as his voice spoke in her ear. She'd never done anything like this before, and felt somehow more sinful than she would if he were actually there touching her. "Joshua, I don't know if I can bear this. I'm getting turned on."

Joshua laughed softly. "That's the point, darling."

"I feel like I'm cheating on you!"

He really laughed then. "But I'm right here."

"I wish you were right *here*."

Joshua gave up the notion of having sex with her by proxy. There was no substitute for her anyway. She was one of a kind, his Erica.

"I'm working on it," he said with a sigh. "Put your top back on, baby. I can see now that there is no deep sexual satisfaction without you in my arms. Tell me what you want to do about the winery instead. Do you want to run it now that your father is retiring?"

"I want to be with you!"

"That's nice to hear," Joshua said. "But there is the real problem of what to do with the family business. Your brother Franklyn has a restaurant to run, and Jason is a lawyer. Has either of them expressed interest in running the winery?"

"No, they haven't," Erica said with regret. "I have no doubt that either one of them could do it. Franklyn has proved he has a head for business. Not everybody can stay afloat in the restaurant business. And Jason has always had a head for business. The desire to make wine is missing, though, it seems."

"And you've got plenty of that."

"Yes, but now I have no desire to be anywhere except with you. And I would never ask you to put off your dreams to come live here with me. That's too much to ask."

"Baby, I would do it for you. But to be honest, I would prefer to build our own legacy to leave to our children one day, just as your mom and dad are doing for you and your brothers."

"That's what I want too," Erica assured him.

"It's awfully tempting to step right into an established business, but it wouldn't be the same for me," Joshua told her. "I feel strongly that I'm the one who should provide for you, Erica. I wouldn't feel like a man if I didn't."

"I understand," Erica said softly. "I do. We *will* find a solution. Franklyn, Jason, and I will find a way to keep the family business going and a way to ensure that we each can find personal happiness."

"I know you will," Joshua said with faith in her. "Listen, you may have to stay on longer than we planned. In the meantime, I'll refurbish the house. I never wanted to bring you there to live in the shape it's in anyway. I hired a local guy to clean up the yard, the attic, and the basement in preparation for the repairs, and he e-mailed me that he'd found a family of possums in the basement. And there were mice in the attic."

"Mice?" said Erica. "I never figured on mice."

Joshua laughed. "So, let me get the house fixed up, and then we'll get married and begin our lives together as vintners."

"The makers of the best pinot noir in the world!" Erica exclaimed.

"Well, the best in northern California, anyway," Joshua said. He sighed. "Well, I'd better go. Go back to sleep, sweetness. And dream about me making love to you."

"Do you think I'm a prude?" she asked, referring to her aversion to phone sex.

Joshua laughed. "Baby, I know you're not. I get hard just thinking about making love to you. I don't want you to do anything you're uncomfortable with. And I want you to always feel as if you can tell me when you don't like something I suggest. Like you just did. Sometimes you might have to rein me in. I want to experience every pleasure imaginable with you. My imagination might tend to be a little out there. Maybe too freaky for your taste. In which case, always let me know, and I'll tone it down a bit."

Erica smiled to herself. Compared to Joshua, her other lovers had been novices.

"The other two men you were with had to be deaf, dumb, and blind not to appreciate you more," he said, as if he could read her thoughts. "You are delectable, every single inch of you. When God made you, he made you with me in mind. He knew I would cherish the graceful way your neck is formed. He knew I would love that beauty mark next to your juicy lips. He knew I would love cupping your behind in my big hands. No, my darling, you are not a prude. You are sex personified."

Erica was so aroused she could not speak for a moment. She had been holding her breath, and she let it out slowly.

Joshua heard her exhalation and laughed. "I see you get me. Better go take a cool shower, sweetness. I'm heading to the shower myself. I love you."

"I love you," Erica said huskily.

After they hung up, Erica lay on the bed, wondering how she was going to survive two weeks or more without Joshua. Then she got up and got better acquainted with the massage setting on the shower head.

In Beaune, Joshua was in the shower allowing the stream of water to wash over his head. He'd decided that a bit of abstinence would be good for him. He was not, after all, controlled by his gonads. A mature male of thirty-four should be able to think about his woman without going into erotic meltdown.

He leaned against the wall of the shower, both hands flat against the tiles. His biceps bulged. His entire body was tense with desire as images of Erica in her shower in Glen Ellen slowly reeled off in his mind like one of those French art films he'd discovered in his youth.

He would not make it two weeks without her. Tomorrow, he would phone the real estate agent with whom he'd listed the house. He would tell him that he'd decided to rent the house after all, as the agent had suggested when he'd gone into his office. Gites, or rental homes, were popular in Burgundy. He could probably earn a nice monthly income on it. The paperwork would be expedited in much less time than it would take to sell a house.

Selling the house had been his biggest task.

If he was lucky, he could be in California within the week.

Chapter Twenty-one

For the next few days, Erica had little time to consult with her brothers about who would be taking over the day-to-day running of the winery. She and Claude, along with six other men, had their hands full. From early in the morning till dusk, with only a break for lunch, they worked in the converted barn that had been turned into a wine press over thirty years ago when Erica's parents had transformed a farm that grew vegetables into an award-winning winery.

Erica and the men were dressed in sturdy pants, long-sleeve shirts (to discourage sticky grape juice from getting on their arms), gloves, and hip boots. The hip boots were a requirement because they had to step down into the big, mechanical wine press and place the bunches of grapes between the press with shovels. It was a taxing job, but since the Bryants stuck to the old ways as much as possible, it was unavoidable.

Right now, Erica and Claude were taking their turn wading among the grapes, pushing a shovel full at a time between the huge presses.

Claude, around Erica's height of five-seven, with dark brown skin, a thick moustache, and no hair on his head, had been more quiet than usual today. In the past, Erica had barely been able to shut him up when they worked together. He talked incessantly about his wife and children. He talked about his childhood in Haiti. Erica rather missed his vivid stories about Les Cayes, his hometown.

"You're pretty quiet today," Erica said by way of opening the conversation. "Is something the matter? There's nothing wrong with Rosaura and the kids, is there?"

Claude's lips were closed tightly, as if he wanted to say something but was forcing it back down. Erica smiled at him. "Of course, if you want to keep your own counsel, that's perfectly fine too."

Claude spoke English with a pronounced French accent. After he'd learned to speak and read English, he developed a love of English novelists, the Brontë sisters, Emily, Charlotte, and Anne. Erica had discovered this one day when he'd whipped out a copy of *Jane Eyre* while they were taking a lunch break under a tree near the vineyards.

He said things like "keep my own counsel" and "I will brook no interference in this matter" all the time. Erica loved his archaic manner of speaking.

His face softened in a smile. "I'm sorry if I'm a bit pensive today. Your father told me what he and your mother plan to do in a couple of months. And I am vexed with concern over it. My family and I have been happy here."

Erica's heart went out to him. "Don't worry, Claude, you will have a position here as long as you want to stay. You're the best foreman we've ever had!" she was quick to reassure him. "No matter who takes over for Dad, you will not be replaced."

"That's what your father said," Claude told her. "But when things change—"

Erica interrupted him. "Look, either I or Frank or Jason will be running things, and all of us care about you and your family. We're not selling the business. It will remain in the family. The only reason you would have to worry is if we were selling it. That's not going to happen. This land has been in the family too long, and we'll fight to keep it!"

Claude peered into her determined eyes. "I pity the fool who gets in your way," he said.

Erica burst out laughing. "Oh my God, you've put down the Brontë sisters for Mr. T?"

"I've been watching reruns of the *A-Team* on TV Land," Claude informed her with a smile. "He's very funny."

Erica laughed again and continued shoveling the grapes into the press.

That night, five days after her return from France, she and her parents had dinner in the formal dining room. Her mother only set the table in there on special occasions, so she knew something was up.

Since Eric's heart attack, Simone had modified all of her recipes into heart-healthy renditions of their former richer versions. Tonight they were dining on broiled salmon, which was naturally good for the heart due to its omega oil content, fresh broccoli, a garden salad, and homemade wheat rolls. Eric was allowed a small amount of margarine made from olive oil on his roll.

Erica glanced across the table at him. He looked good for a man who had "eaten dirt," as he'd put it, a little more than a week ago. She smiled when he ate some broccoli and frowned. He'd never liked broccoli. Her mother made him eat it anyway.

"Erica," her mother said. "Your father and I have something we want to say to you."

Eric put down his fork and regarded his daughter. "We want you to know that we'll understand if you decide to leave the winery in the hands of one of your brothers. We say this because I believe all of us—you, your mother and I, *and* your brothers—thought you would be the one to take my place one day as the big chief around here. Even when you were a kid, you took more interest in the winery than your brothers did. Franklyn wanted to cook since he was knee high to a grasshopper, and Jason always had his nose in a book if he wasn't playing some sport or other. But you, you dogged my steps. You wanted to know everything there was to know about wine-making." His eyes grew misty. "I guess I took one look at you in your mother's arms in the hospital and knew you'd be the one."

"But things change," Simone said as she comfortingly placed a hand over her husband's on the tabletop. "We instinctively know that Joshua is a proud man. He cannot help being a proud man, seeing as how he started out so poor, and has become who, and what, he is today." She lovingly met her husband's eyes. "Your father and I were much like you and Joshua are when we started the winery. Neither of us would give up a moment of that struggle. It made us recognize our strengths and weaknesses. It brought us closer. It strengthened our love. We would be remiss as parents if we tried to prevent you from experiencing that with Joshua."

Erica had tears in her eyes because she had been fearing the moment when she would have to tell her parents she was choosing Joshua over their legacy. Now they had taken that burden from her and set her free to follow her heart.

She got up and walked around to their side of the table and hugged both of them at once. They each placed kisses on her cheeks. "Thank you," she said. "I love you so much. I don't know what I did to deserve such wonderful parents."

"Oh, honey," her mother said. "All you had to do was be born!"

Later that night, just before she dragged her weary

body off to bed, Erica placed calls to each of her brothers.

Jason answered the phone in his usual brusque manner. "Hello, Jason Bryant."

"Well, who else would it be?"

"Erica." He laughed. "What's up?"

"Your time is up. You, Franklyn, and I need to talk business. I take it you're going to come home for the barbecue?"

"Yes, I'll be there."

"Good. I'll phone Franklyn and make sure he's coming. We could talk then. But, Jase, have you given it any thought?"

"I have," he told her, his tone serious. "It would be a big change for me, Erica. I'm a lawyer, not a gentleman farmer. While I've always respected what Dad and Mom built together, as you know, I had little interest in it. Like most boys, I wanted to be something different from what my father was. I guess boys have to carve out their identities separate from their fathers'. Little girls tend to idolize their fathers. I rebelled against him. So did Franklyn. He identified more with Mother's occupation. I don't know whether it's because a father puts more pressure on his sons to conform than he does his daughters, or what. But there you have it."

Erica was disappointed. "Both you and Franklyn are capable of running the winery, Jason. I would remain the enologist here until you hired somebody else. But I'm in love, and I'm going to marry Joshua. One of you has to step up and accept the responsibility of keeping the family's legacy alive and well for future generations. Even if Joshua and I were to stay on, our children would be Knights, not Bryants. You think about that. Let that simmer in your practical lawyer's mind for a while."

"Wouldn't that be a coup for you and Joshua?" Jason asked, grasping at a way out of having to step up and take responsibility as his sister had suggested. "The winery is already a money-making business. You wouldn't have to turn that land in Healdsburg into a winery."

"I would never ask Joshua to give up his dreams!" Erica cried.

"But you would ask me to give up mine of one day heading my own firm," Jason said tightly.

"Is that what I'm asking you to do, Jason?" She sighed. "What about those late-night conversations we've had about your growing tired of representing people who once loved their partners and now want to tear their throats out? You said it was making you too cynical. You were beginning to believe that there is no real happiness to be found in a committed relationship. Is that how you want to end up? Or do you want to change your life, find a good woman, and have children who can grow up on three hundred acres that's a wonderland for kids? Even you have got to admit that growing up on the farm was a good experience."

"Yeah, I had a good childhood."

"You had parents who loved you, and a brother who inspired you, and a sister who was devoted to you."

"Devoted?"

Erica laughed. "Okay, a sister who tolerated you. But who still loved you."

"The way you can monopolize a conversation, you should have been the lawyer in the family."

"Thanks, but no. I'm what I've always wanted to be, a winemaker."

"That's what scares me, Erica. I know you'd do a better job than I ever could."

"Oh, please, I do everything better than you do, but that never stopped you before."

"You're entirely too conceited."

"I got it from you."

"Did not."

"Did too."

They laughed.

"I'm going," Erica said. "I just wanted to see where you were on making a decision. You know I'll always love you, whatever you decide. But I sincerely think you're the obvious choice to do this, Jason. Promise me you'll give what I've said some thought."

"It's already percolating in my brain, sis."

"All right. Good night, sweetie."

"Night," Jason said.

They hung up.

Next, she dialed Franklyn's number. When he picked up, he sounded breathless.

"You're either working out with weights or you have a woman there," Erica said.

Franklyn laughed. "I wish! I couldn't sleep, so I'm doing a few reps."

"Mm-hmm," Erica said. "Tell Elise I said hello."

Franklyn guffawed. "If I had Elise here, I would've let the machine get your call."

"Too bad," Erica said, her tone light.

"Okay," Franklyn said, his breath coming at a near-normal rate now. "Why are you calling? Can't be an emergency, because you took the time to question me about my love life. Which is not dead any longer, by the way. I drove Elise home from work the other night."

"You did?" Erica said excitedly. "What happened?"

"Nothing happened. She took a shift for a waitress who's pregnant and wasn't feeling well, and afterward I put her bike on the back of my pickup and took her home. It was night, and I feared for her safety."

"You're so chivalrous," Erica said, smiling. "What happened when you took her home? Did she immediately jump out of the truck, or did she sort of linger, giving you the impression she wanted to say more?"

"We talked a little," Franklyn told her. "She said she really liked working for me, and she admired the way I ran the restaurant and treated the crew. Then she asked me when I'd started cooking, and I told her about Mom and Dad, and you and Jason. She shared her family's history with me. Her parents live in Sacramento. She has a younger sister."

"No mention of her husband, huh?"

"I think that's still a sore spot for her. I get the impression her marriage didn't end well. Anyway, I asked her if she'd ever been to Sonoma Valley, and she said no. So I asked her to come home with me for the weekend. I told her about the barbecue, and how it's a big celebration of the harvest every year. She seemed fascinated. But she still said no. I think it was the weekend thing that frightened her. She doesn't know me well enough to go away with me for a weekend. I assured her that everything would be aboveboard. I wasn't making a pass at her or anything. I respected her too much as my pastry chef. That's when her eyes took on a kind of sad aspect and she reached for the door's handle and opened the door. I got out and took her bike out of the bed of the truck, carried it up the steps of her apartment building, and we said good night. Where did I go wrong, Erica?"

"Lord, Franklyn, you told the woman you weren't interested in her as a woman, that's where you went wrong!" Erica said with vehemence. "I know you were just trying to put her at ease, but you should have admitted that, yes, you *are* interested in her, but you're a gentleman and she would be perfectly safe traveling to your family home with you for the weekend. Now, I want you to tell her that tomorrow. And I expect to see her on your arm Saturday! She can stay in your old room, and you and Jason can double up."

"I'll try," said Franklyn.

"You'll do it," his bossy little sister ordered him.

"I'll give it my best shot."

Erica sighed. "By the way, the reason I phoned was to let you know that, once you two get here on Saturday, you, Jason, and I have to have a serious talk about who is going to run the winery."

"If I have to, I'll sell the restaurant and move back home," said her easygoing brother.

"I know you would, sweetie," Erica told him, her heart full of love for him. "But we don't want you to have to do that unless it's absolutely necessary. We'll come up with the right solution, I know we will. See you Saturday!"

"With Elise," Franklyn said, and hung up.

Erica replaced the receiver and lay back against the pillows on her bed. She dimmed the lamp on the nightstand and punched her pillow, getting more comfortable. She was still wearing Joshua's pajama top, although she'd laundered it at least once since bringing it home with her. She imagined she was in his arms when she had it on.

As her eyes drifted closed, she wondered what he was doing right now.

Joshua showed the plumber and his helper to the door. The men had done the job to his specifications, and now they were leaving. He was expecting the real estate man in less than half an hour.

He surveyed the living room. None of the furniture was going with him. In fact, he was leaving the house exactly as it was, except for one item. That, he was taking with him to the house in Healdsburg.

Walking toward the hallway, he decided that one more circuit of the house was in order. He wanted to make sure he hadn't left anything behind that he cared about. His bags were all packed. Until he had started packing, he hadn't realized how much he had accumulated in a decade of living in Beaune. The local thrift shops were praising his name he'd given them so much clothing, books he knew he'd never read again, knickknacks, and linens. He and Erica would buy everything new for their home. He thought that was only right. Perhaps she might have some family heirlooms to bring to their home, but he came from a family that didn't have those kinds of things to pass down to subsequent generations.

He paused in the doorway of his bedroom and leaned against the doorjamb. Of all the rooms in the house, this one reminded him of Erica the most. He smiled. They'd certainly baptized the bed in their names. Made it a holy place of their love. If only for a season. He turned away. They would put their indelible marks on the old Victorian house in Healdsburg, too. And wear out a few mattresses before they were done.

After he'd walked through the entire house, he went to the kitchen and made himself a cup of coffee. He took it on the patio and sat in his garden one last time. He was still there when the real estate man knocked on the front door.

"Good news, Mr. Knight," Paul Lignier said upon entering the house. "I've already got a renter for your house. An American writer who wants something quiet and out of the way. He'll be bringing his wife and children with him."

"May I ask who it is?" Joshua asked.

"But of course. His name is Joachim West. He is from San Francisco. Perhaps you have heard of him?"

Joshua smiled when recognition dawned on him. Joachim West was an African-American author. He'd won the American Book Award, among other literary prizes. But it was a popular book West had written that had made a fan out of him.

A book called *Lottie Washington.* It was a woman-scorned story liberally sprinkled with humor. The practical side of him was delighted that the house would be rented by someone who could pay a premium price for the privilege. The constant reader in him was thrilled

Joachim West, one of his favorite writers, would be staying in his house.

"Yes," he told Paul Lignier. "He's very talented."

Paul Lignier smiled broadly. "This is wonderful. You're pleased to have him as a tenant then?"

"Yes, of course," Joshua said, handing him the keys to house. They shook hands at the door. Joshua picked up his suitcase and carry-on bag. "Well, I have a train to catch. Thank you for everything, Monsieur Lignier."

"A pleasure, Mr. Knight."

Joshua left Lignier in the house and walked out to the taxi that he'd requested to be waiting outside his door at a designated time. When he got to the end of the walk, he turned and looked at his little house once more before climbing into the backseat of the cab.

"*La gare, s'il vous plait,*" he said, asking to be taken to the train station.

He relaxed in the back of the cab. In the last few days, he'd said good-bye to his friends and thanked Etienne for his tutelage over the years. While Etienne had not been a good example to follow when it came to how best to treat one's family, he had been an excellent mentor to Joshua. Joshua was armed with the knowledge that Etienne had denied his own son: what it takes to make superb pinot noir wine. Joshua would always be grateful to him for that.

As for whether Joshua thought he was leaving the Etienne Roumier Winery in good hands, time would tell. He believed Henri was a hard worker. And his family was good incentive for him to make a success of his new position. He instinctively knew that Dominique would step in if she saw her brother flailing. Dominique had had a hole in her heart since Christian's death. She would do her level best to get to know her long-lost brother, Henri, and do everything possible to help him.

Therefore, Joshua felt good about this change.

Many hours later, he was checking into a hotel in San Francisco. Tomorrow morning, Friday, he had to see a man about a car, after which there was a woman he needed to chat with in Oakland, across the Bay Bridge. From Oakland, he was going straight to see his woman.

Dee Davis-Wells, sixty-eight, rarely had visitors during the week. Most of her friends and relatives were working people. She would be at work herself if she wasn't on disability due to a bad back. She was in good health otherwise.

As she hurried to the front door of her modest apartment, she allowed that she could afford to lose a few pounds. She was huffing and puffing by the time she stood on her toes to get a gander through the peephole. A good-looking young black man stood on the other side of her door.

"Who is it?" she asked suspiciously. A hunk or not, he could be dangerous.

"Aunt Dee, is that you? It's Joshua, open this door!"

What did he think she was, senile? She hadn't seen her silly nephew in nearly eight years. Not since he'd come from France to attend his stepfather's funeral. She'd seen neither hide nor hair of that boy in so long she wouldn't even recognize him, because she, unfortunately, didn't have any photographs of him as an adult. She had all of the school pictures Antonia had sent her when he was growing up, though.

"Who are you, really?" she yelled at him. "I have a mind to call the police. Showing up at my door telling me you're my nephew! I ain't got nothing you want! I live on Social Security. My house ain't worth robbing."

"When Joslynn and I lived with you, you used to wear a different color wig every day!" Joshua told her. "On Monday you wore a black one; on Tuesday you wore a red one; on Wednesday you wore a blond one."

"Okay, okay, it's apparent you've done your homework!"

"You're my mother's older sister by three years."

Dee harrumphed. "You could have found that out by asking anyone down at the dry cleaner's where I used to work. I talked about my sister all the time."

"Then you ask me a question that only I would know." Joshua was grinning. There he was at his elderly aunt's door, dressed in jeans, a UC Davis T-shirt, white athletic shoes, and bearing gifts, and she wouldn't let him in! It was all his fault. He should have stayed in contact with her over the years. At least she would have been able to recognize him through the peephole.

"All right," Dee said cautiously. "How old were you when you went looking for your no-good daddy?"

"I was eighteen," Joshua answered. "You asked me why I was doing it, and I said I just wanted to look into the face of the man who'd abandoned me. You told me no, that wasn't the reason I wanted to find him. The real reason was that I wanted to punch his lights out! And you were right. He was dead, so I never got the chance to confront him. But I found his family."

"Where?"

"In Boston," Joshua answered, his voice showing no emotion.

His aunt opened her door and flew into his arms. She hugged him so tightly Joshua could barely draw a breath. Afterward she stared up into his handsome face. "You're still upset by the reception your daddy's people gave you. They thought that you wanted something from them."

Chapter Twenty-two

Dee thought her nephew looked kind of uncomfortable perched on her sofa in her small but neat living room. In her youth she had been the type of person who would not rest until she found out everything she could about a person, and then broadcast it in the streets. She'd mellowed with age. Or was it that she no longer had the energy to pry into other people's lives?

She had to admit, he was a handsome devil. But his daddy had been handsome too. A cheating dog, but handsome. Her dear, sweet Antonia had been charmed right out of her good sense when she married him.

He cocked a dark brow at her as he finished drinking her weak tea and placed the cup and saucer on the coffee table. She was busy admiring the demitasse set he'd brought her from France. She'd never seen anything so delicate before. He told her the French made very strong coffee, hence the little cups. One only needed a small amount for a good caffeine buzz. She would have to make some coffee and invite Adele, her friend from across the hall, over for a cup.

He'd also brought her several bottles of wine he said he'd developed at that winery over in France where he'd been working these past ten years. She wasn't a drinking woman, but she told him she would taste it just because he'd made it.

"I guess you're wondering why I've dropped by after all this time," Joshua said.

"Yes, but I was sure you'd tell me when you were ready," Dee said.

Joshua looked into her dark brown eyes. Her eyes were shaped like his mother's. Almond-shaped, turned up at the corners a tad. She wore her gray hair in a short natural style. She was petite. Unlike his mother, who had been tall.

She wore pale pink velour jogging pants and a white short-sleeve top with white athletic shoes as if she were dressed for a walk around the block. He smiled when she said she had been prepared to wait for him to tell her why he'd come. The old Aunt Dee would have pounced on him the moment he'd walked through the door.

People really do change.

"I took a chance coming here," Joshua told her honestly. "I haven't kept in contact with you. You could have moved by now. But I was hoping you were still here."

"Honey, I'm not going anywhere. When I divorced my last husband, I decided that Oakland was fine with me. I was always looking for a man to take me out of here. But I would end up with a man who'd get me even further in debt, preventing me from making any kind of change. Since I kicked Louis out, at least I've gotten outa debt. For once in my life, I actually have a savings account. That's a really sad commentary on a sixty-eight-year-old woman's life, isn't it?"

"No, Aunt Dee, I don't think it is," Joshua said. "There's some satisfaction in being debt-free. And you look healthy, at least I hope you're healthy."

"I can't complain, sweetheart. I can't lift anything heavy because of a back problem, but as long as I remember that, I do fine. And yourself?"

"I'm healthy."

"You look it," Dee said. Although she had lived in Oakland for more than forty years, she still had a slight southern accent from having been born and raised in Georgia. "But then, both you and Joslynn seem to stay healthy. That girl runs every other day. I ask her where she's going, and she laughs and says, 'Around the track, Auntie.' She runs on the track at SFCC. That's where she works as an administrative assistant. She and her husband have two children now. You knew that, didn't you?"

She watched him closely. No, she could tell, he hadn't known he was an uncle.

"No, I didn't know," Joshua said regrettably. "What are they?"

"A boy and a girl. The little boy, Joshua, is five now. The little girl, Tasha, is three."

Joshua had gone still when she told him his sister had named her son after him.

"She named the boy Joshua?"

"Don't look so shocked. Joslynn loves you, she's just stubborn. She got that from your mama."

"I don't remember Mama being stubborn," Joshua said, a little peeved she was bad-mouthing his mother.

"Oh, you didn't know her like I did, and I'm not one to lie about folks just because they're no longer with us. Antonia wouldn't want me to lie and say she was a saint, when she was only human. Humans make mistakes. Now, Joshua, I can see you're gonna make me revert to my old self and dig to get the real reason you're here out of you. What brings you here? What's happened to make you want to do something about your past?" She waited a heartbeat, then continued. "Because you didn't just get it into your head that you had to see your dear, sweet aunt Dee again for no reason at all."

"I'm getting married," Joshua said.

"Your first marriage?"

"Yes, Aunt Dee."

"Well, you've been gone a long time," she said, defending her question. "You could've been married and divorced three times over by now." She smiled mischievously. "I had been by the time I was your age. What are you now, thirty-five?"

"I will be in October."

"October what?"

"Thirtieth."

"The day before Halloween," Dee said speculatively. Then she changed the subject altogether. "What's your fiancée's name? Where does she come from? How did you two meet? Is she French or American?"

Joshua laughed. "Would you please ask one question at a time? I'm a little jet-lagged. I can't keep up with you."

"That's what all the men say," Dee told him. "Okay. Her name?"

"Erica Bryant."

"Where's she from?"

"Glen Ellen, California."

"Where's that? I've never heard of it."

"It's in Sonoma Valley. They're known for their wine, like Napa Valley."

"Yeah, I've heard of Sonoma Valley, it's not too far from here. Is that where you two are going to settle down, in Sonoma Valley?"

"Yeah, we're going to start a winery of our own," Joshua said, enjoying watching her animated face. She was at her best when she was digging into somebody's life. She could have been a private investigator.

"So you're not going back to France?"

"Not to live," Joshua said. "I've accomplished what I wanted to over there. I've learned how to make fine wines."

"Are there any black winemakers in California?" Dee

wanted to know. "Not being a wine drinker, I've never looked into the subject."

"There are around ten wineries owned by black folks in California," Joshua informed her. "Erica's family owns a winery. That's how we met, we're in the same business, and she came to a tasting my winery was hosting in Paris."

"Paris!" said Dee wistfully. "I envy you your travels, sweetheart."

"Don't," Joshua told her. "I envy you your family connections. I've let mine fall by the wayside."

"Then that's why you're here," Dee said with a short laugh. "You're trying to reconnect with your family. Well, honey, we never gave up on *you*. We thought you'd given up on *us*!"

"But Joslynn had practically nothing to say to me at Dad's funeral," he said.

"Joslynn was grieving. She didn't have much to say to anybody. It's funny how our own preconceptions can lead us to the wrong conclusions. Joslynn has wanted to get in contact with you. She told me so. But she was afraid you had no use for her since you've come up in the world. Living in France and associating with millionaires and all that! She figured she was too lowly a person for you to bother with."

Joshua grimaced. He'd made the same assumptions about Erica's mother and father. That they would think he wasn't good enough for her.

"Where does she live? I want to tell her she was wrong. I've missed her. I've missed her a lot!"

Dee laughed. "Antonia, God rest her soul, is probably shouting in heaven right about now. I'd better give you Joslynn's home address and her work address."

She happily gave him his sister's addresses and sent him on his way, but not before giving him *her* phone number so he could call her and give her the skinny on everything that happened at their reunion. The *gossip* was back, and she needed to be fed!

It was after noon by the time Joshua tracked his sister down at a park not far from the campus of San Francisco Community College. He was ashamed that he could not glance at the young black women, of whom there were several, sitting on benches eating their lunches, and instantly identify Joslynn. He actually had to walk up to a couple of them and ask, "Joslynn Jenkins-Adams?"

The second woman he asked knew Joslynn and pointed to an attractive woman sitting alone several benches over. "That's Joslynn." She gave him the once-over. "You can come back here once you're finished talking with her."

"Thank you," Joshua said politely. "But I just got engaged."

"I don't want to marry you, I just want to borrow you," the woman, a tall blonde with brown eyes, joked. "She can have you back when I'm through with you."

Joshua laughed shortly. "That's a generous offer, but I'm going to have to decline. You have a good day."

"You too, honey," said the blonde good-naturedly, whereupon she returned to her low-carb lunch.

Joslynn was in the middle of the closing chapter of a Melanie Schuster novel and her eyes were rapidly scanning the page. The hero was about to admit he'd made a huge mistake when he broke her heart, and ask her forgiveness; and the heroine, sassy diva that she was, was probably going to make him beg! Joslynn loved Ms. Schuster's characters.

"A little begging is good for a man's soul," she said under her breath as she continued to read the delightful novel.

"Good book?" asked a male voice.

Joslynn glanced up, irritated. Some stud in a UC Davis T-shirt and jeans was standing in front of her with shades on, wearing a devastating smile. Happily married for seven years now, she was immune to studs.

She calmly put a bookmark where she'd left off, closed the book, and placed her left hand atop it so that her wedding rings were prominently displayed. "Yes, it is a good book."

The guy had the temerity to sit down beside her without being invited. Then he removed his sunglasses.

Her eyes bugged out. "Joshua?" she croaked.

"Hello, sis, Aunt Dee told me where to find you. I hope you don't mind my disturbing you on—"

He wasn't able to get the rest of the words out, because Joslynn had thrown herself into his arms and was hugging him so tightly around the neck that no words could make it through his windpipe.

She was screaming so loudly the others in the park looked in their direction, determined that she wasn't being attacked, and returned to what they were doing.

Joshua was laughing as he rocked her in his arms.

Joslynn was laughing *and* crying.

Finally, he managed to hold her far enough away from him so that he could clearly see her face. "My God, you look just like Mom."

Medium brown skin, a heart-shaped face, dimples in both cheeks, dark brown almond-shaped eyes with an almost Asian cast. Full lips, short nose with that little dent in the tip. He had that minuscule dent too.

Her dark brown hair was long and lay in waves down her back. Their mother had had lots of hair. He remembered she always wore a hair band that kept it out of her face.

"Please forgive me for staying away so long," Joshua said as he continued to hug her. "I'm sorry. I'm sorry I hurt you. I'm sorry I wasn't a big enough man to admit my feelings were hurt when you told me I was betraying

Dad by looking for my biological father. I loved Dad. He's the only father I've ever known. And I'm sorry I didn't recognize that you were in pain the last time I saw you, and your ignoring me wasn't personal. You were just dealing with grief in your own way."

"I'm sorry too," Joslynn said between sniffles. "I let pride keep me from contacting you. I thought you were ashamed of where you came from and didn't want to be reminded of it. That's why I thought you stopped calling, or coming for visits."

"No, nothing of the kind," Joshua assured her. "I thought you were still mad at me!"

"I was never really mad at you, Joshua. I took it personally when you went looking for your dad, because I thought you felt we weren't good enough for you. But I realize I was wrong. You simply wanted to know where you came from."

"It was a dead end anyway," Joshua told her. "I never found my father. He'd died years before I tracked his relatives down. What's more, they were suspicious of me and wanted to know why I'd contacted them when I was getting ready to go to college. They thought I wanted them to pay my tuition or something. I haven't seen any of them since then."

Joslynn hugged him again. "I'm sorry it didn't work out for you."

"Thanks."

They both exhaled as if they'd finally come to the end of a very long journey and found peace there waiting for them.

Joshua looked down into her eyes. "Aunt Dee told me that you're married now and that you have two children."

Joslynn beamed at him and mimicked the character Sugg Avery in *The Color Purple.* "Yeah, 'I'se married now!'" She laughed and continued. "Jack's a policeman with the Oakland Police Department." She smiled up at him. "We named our son after you. Jack insisted. He said it was kind of a peace offering to mend things between you and me. I didn't know what he meant by that when he said it, but I think I do now. It was to be proof that I loved you and I never stopped loving you."

"I can't wait to meet your family," Joshua told her.

"Let's go," Joslynn said as she rose. "I'll take the afternoon off and you can meet your niece and nephew. I'll phone Jack and let him know you're in town, and we'll all have dinner together when he gets off from work at around six."

Joshua immediately accepted.

Elsewhere in the city of San Francisco, a shy man was trying to get up the nerve to walk across the kitchen of his restaurant, a short distance in actuality, but a great distance for one whose life depended on the outcome of that trip, and speak to a lovely young maiden who had her hands in the dough of what would soon be cinnamon buns so good they would melt in your mouth.

Franklyn's mouth was dry.

Elise had been avoiding eye contact with him all day. From her behavior he deduced that Erica had been right. He should have made it plain to Elise from the beginning that he was smitten with her.

His problem now was, how could he let Elise know he was interested in her without appearing to be *too* interested in her? He didn't want to scare her off.

Elise had been watching him out of the corner of her eye all day. She wondered why, if he was only interested in her skills as a chef, he kept giving her soulful looks as if he were in a state of constant craving. Well, whatever was going on in his mind, she would not play games with him. If he wanted her, he was going to have to say so and say it in such a way that she could not possibly construe his meaning to denote anything else. First, he'd invited her away for the weekend, then he'd said she needn't feel as if she wouldn't be safe from any advances from him, because he valued her skills as a chef! That had made her mad initially, then it had made her sad.

She didn't want him to desire her because she was a good chef, but because she was a good *woman.*

She should quit, that's what she should do! Then he would miss her presence and come see her and beg her to come back to him. The thought excited her and she punched the dough back down so that it could rise for a third time.

She then wiped her hands on a clean dish towel and covered the bowl with the dough in it. As she turned to go to the pantry in the back of the big kitchen to get the ingredients she'd need to complete the recipe, she walked right into Franklyn's rock-hard body.

She had to grab hold of his arm to steady herself, and she felt his biceps in his arms as she did so. A thrill of sensual awareness shot through her. She raised her gaze to his. "I'm sorry."

Franklyn tenderly grasped her hand, his eyes never leaving hers. "Elise, I bungled what I was trying to say to you the other night. Please believe me when I say I value you as a person, not just as a chef." His eyes swept lovingly over her face, and this time there was no mistaking his meaning. "I like you a lot. I think you're wonderful. And I wish you'd reconsider coming home with me tomorrow, because I'd really like you to meet my folks. I know they're going to like you too."

Elise was trembling inside. She hoped Franklyn wasn't able to detect it. He still had hold of her hand. "I'd love to," she said softly.

Franklyn's heart beat a loud drum in his chest. "Yes?"

Elise nodded. "Yes."

He briefly brought her hand up to his thudding heart. Elise felt the beat and thrilled to it. She had not been alone in her feelings for him, after all. He'd craved her too.

"I'll pick you up at eight in the morning," Franklyn told her. "The barbecue is usually a jeans type of event. But you might want to bring something dressier for Sunday dinner. We primp a little for that."

"All right," said Elise, smiling up at him.

Neither of them had noticed several others in the kitchen had stopped what they were doing to watch them. Lettie had a huge grin on her face.

Franklyn reluctantly let go of her hand. "Okay, then. I'd better get back to work."

"Me too," Elise said.

After another longing look, they went in opposite directions.

In Glen Ellen, Erica pushed the door open to Aminatu's Daughters and strode inside. She removed her sunglasses and allowed her eyes to adjust to the lighting. The day was exceptionally sunny.

She spotted her prey standing in the children's section before an audience of twenty or more children whose ages appeared to range from two to seven. She was animatedly reading them a story. They sat in miniature molded plastic stacking chairs in various bold colors.

Erica went to stand nearby and listen.

"A friend," Sara read, "is someone who will listen to you when you're sad. Celebrate with you when you're glad. Calm you down when you're mad. And scold you when you've been bad. A friend will always tell you when you're wrong. Because facing up to your faults makes you strong."

Many of the kids obviously knew the story by heart, because whenever Sara got to the last word in a sentence, they chanted it along with her.

Erica looked into their sweet faces. Black or white, brown eyes or blue eyes, dark-haired or towheaded. They were all beautiful.

They sat, rapt, listening to the melodic sound of Sara's voice.

When she was finished, the kids scattered, some running to their parents who stood on the edges of the children's section waiting for them, some to other parts of the store.

Sara didn't ask them not to run. She seemed at peace with their energetic behavior.

When she began straightening the chairs, Erica walked over to her and helped.

"Hi, Sara," she said, smiling warmly.

Sara's eyes brightened. "Erica! I'd heard you were back from abroad. Do you have time to sit and chat awhile?"

"That's why I'm here," Erica told her. "That, and to ask you to join us tomorrow night for the barbecue. I sent you an invitation, but I didn't get an RSVP from you, so I wanted to make sure you'd gotten it."

"I'm sorry," Sara said, looking chagrined. "I meant to phone you. I won't be able to make it."

Erica gave a little disappointed moan. "I'm sorry to hear that. I thought you might like to come out and get reacquainted with some of your classmates. Lots of people you went to school with will be there."

Sara laughed softly. "I know. Some of them have been calling to let me know they're going and to ask if I'll be there. But I've already made plans for tomorrow night."

"Well, the barbecue will be from seven till the wee hours of the morning. So, if by some chance you do get a minute or two, drop by. We'd love to have you. And feel free to bring a date."

Sara considered that. It would show Jason Bryant that she didn't fear being around him anymore if she showed up on the arm of a gorgeous man. Plus, the guy would serve as a buffer between her and Jason. She had seen the keen interest in his eyes when he had looked at her. Maybe he thought that ex–fat girls were easy. Especially an ex–fat girl who'd had a crush on him for years.

It had not been the fact that he had stood there and not done anything when she was being picked on. It was his refusal to even smile when she was being roasted alive by his friends. He had not enjoyed it. Yet, he still had not spoken up for her. When their eyes would meet, she would see the pity he felt for her in them. It was his pity that was unforgivable. She didn't need his pity! She would show him that she was a woman to be coveted, not pitied.

"Maybe I *will* get the chance to drop by," she told Erica as they walked across the store to the coffeehouse.

They sat at a booth replete with a miniature jukebox at the table. Sara smiled at her. "What will you have? We have thirty varieties of coffee, and we've just put in an ice cream parlor. So now you can have a banana split if you like."

"Mmm," said Erica. "That sounds good, but I'm watching my calories right now. I want to fit into my wedding dress." She showed Sara her ring.

Sara stared at it and reached over to grasped Erica's hand to turn it this way and that way. "You've only been gone three months and you returned engaged? I guess word hasn't gotten around, because I didn't get that bit of news with the gossip of your return. Who is he? Where did you meet him?"

Erica gave her a quick rundown of how she and Joshua had met, putting the emphasis on the fact that they'd known each other years ago, and had met and fallen in love after they became adults.

She wanted Sara to mentally compare her and Joshua to herself and Jason.

Sara sighed wistfully. "That is so romantic!" She was silent a moment, then added, "The problem with my meeting someone I knew when I was a child and falling in love with him is all he'll remember about me was that I was fat. And if we started dating, and he took me out to dinner, he would watch everything I put in my mouth and wonder when I would start ballooning again. No, I prefer to date men who didn't know me back then. They have no expectations."

Chapter Twenty-three

"They fit so well together," Simone said in Erica's ear as they stood watching Franklyn and Elise on the dance floor. The couple was gazing into each other's eyes and barely moving. It was as if they were just happy to be in one another's arms.

There were tents and tables set up in the big front yard. The party planner and her crew had strung lights high between the tents, so there was good visibility. In the center of the square the tents formed was a raised wooden dance floor and attached to it, higher still, was the bandstand.

The band, which played mostly rhythm and blues, was in the middle of its tribute to Van Morrison. The male lead singer was doing a pretty good rendition of "Moondance."

"It's a marvelous night for a moondance . . ." he sang.

Erica had to agree. There was a half-moon tonight. It hung like a sickle in the velvety night sky. Any minute now, she expected to see a beautiful woman adorned in a slinky white dress, somewhat like the one *she* had on, appear on it with her long legs dangling.

"How many years has she been working for him?" Erica asked.

"Three, I think," Simone answered.

"My big brother sure is a patient man. The way he's looking at her, it's a wonder they're not already married with two children."

Simone laughed, and they continued their stroll through the revelers.

More than three hundred people had accepted their invitation to come party with them tonight. Erica kept running into old classmates, some of whom lived out of town but who'd been invited by other classmates who'd gotten invitations.

"Oh, my," said Simone. "Vincent Anderson at twelve o'clock."

Erica looked straight ahead of them and burst out laughing. Vincent was walking toward them as if he were falling-down drunk. His legs were wobbly, and he had a bottle of Corona in his hand. Anyone who didn't know Vincent might believe he was actually drunk, but Erica and her mother knew him for the prankster that he was.

Since elementary school, Vincent had reigned supreme as the class clown. No matter where he went, he made people laugh. It was little wonder that he now made his living as a highly paid comedian.

He stumbled over to Erica and Simone. "L-ladies, you look b-beautiful tonight. All f-four of you!"

Laughing, Erica stepped forward and took the bottle of Corona from him, while her mother opened her arms to the tall man for a hug. Vincent obliged, and she gave him a quick kiss on the cheek. "Great to see you again, Vincent. Give your parents my best. I'm going to make sure Eric's not sampling the barbecued ribs." She smiled up at him. "See you children later."

She left them.

Vincent, having already abandoned his drunk act

when he'd hugged Simone, grabbed Erica about the waist and pulled her close to his side. "Do you think your mother will ever stop calling us children?" he asked as he smiled down into her upturned face.

"Not in this lifetime," Erica told him.

Vincent had black, curly hair. A lock of it often fell across his handsome forehead. Women found the combination of dark good looks and a killer sense of humor very attractive, and he was never short of admirers.

They began walking away from the dance floor. "I'm glad you could come tonight," Erica told him. "When I sent you the invitation on such short notice, I figured you would be on the road, as usual."

"I'm off the road for a while," Vincent told her. "My partner and I are in negotiations with a network to develop a sitcom based on my life in a small town."

"You mean Glen Ellen is going to become a sitcom?" Erica asked, intrigued.

"Well, we're not calling the town Glen Ellen," Vincent said. "We're calling it Glen Falls."

"Big difference," Erica said, laughing softly. "If you write me into it, be sure you get an African-American actress to play me. I don't want to be turned into a blonde with blue eyes."

Vincent grinned at her and gave her a sensual perusal. "You might look good as a blonde."

"In your dreams!" She bumped hips with him, breaking his hold on her waist, and punched him in the arm. "Don't go Hollywood on me, Vincent Anderson. I knew you when the other boys were giving you wedgies. Who used to help you fight them off?"

Vincent laughed. "You did."

"And don't you forget it. If you're going to write me into your show, get Sanaa Lathan to play me!"

"Yes, ma'am!" Vincent promised, his right hand held up as if he was willing to swear to it.

They hugged.

Afterward, he held her at arm's length to gaze into her eyes. "I'm told congratulations are in order. You're getting married. Who's the lucky guy?"

Erica told him as they continued walking.

"I always thought you'd marry some hometown guy," Vincent told her. "Unlike a lot of us, you didn't catch the first Greyhound leaving town after graduation."

"He's not a hometown guy, but he's definitely the right guy for me."

Vincent looked around them. "Where is he, is he here tonight? I'd like to meet him."

"No, he's wrapping up loose ends in France, and then he'll be coming to the States."

"Well, I'm happy for you," Vincent said sincerely.

A tall buxom redhead in skintight jeans and a crop top was swiftly walking toward them. "Vincent, there you are!"

Vincent grimaced. "My date," he said to Erica under his breath.

The redhead stalked up to them. "How dare you leave me alone! I don't know anybody here." She eyed Erica with curiosity. Her delicate brows rose when she turned her gaze on Vincent as if to say, *Who is this?*

"Tracy, meet Erica Bryant. This is her family's winery. Erica and I have been friends since kindergarten."

Tracy smiled warmly. "Hello, Ms. Bryant. You have a lovely home."

"Thank you," said Erica. "Welcome. I hope you're enjoying yourself."

Erica playfully pushed Vincent toward Tracy. "Go dance with the lady, Vincent!"

Tracy gave Erica a grateful look as she pulled Vincent back toward the dance floor. Vincent glanced back pleadingly at Erica as he allowed himself to be led away.

Erica laughed and continued on her way.

She looked around her. There had been no sign of Sara all night. It was now past ten, and she'd noticed

Jason working the crowd as she was doing. She had a sneaking suspicion he was keeping an eye out for Sara.

Jason was having better luck than his sister in his search for Sara.

He spotted her the moment she arrived, on the arm of the same guy he'd seen her laughing with in Aminatu's Daughters over a week ago. She had on a long, summery purple skirt made of a material that seemed to flow over her long limbs and a sleeveless lilac blouse that accentuated the exquisite curve of her long neck and the enticing shape of her breasts, although very little cleavage was visible. Her healthy, shiny braids fell down her back in a dark cascade. Her date was wearing a suit.

Jason immediately started across the lawn to where she and Mr. Suit stood.

The band was doing "Into the Mystic."

"You made it," Jason said to her once he reached them.

The two of them regarded him as if they were surprised he'd addressed them.

Jason chose to ignore their attitudes. "Erica told me she'd invited you," he said to Sara. He offered the guy his hand. "Hi, Jason Bryant."

The guy stiffly shook his hand. "Gary Pruitt."

They allowed their hands to fall to their sides.

Jason turned his attention back to Sara. "Sara, there's something I need to talk to you about, in private." He glanced at Gary to see if he had any objections. Gary was looking at Sara to see if *she* had any.

Sara, who'd been taken by surprise, nodded her assent. "All right. Gary, this won't take long."

"Thanks, Gary," Jason said.

He and Sara walked over to one of the empty tables. Jason held out a chair for her. Sara sat down. He pulled another chair close to her and sat beside her.

Sara was intently watching him as if she felt he might

grab her, suddenly, and kiss her. She wanted to take every precaution in case he tried something funny.

"Sara," Jason said quietly. "There's no easy way to say this, so I'm just going to say it. I was an immature jerk back then. I should have spoken up for you. I should have made them stop picking on you, but I was afraid that if I defended you I'd no longer be welcome in their crowd. I'm not making any excuses. I was raised better than that, as my mother reminded me when I told her what I'd done."

"You told your mother!"

"Yes, and my sister. They were both disappointed in me, and I'm disappointed in myself. I knew better. Every time I looked into your face, I wanted to tell you how sorry I was for being such a coward." He sighed. "Is there anything I can do to make it up to you?"

"I thought you were looking at me that way because you pitied me," Sara said, her big brown eyes glistening. "I thought you felt sorry for the poor fat girl, who couldn't stop eating even when people made her feel lousy because of her weight."

She lowered her gaze.

Jason bent his head so that he could see her eyes. "Sara."

She met his eyes.

"I never pitied you. In fact, I marveled at your strength. I wondered how you could continue to come to school, day after day, when you knew what would be waiting for you. I wish I'd had your strength."

Sara got up suddenly. This wasn't turning out the way she'd planned. She'd wanted Jason to see her with Gary and intuit that he didn't have a chance with her. She would ignore him at every turn. Make him wonder why she was being so cold to him.

But he had to apologize for his past behavior! He sounded genuine, too. Like he meant every word. What was more, she was still so drawn to his rugged good looks that every time their eyes met, a sharp pain clutched her stomach and squeezed. It was a bittersweet feeling of what might have been.

Jason slowly rose too and faced her.

Marshalling all her strength, Sara said in her most formal voice, "How kind of you to apologize to me after all this time, Jason. When we met again a few days ago, I could have sworn you didn't remember me at all." She paused. "Well, all right. If it's forgiveness you're after, I forgive you."

Jason smiled and placed one big hand on her arm. She recoiled. He knew then that she had not forgiven him at all, but was just being civil. "Maybe your hurt goes deeper than you're willing to admit," he said tightly.

"Why, because I don't want you touching me?" Sara asked tightly. Her eyes raked over his face. "You would never have approached me if I looked the same way I used to in high school, Jason. So don't get an attitude with me. Let's leave the past where it belongs, in the past. You've apologized. I've accepted. All's well that ends well."

"But I thought that we could—"

"Go out sometime?" Sara asked. She actually smiled, although it didn't reach her eyes. They were cold as she continued. "When hell freezes over!"

Jason surprised himself with his cool detachment. Why she was so angry he didn't know. But the fierceness with which she had yelled at him served only to intrigue him. He wanted to know what else lay underneath her cold exterior. In his experience, angry emotions were kindled by strong feelings. Could she be attracted to him and she was trying to hide it by behaving like a shrew?

"Is that a challenge?" he asked.

Sara was bewildered. "What?"

"A challenge," Jason said calmly. "You say you won't go out with me until hell freezes over. I believe you *would* go out with me if I stated my case convincingly enough."

He moved closer to her.

Sara did not move an inch. She didn't want him to think he intimidated her.

Jason bent toward her until their faces were a mere inch apart. He inhaled her scent. She smelled of citrus and cocoa butter. He wanted to lick her skin.

He heard her sharp intake of breath. She held it.

He stepped back and regarded her like a great white shark might regard an ignorant surfer who'd had the bad luck to be at the wrong place at the wrong time. "It's a woman's prerogative to change her mind, Sara. I don't think you're as indifferent to me as you say you are."

Sara sighed. Her eyes bored into his. "Just stay away from me, Jason Bryant!"

She abruptly turned and left him standing there.

Jason enjoyed the gentle sway of her hips as she walked away.

He smiled. She hadn't seen the last of him.

Joshua almost missed the turnoff to the Bryant Winery. It had been years since he'd been in this area, and it didn't help that it was dark along these country roads. But he found it and soon was on the half-mile paved road that led up to the low-slung hacienda-style house. He slowed. The house was sprawling, as he'd remembered it. Sometimes the things you recalled in your childhood didn't measure up once you saw them again when you became an adult. The Bryant property was as majestic as he'd recalled.

The house, the barn, the stables, and the land that surrounded it all.

He smiled. He wasn't getting cold feet now, was he?

It had been his plan from the beginning to surprise

Erica by showing up so soon. She had been so good in keeping him informed via e-mail about the goings-on at the winery that he knew when he arrived the harvest party would be in full swing. He had gotten a room at the Glen Ellen Inn and freshened up. He would have arrived earlier if he hadn't been persuaded to stay for a picnic with several relatives. Joslynn and Aunt Dee had phoned and told everyone that Joslynn's long-lost brother was finally home and they'd better come get a gander at him before he went off and stayed another eight years. He laughed. That part had been Aunt Dee's contribution.

He had been gratified to get to meet Joslynn's husband, Jack, and their kids, Joshua and Tasha, though. The children were so unspoiled. They asked him all sorts of questions about his absence from their lives. He'd answered them as best he could. And he had assured them that he'd visit them much more often in the future, which, to his delight, had made them happy.

Joshua found a parking spot among the other hundred or so vehicles and got out. He stretched his long legs. Wearing jeans, a denim shirt, and black motorcycle boots, he felt he would fit right in at the hoedown as Erica had described the party in her last e-mail.

He locked the door of the brand-new Ford Explorer. He'd bought it for its toughness and reliability; plus it was a sight cheaper than some of the other sports utility vehicles he'd test-driven. It was black, with a tan interior. The Mercedes had had the same color combination. Erica had liked the Mercedes. He hoped she liked the Explorer too. After all, she would be driving it as much as he would.

He heard a male voice singing "Crazy Love," an old Brian McKnight song. He peered closer. They had a live band. The dance floor was crowded, and so was the area surrounding it. He looked for a familiar face, wondering if he'd recognize Erica's parents or her brothers without being introduced to them. He sincerely doubted it. It had been seventeen years.

He strolled among the guests for at least ten minutes before he paused at one of the refreshment tables and ordered a glass of Bryant Winery chardonnay. The waiter handed him the glass of chilled wine.

But before he raised the glass to his lips, his eyes were drawn to a woman's figure about eight feet away. Her back was to him, and she was wearing a formfitting white dress that, he swore, he could make out the curve of her butt in. His eyes lowered to her legs. He knew the backs of those knees, calves, and ankles intimately. He'd kissed them enough times.

He set the glass of wine on the table and strode across the lawn to the woman. She was talking animatedly with a group of about six people, three men and three women, who appeared around her age. Of course some of them saw Joshua approaching her from behind. He placed a finger to his mouth in the universal gesture of "shhhh." No one gave him away as he quickly covered the woman's eyes with his hands.

Erica, always game, smiled when she saw the big hands about to cover her eyes. She assumed it was yet another one of her old classmates. The people around her laughed when her assailant said in a deep voice, "Guess who?"

Erica immediately knew it was Joshua. She screamed and started jumping up and down like a crazy woman. Joshua had no choice but to remove his hands. Erica spun around and threw her arms around his neck. Their bodies pressed close and Joshua bent her backward for a deep kiss.

"I guess she knows him," one of the women commented, to gales of laughter.

"She didn't kiss me hello like that," said a man enviously. More laughter.

A bigger crowd gathered around the kissing couple,

who did not seem likely to come up for air any time soon.

They started rooting them on with clapping, and hooting, and shouts of, "Erica, Erica, Erica." Because no one knew the name of the kissing bandit.

Hearing the commotion, Eric and Simone went to investigate. When Simone saw Erica's familiar figure in her pristine white off-the-shoulder dress, all bent over like that, her arms wrapped possessively around a stranger's neck, her mouth pressed firmly against his, she cried, "Erica!"

"Young man, take your hands off my daughter!" bellowed Eric.

The crowd began to disperse at the sound of their host's belligerent tones.

Erica and Joshua slowly drew apart. Erica looked dreamily at the crowd that had gathered. Her eyes settled on her parents. She smiled. "Mom, Dad, this is Joshua."

Joshua stepped forward and nodded respectfully in Simone's direction. "Mrs. Bryant, so good to see you again."

Simone smiled at him. "You certainly have filled out since I saw you last."

She crooked a finger at him. "You're going to have to bend down for a proper welcome."

He bent, and she planted a kiss on his cheek. He blushed. "Thank you."

From the irritated expression on Eric's face, Joshua certainly didn't expect a kiss from his future father-in-law. However, he hoped he wouldn't get punched in the face.

He stepped forward and offered Eric Bryant his hand. "Sir, it's a pleasure to see you again."

Eric grudgingly took his hand, his lips forming a thin line. "Boy, I would appreciate it if you wouldn't slobber all over my daughter in front of everybody like that. It's disrespectful. Furthermore, your technique is all wrong. Come here, Simone."

Simone walked into her husband's embrace. "This," said Eric, "is how you should kiss a woman." And he bent Simone over backward and laid a good one on her.

The crowd roared with laughter and applause.

Joshua laughed. For a second there, Eric Bryant had had him trembling in his motorcycle boots. But with one gesture, he'd lightened the mood and made him feel welcome.

Eric released Simone and clasped her hand in his. He also took one of Erica's hands and placed it in Joshua's with a mind to formally announce their engagement.

"Friends," he said to those gathered around them. "Meet Joshua Knight, Erica's future husband."

Murmuring ensued, and then everyone started offering congratulations to the happy couple.

A few minutes later, after her father had retired for the night and the guests had started saying their good nights, Erica and Joshua got the opportunity to sneak off.

They climbed into the Explorer and Joshua drove them to the Glen Ellen Inn where, after they arrived at the door to his suite, he scooped her up in his arms and carried her across the threshold.

Joshua set her down, and Erica shut and locked the door behind them. She leaned against the door, regarding him with fiery desire in her eyes. Indolently pushing away from the door, she walked up to him and began unbuttoning his denim shirt. "How many days has it been?"

"Nine," Joshua said.

Erica finished unbuttoning his shirt and spread her hands across his pectorals, and ran them lower across his washboard stomach. She raised her eyes to his. "Did you miss me?"

Joshua took her hand and put it on his crotch. "What do *you* think?"

"I think you should be making love to me by now."

He was a fellow who liked doing as his woman asked, so he wasted no more time on witty repartee. He was out of his clothes in record time, and had Erica out of hers shortly thereafter.

He tossed her, bottom-first, onto the bed.

It was at that point that Erica said, "Okay, slow it down. I want you to lie on your back for me."

Joshua slowly went to the bed and lay down on his back. He kept his eyes on Erica. Her skin seemed to be a darker shade since he'd last seen her nude. "You've gotten some sun, I see."

"Three days back home and I had a tan," Erica told him as she came and lay on top of him. Joshua cupped her butt, pressing her firmly against his erection. Erica opened her legs and felt his penis throb at the opening of her sex. She was already aroused, but that turned her on even more.

She sat up, straddling him. Joshua raised his hands to her breasts. He felt the weight of them in his palms, then he began to gently rub the nipples between thumb and forefinger as he liked to do. He felt the hot, moist response to his efforts between Erica's legs. "Where are the condoms?" Erica asked.

"Top drawer," Joshua said. "Hold on." He sat up a bit, reached over, opened the top drawer of the nightstand, and got a couple of plastic-wrapped condoms. He tore one of them open and handed it to Erica. She grasped the latex condom inside and left him with the plastic wrapper held between his fingers. He tossed it onto the nightstand.

Erica scooted back a little until she was no longer sitting on his penis. She grasped him and gently rolled the condom onto him, then she raised herself up, positioned his penis at the opening of her vagina, and gently pushed.

She slowly lowered her body onto him until he was deep inside her. She sighed with satisfaction. Joshua's moist lips enticed her and she bent to kiss him. She kissed each cheekbone and the tip of his nose. She then kissed his forehead and those fly sideburns of his. She ended with his chin, which had stubble on it, but she didn't care.

All the while, Joshua seemed to be expanding inside her. She felt she could go slowly as long as Joshua didn't speak to her. His voice was such an erotic stimulus to her that the sound of it in her ear often made her lose control when she was in the throes of passion.

She began pushing a bit harder. Joshua squeezed her buttocks. Erica thrust harder. With each movement his penis brushed against her clitoris, giving her immense pleasure.

"God, I missed you," Joshua said at that moment, and an instant later, Erica cried out in release. She lay on his chest, and Joshua felt her entire body quiver as she came down. He kissed her forehead.

Erica laughed.

"What?" he asked.

"I was trying to prolong that wonderful feeling, and then you spoke to me and the.sound of your voice sent me over the top."

"Well," he said, pulling her firmly against his chest, "we're just getting started."

She felt his hard penis move inside her. She smiled down at him.

"I want you on your back," he said. "And your feet in the air."

They gingerly reversed positions and Joshua held himself up so that his entire weight would not be on her. Erica's hands grasped the backs of his powerful arms. She thrilled at the feel of him.

With each thrust of his hips, her breasts shook in response. Joshua could not tear his eyes away from her sweet face, her plump lips. He paused long enough to bend his head and kiss her beauty mark. "Girl, you had me running around Beaune like a crazy man getting rid of my possessions so that I could come to you as fast as possible."

Erica met him thrust for thrust. "My dreams about you were so erotic I'd wake up with a thin layer of perspiration covering my body," she told him. "With the memory of the taste of your kisses in my mouth. Then it would fade, and I'd feel like crying."

Her words, so sincere, so sensual in his ear, brought him to the peak. He climaxed, pulled her close, buried his nose in her hair, and whispered, "I love you!"

Chapter Twenty-four

The next morning, after breakfast, Erica, Jason, and Franklyn gathered in the solarium, adjacent to the kitchen, to talk. Erica could feel the tension in the air. What they needed to decide would change all of their lives forever.

Franklyn lightened the mood by saying, "Erica, have you no self-control? Have you no will of your own? Have you no sense of decorum where Joshua is concerned? I wasn't there to witness that kiss, but several guests were more than happy to fill me in on what I missed." He gave her a stern look.

"Yes," said Jason. "It was embarrassing to say the least!" Humor lurked in the depths of his eyes.

"If Mom and Dad weren't embarrassed," Erica told them, "I'm definitely not worried about you knuckleheads! And no, if you must know, I don't have any self-control whatsoever where Joshua is concerned. So there!"

Franklyn and Jason laughed.

Erica scowled at her brothers, both of whom looked refreshed this morning in their jeans and T-shirts, Franklyn's with the skyline of San Francisco at night on a black backdrop, and Jason's a plain white Fruit-of-the-Loom. They both wore athletic shoes. She was attired in jeans, layered T-shirts, one pale pink, one lime green, and was barefoot. Even when she was a child, her mother often had to remind her to put on her shoes before going outside.

"And where did you two go shortly after he arrived?" Jason asked, still smiling. "You came back home at around two in the morning with your dress on backward."

Erica laughed. "It was not! The party was just ending then, anyway. I wasn't even missed. What I want to know is, did Sara ever show up last night? I didn't see her."

"Yes, she came late and left early," Jason told her. "She was with some guy who looked so uptight I'm sure he sleeps in those expensive suits he wears so he can save time getting dressed in the morning."

Erica's smile broadened. "You didn't like him? Or you just don't like seeing Sara with anyone else?"

"Probably the second choice," Jason said truthfully. He sighed, his expression turning serious. "I apologized for my past mistakes, and she accepted. Then, when I was about to ask her if we might try to get to know one another better, she rounded on me and told me in no uncertain terms that, and I quote, 'hell would freeze over' before she would go out with me!"

Erica and Franklyn made valiant efforts not to laugh, and failed miserably.

"I don't see what's so funny," Jason said. "The woman spoke to me like I was the scum of the earth. I happen to be a pretty good catch, even if I do say so myself."

"Which you have, on several occasions," Erica commented dryly.

"Every chance you get," Franklyn added.

"But, apparently, Sara doesn't like fish," Erica quipped.

"Before I'm done with her, she'll be eating crow!" Jason exclaimed.

Excited by his determination, Erica leaned toward him on the couch. She and Jason were sharing the wicker couch, the seat cushions of which were bright green, on the solarium, while Franklyn sat across from them in the matching chair.

"What do you mean?" she asked, curious.

"I mean, I'm going to be pretty hard for her to ignore when I'm living here and not having to come all the way from Bakersfield to court her!" He continued, awed by his decision himself because it had just occurred to him. He glanced at Franklyn. "Franklyn, you told me that your restaurant is doing better than you ever imagined it would. You're happy where you are. And you're in love with Elise, I can see it all over your face whenever you look at her." He turned his gaze on Erica. "Erica, you and Joshua are building a life together. It's going to be pretty hard to do that if you ask him to live in your family's shadow. Me? I have no one special in my life. I'd *like* to have someone special, but love has always eluded me—"

"Or you were too slick for it to catch you," Erica put in.

"Maybe," Jason allowed. "At any rate, lately practicing law has started leaving a bad taste in my mouth. I feel like I need a change. *I'm* the one who should come home and run the winery. But," he continued, "I'm going to need some time to make a smooth transition. I'll need to give notice at the firm, among other things."

"Take all the time you need," Erica told him. "Joshua wants time to repair the house in Healdsburg before we move in anyway, and we plan to live separately until the wedding."

"You don't say!" Franklyn laughed, recalling his parents' views on cohabitation without the benefit of marriage. They didn't advise it for their sons, or their daughter. They saw it as a lack of commitment. "I'm glad to see you were actually paying attention to what Mom and Dad were saying while you were growing up."

"Yeah, I've learned to appreciate them more and more recently," Erica told him.

She was remembering how understanding they'd been last night when they caught her and Joshua in that lip-lock. They could have reacted badly. Instead, her father had turned it into an occasion for laughter.

"We definitely lucked out in the parent department," Jason said, holding out his hand for their special handshake. Franklyn's right hand would be the first, then Jason's on top of his, then finally Erica's on top of Jason's.

"Brothers and sister, through thick and thin," they chanted. "Bryants until the end!"

It was corny, and they hadn't done it in a long time, but somehow they felt it fit the occasion. Jason would assume leadership of the family business. He was to be the guardian of the future of the Bryant line.

With that settled, Erica threw herself into planning her and Joshua's wedding. Her parents had been looking forward to giving her a wedding for years now, and they all enthusiastically embraced the idea of a December wedding.

Joshua wanted at least three months to work on the house. Even with an excellent contractor, there was only so much one could do in inclement weather. They say it never rains in southern California, but they were in northern California and it rained practically every day in September. In October it began to dry out. In November the major work was done on the house. All that needed doing was the painting of the rooms and furnishing it.

It was at that point in the house's refurbishment that Joshua went to collect Erica and bring her back for her first-ever walk-through of their new home. He had not wanted her to see the house before then. Erica had protested, but she was learning to compromise. Joshua would always retain some of his prideful thinking, only wanting her to have the very best, and it wasn't up to her to change him. The way she saw it, he'd already made some significant changes due to her coaxing. He regularly spoke with his sister and aunt over the phone. Joslynn and her family and Aunt Dee had spent Thanksgiving Day with Erica, Joshua, and Erica's parents at the winery. Erica had been delighted when the kids had called her Aunt Erica even before she and Joshua were officially wed.

On the day Joshua arrived to take her to the house, Simone and some of Erica's girlfriends were throwing her a bridal shower at the winery. Joshua had known the bridal shower was to take place that day, but Erica had told him the party would be over by seven o'clock. When he arrived at seven thirty, the party was still going on.

Simone met him at the door attired in a royal-blue pantsuit, and barefoot. Joshua looked down at her red-lacquered toenails. "Hot, Mrs. B," he joked.

Simone blushed and hugged him briefly. "Eric likes them." She pointed to the den. "Erica's back there. I'm sure the ladies are going to get a kick out of you."

Joshua, in jeans, a black T-shirt, a brown leather jacket, his favorite black boots, and a black cowboy hat, grinned. "I'm not looking forward to it." A roomful of women discussing the intimacies of marriage tended to make a man nervous.

As soon as he entered the large room, the women uttered a collective sigh of appreciation. He walked farther into the room after he spotted Erica sitting on the couch amid piles of boxes and wrapping paper. She abruptly got to her feet, upsetting a box with various-colored pairs of panties that had been on her lap. The panties scattered at her feet, and one of her friends bent to pick them up.

"Thank you, Helen," Erica said, grateful.

She met Joshua's eyes across the room. She smiled.

He smiled back. They hadn't seen each other in about a week, what with his living in Healdsburg and her there at the winery.

"Ladies," she said, her eyes never leaving his face. "This is my husband, I mean, my soon-to-be husband, Joshua Knight."

Joshua politely tipped the brim of his hat in their general direction. "A pleasure."

In the cacophony of excited female voices, Joshua thought he heard several hellos. However, as it was apparent he was causing them undue distress, he decided it would be wise to beat a hasty retreat. Once, that is, he got what he came for.

Erica might have sensed his purpose if she had gotten a good look at his eyes, but he'd adjusted the brim of his cowboy hat so low on his forehead that she wasn't able to see them until he was upon her. In them she saw quiet determination, and mischief, plain and simple.

Before she could stop him, he picked her up in his arms and began walking from the room with her. "Ladies," he said, "I'm sure you won't mind if I take my fiancée for a little ride in the country."

Helen spoke up, laughing. "No, go right ahead."

"I love you all!" Erica called. "Thanks for coming, and thanks for the lovely gifts!"

When they got outside the room, Joshua continued through the house. Simone came from the kitchen, drying her hands on a dish towel. She held the front door for them. "Should I expect you for dinner?" she asked.

"I doubt it, Mom," said Erica.

Joshua bent to plant a kiss on Simone's cheek. "I'll have her back before dawn."

Once he was walking to the waiting car, Erica pretended to be upset with him.

"That was rude, taking me away from my guests like that."

"You told me the party would be over with by seven," he reminded her.

"I didn't know you were coming by today. It's Friday, and we usually see each other on Saturday."

"The house is finished, and I didn't want to wait until tomorrow to show it to you. I waited until well after seven o'clock."

"The house is finished!"

"Yeah, and now all it needs is your special touch, and you can't very well do that from Glen Ellen."

He set her down in front of the passenger-side door. "Get in, woman!"

At the house, Joshua explained that he and the workmen had opened up the small rooms of the Victorian by moving walls and eliminating hallways. The result was large, airy rooms with hardwood floors and intricate molding. The walls were all white because, "I figured you wanted to pick out the colors for the rooms yourself."

Exterior redwood timbers were retained because they were of good quality, but they had to be removed, reapplied, and repainted. The house needed new wiring throughout, and the kitchen had been totally remodeled as well as the bathrooms.

Erica loved the big front porch that was painted white and had gingerbread detailing. In the backyard, Joshua had built a walled garden replete with a hot tub. "For those evenings you need to relax," he said.

Erica looked at it all with awe-filled eyes. The amount of work that Joshua had done was amazing. "It's beautiful!" she said truthfully. "It's a home any woman would be proud of."

That made him beam.

She walked into his arms, tiptoed, and kissed him.

When they parted, Joshua said, "There's one more thing you haven't seen yet."

He took her hand and led her upstairs to the master bedroom.

"I've already seen our bedroom," Erica said.

"Yeah, but when we came up, I distracted you and you didn't go into the master bathroom."

He allowed her to precede him. Erica walked through the large bedroom to the back and turned the doorknob. When she opened it, she was rendered speechless. Their big claw-footed bathtub, all the way from Beaune, was waiting for her. She immediately went over to it, put the stopper in, and began running water into it.

Laughing as he walked into the room, Joshua asked, "Baby, what are you doing?"

She smiled up at him. "I'm getting ready to christen our new home. Get naked, boy!"

Dear Reader:

I hope you enjoyed Joshua and Erica's story. I purposely introduced you to Erica's brothers, Franklyn and Jason, because both of them will be getting books of their own in the near future. Franklyn will be wooing Elise in *Constant Craving* next year, and Jason will still be in hot pursuit of Sara in the final book of the Bryant Winery Trilogy, *One Fine Day*, a few months later.

If you'd like to drop me a line or two you can do so by writing me at P.O. Box 811, Mascotte, Florida 34753-0811; or e-mail me at *Jani569432@aol.com.*

Please check out my Web site at *http://www.janicesims.com.* And don't be shy when you visit, leave me a message!

Continued blessings to you and yours,
Janice Sims

ABOUT THE AUTHOR

Janice Sims is the author of eleven novels. She has had stories in five anthologies. During her career her work has been critically acclaimed, and she is deemed a favorite among readers.

She is the recipient of the 2004 Emma Award for Favorite Heroine: Katharine Matthews in *Desert Heat*. She has also received an Award of Excellence from Romance in Color for her 1999 novel *For Keeps*. In 2000, she won the Novella of the Year Award from Romance in Color for "The Keys to My Heart," her contribution to the Arabesque Mother's Day anthology, "A Very Special Love."

Romantic Times Book Club nominated her for their Career Achievement Award in 2000. She was nominated again in 2002.

She lives in central Florida with her husband and daughter.

MORE SIZZLING ROMANCE BY

Janice Sims

__WAITING FOR YOU	1-58314-626-1	$6.99US/$9.99CAN
__TO HAVE AND TO HOLD	1-58314-421-8	$6.99US/$9.99CAN
__DESERT HEAT	1-58314-420-X	$6.99US/$9.99CAN
__FOR YOUR LOVE	1-58314-243-6	$6.99US/$9.99CAN
__THIS TIME FOREVER	1-58314-242-8	$5.99US/$7.99CAN
__A SECOND CHANCE AT LOVE	1-58314-153-7	$5.99US/$7.99CAN
__ALL THE RIGHT REASONS	1-58314-231-2	$5.99US/$7.99CAN
__A BITTERSWEET LOVE	1-58314-084-0	$5.99US/$7.99CAN

Available Wherever Books Are Sold!

Check out our Web site at **www.BET.com.**